Chris has always known he would become the next alpha. It's his duty, and there's no getting out of it.

Or is there?

Jacob and Chris fell in love during the time Chris spent hiding in cete territory. They couldn't find a way to make things work long term because neither of them was ready to compromise.

Now, they are.

Chris is starting to realize he can't live for his father. He has choices to make, and for once, he wants to think only of himself. Jacob never stopped loving him, and together, they can build a life that will make both of them happy.

When tragedy strikes, it tears Chris and Jacob apart for a second time. Will they make the right choice and find their way back to each other—forever this time? Or will they allow circumstances to make them miserable?

The Only Right Choice
Copyright © 2020 Catherine Lievens
ISBN: 978-1-4874-3128-0
Cover art by Angela Waters

Published by eXtasy Books Inc or
Devine Destinies, an imprint of eXtasy Books Inc

Look for us online at:
www.eXtasybooks.com or www.devinedestinies.com

THE ONLY RIGHT CHOICE
ALLEGHENY SHIFTERS 7

BY

CATHERINE LIEVENS

CHAPTER ONE

For some reason, all of Chris's sisters had decided they had to be home since he and Nico had come back. He didn't understand why they'd been hanging around, and he wished they would stop. He wanted to get used to being home again the way he had been before, and it wasn't possible when his three sisters were there.

They were all married, for fuck's sake. Didn't they have better things to do? Instead of being home with their husbands and children, they were hanging around Chris and Nico, staring at them as if they'd never seen them before.

Chris glared at them from his favorite armchair. They didn't seem to care, though. They kept on staring, and Chris had to look away.

He wished he was back at the Bishop house. He wished he'd never left it. He missed Jacob, even though Jacob had rejected him.

He had to stop thinking about Jacob. Nothing would come out of it, and it was in the past now. Chris would probably never see him again. He didn't have a reason to. Chris was back home, and now that he'd started working with his father again, there was no way for him to see Jacob. Jacob was no one important. Well, he wasn't important in the big picture. For the badgers, though, he was the head of their security, so he *was* important.

He was to Chris, too.

"They're just trying to cheer you up," Nico murmured.

Nico was sitting on the couch with his legs crossed as he

1

read a book. Their sisters weren't bothering him, probably because he was faking being busy — or he *was* busy. Chris wasn't sure.

Chris, on the other hand, wasn't doing anything. He was staring out the window, thinking about what he'd lost and what he hoped he could get back.

He knew there was nothing he could do about the situation. He was a bobcat, and he belonged with the clowder. More importantly, he was a future alpha, which was why he should stop thinking about the Bishop house and the time he'd spent there and focus on the future.

The future he wouldn't be spending with Jacob.

He'd fallen in love. He'd thought Jacob loved him back enough to follow him home once he left. He'd always known his time at the Bishop house and in badger territory would be short-lived. He'd had more of it than he'd expected, and he couldn't regret it. He *did* regret putting his heart in jeopardy, though. Now, it was broken, and he didn't know how to fix it.

Nico sighed and closed his book. "They're not wrong, you know. You've been pouting since we came home."

"We've only been back a few days," Chris pointed out.

"And you haven't done anything to get back to our old life. You're still living in the past. You're still living in the Bishop house."

Chris stiffened. His brother had always been able to read him better than anyone else, and he was right. Chris couldn't stop thinking about the Bishop house, but even more so about Jacob. Who would blame him? He was in love with Jacob, and he'd thought Jacob loved him. Maybe he had, but it wasn't enough. When Chris had asked Jacob to come with him, Jacob had refused. He couldn't see himself as an alpha mate, and he'd stayed behind, breaking up with Chris.

And now Chris was alone, and he was facing the rest of his

life that way.

Okay, so maybe he was a tad dramatic. Still, it felt that way, and he thought he had an excellent reason to mope, at least for a bit.

The front door opened, making all of them jump. Chris glared at his sisters again, but they still didn't seem to care. The three of them were sitting on the couch, whispering to each other, peeking at Chris every so often. He was sure they were talking about him, and he didn't understand when he'd become so interesting. He was very young compared to them. He was nineteen, he and Nico being the babies of the family, while his sisters were thirty-two, twenty-nine, and twenty-four. Why were they were so focused on him?

"Chris?" their father called out from the entrance.

Chris jumped to his feet and rushed to him. At least he wouldn't be on display for his siblings anymore. "Dad. I'm here."

His father turned to look at him, smiling. "Good. We have to go talk to the fox alpha."

Chris blinked. He knew he was supposed to start working with his father again, but he hadn't expected it to be this soon. That wasn't a bad thing, though. At least he'd be able to think about things that weren't Jacob. "Of course. Are we leaving right away?"

"We are. Are your sisters still in the house?"

"They're in the living room with Nico."

Chris's father rolled his eyes. "Those girls, I swear. Don't they have anything better to do?"

That was what Chris had been thinking, but he didn't mention it. "I can be ready in five minutes," he said instead.

His father nodded at him. "Good. I'll be waiting here."

Chris wasn't sure why his father was in such a rush. He supposed he was going to find out on the way to the skulk, hopefully. It wouldn't be like his father to make it a surprise, especially after everything Chris had gone through. He didn't know if his dad knew about Jacob, but he suspected that was the case.

He wouldn't be surprised if his father was trying to distract him. It would be just like him. He wouldn't want Chris to focus on what he couldn't have, but rather, on what he was supposed to do.

Chris was the alpha heir. It didn't matter that he was a carrier, that he was only nineteen, or that he was in love. All of that had to take a step back to his future job.

Chris washed his face, put his shoes on, and headed back downstairs. His father was still there, but he wasn't alone anymore. He was talking to Nico, and when they heard Chris, they both snapped their mouths shut and looked up.

Chris hated it when people talked about him, but he supposed he should get used to it. He forced a smile on his face. "I'm ready."

His father gestured at the door. "Let's go, then." He squeezed Nico's shoulder, then headed out.

Chris walked past his brother, ignoring him. Nico wouldn't have any of it, though. "Are you sure you should go?" he asked.

Chris paused only long enough to nod tightly. "Of course I am."

"You should get some rest. Think about other things. We both know you're not in the mood to do anything like this."

"What I'm in the mood for doesn't matter. It's what I have to do. It's what I came back for." Chris stepped outside and closed the door. He took a deep breath. Then he followed his father to the car. He climbed into the passenger seat, put his seatbelt on, and waited.

"I'm glad to have both of you back," his father said as he drove out of their territory.

"It's good to be back," Chris said, even though it was a lie.

"I know you fell in love with a man," Chris's father began.

Chris couldn't listen to this. He didn't want to. "I did, but it's in the past. I'm back home now."

"I know that. It doesn't mean you can't be in pain. It doesn't mean you can't want something else, something different."

"I know being here is my duty. You don't have to worry about me. I can focus on that. Jacob is in the past, and I'll be fine."

"All right."

Chris suspected his father wasn't sure of that, but it was enough to make him stop talking about it, and Chris relaxed.

If he could, he would never think about Jacob again. He couldn't, but at least he could make sure people around him didn't talk about him. It made things harder on Chris, and he didn't need that right now.

"We can reassign the bears to the sleuth," Jacob said.

Eden nodded. "I'll talk to Morris about it, but he'll be fine with it. It's a pity, though. All the guards have gotten used to living here. They like it."

"I should talk to Thomas, too. If the bears want to stick around, I doubt it'll be a problem. Our two groups have become so intertwined that it's almost like a gigantic cete."

Eden grinned. "You mean a gigantic sleuth."

Jacob laughed. "Whatever you want. But yes. I'm sure that if they want to stay, it won't be a problem. We'll have to clear it with the alphas, but I doubt they'll say no. Just get the names of the people who want to stay."

"I'll do that. What about the badgers? Where will you reassign them?"

"Well, I want at least a few of them to stay at the Bishop house, since some of the carriers are still there. They shouldn't be in danger, but just in case, I don't want them to be alone."

Eden nodded and made a note on her phone.

Jacob looked at the Bishop house. It felt empty in a way it hadn't been in a while. When all the carriers had been staying there, it was lively with voices, sounds, and music. Now it felt dead, and Jacob didn't like it.

He also didn't like the fact that Chris wasn't there anymore. He missed his ex, and he wanted him back. He knew that was impossible, though. Chris had gone back to his life, the life he never should have left. Things were back to the way they should be, and Jacob had to stop thinking about him and what they'd shared.

"Jacob?" Eden asked. She sounded like she'd called him a few times already.

He turned his attention back to her. "Yes?"

"I said, who are you keeping here? Not that it matters, but I'm curious."

"Oh. I was thinking about Darrell and Graham, although Robin mentioned sticking around, too. I don't know. I want to keep a rotation, but it's not as important as before."

Eden nodded, but she was still staring, and Jacob knew what was coming before she even said the words.

"Are you all right?" she asked.

"I'm perfectly fine."

She rolled her eyes. "You should try harder. I don't believe you."

Jacob would have been offended, but he and Eden had been working together since the first carriers had started arriving in cete territory, and they were more friends than coworkers by now.

"You can talk about him if you want. I know you have to be sad," Eden said.

Talking about Chris was the last thing Jacob wanted to do. "I don't want to talk about him. What's done is done, and it's in the past. We should focus on the future and on our jobs."

"I'm not saying you shouldn't. I'm just saying that even though Chris didn't die, you still lost him, and you have the right to grieve." She huffed. "I don't understand why he left. It was so obvious he was in love with you."

"I wasn't enough. I came to terms with that, and so should you." It wasn't her business, but Jacob wasn't going to tell her that. He didn't want to lose her friendship or hurt her feelings.

"I still think you two should have worked harder at finding a compromise. That's what being together is about, and you didn't have it in your relationship."

"Duly noted. Can we go back to the planning now?"

"Sure. You were the one daydreaming, though."

Jacob shook his head and looked back at his list of guards who had worked at the Bishop house. If some of the bears wanted to stay, he was going to have to find a way to integrate them into cete security. It wouldn't be a problem. He'd been working right along with them, so he knew they were good at what they did. All of them had their weaknesses and strengths, of course, and Jacob would use them.

His thoughts drifted back to Chris. Was he safe now that he was back home? Jacob doubted Chris's father would put him in danger, but Dan might not realize Chris needed to be protected. As far as Jacob knew, not a lot of people knew Chris and his twin brother were carriers, but if someone outside the clowder and the people who already knew found out, it would be a scandal. Dan had been working on teaching Chris to be his heir since Chris was a teenager, and everyone knew he would be the one taking the alpha's place once Dan stepped down. There had never been a carrier alpha, though, and people would have a lot to say about it. Jacob wouldn't be surprised if some of them tried something, and he hoped Dan knew that.

But then, Dan had been living with this knowledge since

Chris was born. He'd been working toward it for nineteen years, so he no doubt knew what he was doing. It wasn't Jacob's job to protect Chris anymore, and he had to remember that. He had to let go.

It was hard. He was in love with Chris, and he doubted that would ever change. He also knew Chris was in love with him, which made everything harder. If his love had been unrequited, he could have put it away in the back of his mind and focus on other things. As it was, he knew what he was losing. He and Chris had been together while Chris was still living in the Bishop house, but now they weren't. Chris was home, and so was Jacob. The fact that their home wasn't the same place meant they could never be together.

So did the fact that Jacob couldn't be what Chris needed.

He would never be a good alpha mate. He didn't have it in him. He might be head of security and have people who obeyed his orders, but it wasn't the same. That was an alpha's job. An alpha mate's job was to take care of people, and Jacob didn't think he could do that. That was why he'd let Chris go, and while he regretted it every second of every day, he also knew he'd done the right thing.

"You're daydreaming again," Eden said.

Jacob shook himself. He had to stop this, and not because of the teasing. He couldn't think about Chris anymore because he'd lost him, and he would never get him back. He had to focus on his new life without Chris, even though it was hard.

He cleared his throat. "Well, let me know when you've talked to the bears and you know what they want to do. I don't think we can plan anything else until we know who wants to go where."

Eden nodded, but she was still staring at Jacob. "I will. You're sure you're all right?"

"I'm sure. I have to go, though. Call me when you have the

answers we need, and we can meet again to decide who goes where and does what."

"All right. But, Jacob?"

Jacob paused. "Yes?"

"I know we're not exactly best friends, but I do believe we *are* friends, right?"

"We are." The guards and the carriers who lived in the Bishop house had started feeling like a huge family.

A family Jacob had lost.

"Well, if you need anything, even if it's only to rant about Chris, I'm here. Just call me."

Jacob was touched, but he knew he wouldn't do it. He couldn't. He couldn't talk about Chris to anyone, not even Eden.

Chris wasn't in his life anymore, and the less he talked about him, the better it would be, at least for him.

"Dan and I will talk in my office," Jerome, the fox alpha, said. He stared at Chris and Gwen, his daughter.

When Chris and his father had arrived at the alpha's house, he and his daughter had been waiting. Chris didn't understand why she was there, but he hadn't asked. He didn't want to make anyone uncomfortable, and he knew how to behave when he was with other alphas. Still, he'd thought his father had wanted him there to include him at the meeting, not to leave him with Jerome's daughter.

He looked at his father, but his dad was looking away as if avoiding his gaze. That was strange, and Chris would make sure to ask him about it once they were back in the car. In the meantime, he could wait in the living room with Gwen. They didn't know each other, but they were about the same age, so they could probably find something to talk about.

"Of course, Dad," Gwen said. She looked down—the

perfect image of the submissive daughter.

Chris didn't like it. His sisters had never behaved like that with their father. He was their alpha, but more importantly, he was their dad, and they'd always talked back to him and told him what they thought about his orders. Gwen didn't seem to have the same fire in her, and it made Chris wonder how she'd been raised and what kind of father Jerome was.

She was pretty. Even though Chris was very much gay and in love with Jacob, he could see that. Her long blonde hair was braided, with wisps escaping from it and framing her face. Her cheeks were pink, and her blue eyes glittered. Any other guy would have been all over her.

Jerome blinked at her. "All right. We'll go to the office, then," he said. He exchanged a glance with Chris's father before they both disappeared down the hallway.

Chris looked around the living room. He supposed he and Gwen could watch TV or something like that.

They both heard the office door close in the distance, and Gwen's demeanor changed. She went from submissive to standing tall and glaring at Chris, and Chris didn't understand what was happening.

"I am *not* marrying you," she snapped.

Chris had no idea what she was talking about. "Good. Because I haven't asked you to marry me." And he wasn't going to. He and Jacob had broken up, but it was too soon, and besides, he was only nineteen.

Gwen crossed her arms over her chest. "That's why you're here, though. You want to marry me. You want to unite the fox and the bobcats."

"I have no idea what you're talking about. I swear." But he didn't like the sound of it.

"Why should I believe you?"

Chris hesitated, but he knew the best way for her to believe him was to tell her about Jacob. "Because I'm in love with someone else. We broke up, and I know there's no going back, but I still have feelings for him, and I can't think of marrying anyone else right now. Why do you think I want to marry you?"

Gwen looked like she wanted to ask more about Jacob, but instead, she dropped her arms. "Because my father asked me to consider it. Your father didn't?"

"No." Hell, he'd been talking about Jacob in the car as they came here. "Can you tell me what happened?"

"Nothing much." She huffed and flopped onto the couch. She looked nothing like the submissive woman she'd been only minutes ago. "My father came to me yesterday. He said he wanted to talk, and when I agreed to listen to him, he explained that he wanted me to consider marrying you. He talked about you, told me that you're nineteen, the future alpha, and that it would be good both for the clowder and the skulk to be united. I don't want that, though. I don't know why my brother can't marry one of your sisters. He's the alpha heir, not me."

"Probably because they're already married." Chris sat on the edge of the couch, giving Gwen space. He was angry at his father. He couldn't believe he was doing this right after asking about Jacob. He'd acknowledged how much Chris loved Jacob, yet he'd turned around and had suggested a wedding. Hell, he hadn't even talked to Chris about it. He'd left that to Gwen, and Chris would make sure he knew what he thought about this once they were back in the car.

"So you're not okay with this?" Gwen asked.

"I'm not. Even if I wasn't in love with someone else, I'm only nineteen, and you're what? The same age?"

"Eighteen. And yes, that's way too young to get married."

"I understand why our fathers want to unite the clowder and the skulk, but I don't think it's a good idea to do it this way."

"You're right. Even if I had agreed to marry you, I don't want to get married to someone who's in love with someone else. No offense, but I don't want to get married just to make sure the skulk is okay. I deserve more."

"I agree."

Gwen sat up, crossing her legs under herself. "Do you want to talk about the guy? The one you're in love with?"

"Not really."

"You said you broke up with him," Gwen said, ignoring what Chris had just said.

Chris sighed. This was going to be a long meeting, and he knew Gwen would stay with him the entire time. "We did. But I don't want to talk about it."

Gwen shrugged. "Pity, because I don't have anything else to do. Come on. Tell me his name."

Chris could have kissed his father when he heard him and Jerome come down the hallway about an hour later. Gwen had tried to get details about Chris's relationship with Jacob the entire time, and Chris had had a hard time rebuffing her. He might have talked to her if they'd been friends, but they weren't. He didn't know Gwen, even though their fathers thought they should get married. He doubted he would ever see her again, unless their fathers insisted. He was pretty sure his dad wouldn't, though, not after Chris was done with him.

Chris got to his feet, nodding when his dad and Jerome walked into the room. They both looked on edge, probably expecting Chris and Gwen to say something about the situation they'd been dumped in.

Chris only narrowed his eyes at his father. His father sighed heavily, then turned to Jerome. "Well, we're going to head out. I'll call you once I know more."

"You do that." Jerome looked from Chris to Gwen. "Everything okay while we were gone?"

"Of course," Chris said. Gwen was back at playing

submissive, and she was looking away. Chris could see her vibrating with anger, though, and he suspected her father would be yelled at as soon as he and his dad were gone.

He felt quite smug at the idea.

He waited until he and his father were back in the car to turn to him. "I can't believe you did that to me."

His dad sighed again. "I'm sorry. I should have explained why we were coming, but I knew you would refuse if I told you about it."

"And you know exactly why. I can't believe you asked me about Jacob only to throw me in Gwen's arms ten minutes later. You know I'm still in love with him." The words made Chris choke, but he had to say them. "Look, I realize that me and Jacob can never be together. It's the reason I came back home. I knew there was no hope. It doesn't mean you have to push me toward someone else, though. I'm not ready for another relationship, and I'm nowhere near ready to get married. I'm only nineteen, and I'm still trying to learn everything I need to know to take your place when you retire. Don't force this on to me, too."

"Is that what I did? Force the alpha position onto you?"

Chris couldn't answer that. He pressed his lips together and shook his head. "That's not what I'm talking about right now. Promise me you won't try to arrange another marriage for me. Even if you want me to marry someone for the good of the clowder, I want a say in it. I don't want it to be a secret or a surprise."

His father peered at him before turning his attention back to the road. "Fine. I promise I won't do it again."

Chris leaned back in his seat and looked out the window. It was a victory, albeit a tiny one. He'd sorely needed it, and he was relieved he wouldn't have to see Gwen again, not like this anyway.

It didn't solve any of his other problems, but it was a start, or at least, he hoped so.

"See you tomorrow," Thomas said as he closed his front door.

Jacob smiled at him, then turned around to head to his truck. His day was over, and he was headed home to have dinner and relax.

Except he didn't want to go home.

His house didn't feel like home anymore. He'd spent so much time at the Bishop house with everyone else that it felt more like home than his own house. He didn't understand why, yet he did. The Bishop house was the place in which he'd fallen in love with Chris. It was the place in which they'd been together. It was also the place in which Jacob had friends. All the carriers except a few had been friendly, and even though they weren't best friends, they were still part of Jacob's family now. A lot of them had left, but five were still there, and Jacob decided to head over to them rather than go home to an empty house. He could have dinner with them, talk, and make sure they were okay. It had to be a big change for them to be almost alone in a big house after sharing it with so many people. It was emptier than it had been, but still fuller than Jacob's place was.

He drove to the Bishop house, smiling when he saw the lights on inside the house. The five carriers who remained weren't alone. A few guards were still there, too, and they always ate with the carriers. They were like a big family, and just being here made Jacob feel better.

He couldn't have Chris back, but this, he *could* have.

He turned the engine off and rushed out of the truck, climbing the porch steps two by two. He knocked on the door, and he heard the conversation in the kitchen stop before someone moved to open the door.

He beamed when Hector opened. Hector blinked, clearly

surprised to see him, but he stepped aside to let him in. "We didn't expect you."

"Do you want me to leave?" Jacob asked because he would never force his company on anyone.

Hector laughed and shook his head. "Of course not. You're part of the family. Come in. You're just in time for dinner, but then, I suspect that's why you're here."

"You're right. I didn't want to cook tonight."

"I see."

Jacob suspected Hector knew why he was here and that it wasn't because he didn't want to cook, but thankfully, he didn't say anything about it. Instead, he led the way to the kitchen, where the other four carriers and the two guards were sitting and cooking. Jacob nodded at Gail and Darrel, the guards, and sat at the counter with Burnell and Lennox. Redley, Hector, and Turner were cooking.

Jacob relaxed. It was familiar. It was *family*.

"We didn't expect you," Redley said. He was using a wooden spoon to mix something in a pot.

"I just finished work, and I was too tired to cook," Jacob said, using the same excuse he'd used before.

"Well, you're always welcome here. All of you are. We're grateful you're allowing us to stay in this house, and we want to make life easier for you, if it's at all possible."

"You don't have to do that. You know you're welcome to stay for as long as you want, regardless of what you do."

Redley grinned. "Careful. I might decide to stay for the rest of my life."

"That wouldn't be a problem. You can stay if you want. Thomas was clear." But Jacob wondered why Redley hadn't gone home. He was a fox shifter. The clowder was safe for carriers now, and Nico and Chris had left. Redley was still here, though. "I'm surprised you stayed," Jacob said. It might not be the right moment to ask, but everyone here had learned to be honest with each other. It was the only way they'd managed to make it work with so many people living together.

Redley sighed. "I don't know. I don't hate the clowder or anything like that. I just never felt like it was home, you know? Everyone there knew I was a carrier, and they treated me differently for it."

"Do they treat Jacob and Chris differently, too?" Lennox asked.

"Not really. But then, they're the alpha's sons. Chris is going to be the next alpha. I'm no one. I'm just a carrier, and it showed. I'd rather not go back to that if I have a choice."

"Well, you do. You can stay here," Jacob told him.

Redley smiled. "And I'm grateful for that. Truly. The clowder has never felt like home, but this place does. I'm grateful for everything the cete did for me."

"Don't even mention it." The cete had done what they had to do, what anyone else would have done in their place. They'd had a safe place for the carriers, and they'd made sure none of them got hurt. They'd helped those who had been imprisoned, and now, they were free.

"Have you heard about Chris?" Hector asked.

Jacob could have sworn everyone in the room winced at his words. "I haven't. He hasn't called me, and I'm not going to call him," Jacob told him.

Hector bit his lower lip. "Look, I know everyone is walking on eggshells around you when it comes to this, but I have to say it. I think it's a pity the two of you broke up."

"I agree. It is."

"But it's not going to make a difference, is it?"

Jacob sighed. He didn't want to talk about Chris, but he understood why the others were asking. His and Chris's fights had been loud, so everyone knew why Chris had left without Jacob and why things couldn't work between them. Jacob wasn't surprised they were asking, though. They had hope, just like Jacob had in the beginning. "He needs an alpha mate. That's not me. It can never be me."

"Pity. You would have been a good alpha mate."

Jacob snorted. "I doubt that. I'm way too selfish to be an alpha mate." Which was why he'd been with Chris even though he'd known things wouldn't work. He'd hoped Chris would leave his clowder and the alpha position, but of course, he'd been wrong.

"Well, even though you don't have him, you have us," Turner said. "It's not the same thing, but we're still family, aren't we?"

Jacob forced himself to smile at him and nodded. "We are."

Turner was a skunk shifter. Even though things were getting better for most of the shifters in the forest, some groups resisted change, and the skunks were one of those. Turner still didn't feel comfortable enough to go home. That was fine with Jacob, and with everyone else. The Bishop house was these men's home now, and that would never change.

It was also Jacob's, but he knew that *would* have to change. He had a house. Eventually, he would have to stop coming to the Bishop house so often. The five men who lived here deserved to learn to live on their own, and that wouldn't happen if Jacob was always around. In the meantime, though, Jacob was going to do his best to make them see they were welcome in the cete for however long they wanted to stay. No one expected them to leave or to do anything. They could be themselves in a way they couldn't have been if they'd went back home. Hell, for a few of them, it would be too dangerous to go back.

But they didn't have to. They had a home and a family, something they'd never had before, and the same went for Jacob. It complicated things, but Jacob wouldn't change it for anything in the world.

CHAPTER TWO

Things between Chris and his father were still tense, and he wished he could just stay in his room and pout. Instead, he had to work with his dad, which was why he was in his office.

He already knew everything his father was telling him. He'd been training with him and learning since he was fifteen, and even though he'd had to leave the clowder and spend time at the Bishop house, it wasn't like he'd forgotten anything. His father acted like he had, though, and it took a lot of patience not to snap at him, especially considering what he'd done with Gwen and the foxes.

"You're not listening," his father said.

Chris sighed. "I'm sorry. I have a headache." It was a lie, but Chris was bored.

His father frowned. "Why don't you go to the kitchen and get something to drink?"

"I will. Do you want anything?"

Chris's father looked surprised at his offer, but even though Chris was still angry at him, he didn't hate him. "A glass of water, please."

"I'll be right back."

Chris was relieved to escape the office. He loved his father, and he understood why he'd wanted Chris and Gwen to see if they could work something out, but he was pissed. He was angry at his dad for assuming that he wanted to marry someone he didn't even know. He was angry at him for asking about Jacob and then dismissing it even though he knew

Chris was still in love with him. He was angry at the world for not allowing him and Jacob to be together. He was angry at Jacob for not choosing him instead of his own comforts and his wants.

He sighed. Yes, he was angry at Jacob, but he understood why Jacob had made his decision. If Chris had a choice, he would have stayed with Jacob. Even though he was the alpha heir, he'd never *wanted* to be alpha. It was his duty, though, and he would do it.

"Chris. How's everything going?" Chris's mom asked when he walked into the kitchen.

He cringed, knowing what she was referring to. "We'll patch things up," he said.

She smiled. "Good. I told him it was a bad idea to spring that on you, but of course, he didn't listen. He never does. You boys took that from him."

"He shouldn't have sprung it on me, but we're fine. I promise."

"Good. I just got you back. I don't want to lose you again."

"You won't." Because there was nothing left at the Bishop house for Chris, it wouldn't make sense for him to go back.

"How are you feeling? I know things haven't been easy for you."

Chris didn't want to talk about this, either. He didn't want to talk at all, but of course, no one realized that. "I'm fine."

"Are you sure? I know what heartbreak feels like. I went through it before I met your father. It's never easy, but it has to be especially hard in your situation."

"I'm okay, Mom. I promise. I don't want to talk about it because I don't want to think about Jacob. That's all."

His mom looked skeptical, and Chris knew she didn't believe him. He wasn't surprised. Chris spent a lot of time with his father since he was training, but his mother had always been able to read him much better than his dad.

"I know I'm your mother and that it's probably awkward, but you can talk to me if you need to," she said.

"Thank you." He wouldn't take that offer, though.

There was nothing either of them could do. The only thing Chris could do was forget everything about Jacob and act as if he'd never been in his life. It would be hard, but moping around wouldn't help. Jacob had made his choice, and so had Chris.

They both heard the office door open, and Chris turned around. When his father stepped into the kitchen, he frowned. "I wasn't taking that long to get you a glass of water."

His dad shook his head. "I know. But we have a meeting."

"You didn't tell me about it."

"I know. I wasn't sure it was a good idea to have you come with me."

"Why not?" Chris always went to meetings with his father. He didn't have a say in what was happening, but it was his duty.

His dad hesitated, and Chris knew what he was going to say before he said it. "It's with Thomas, the badger alpha."

"I see. I'll be ready as soon as you are."

"You don't have to come if you're not comfortable with it. I'll understand."

"I'm fine. I promise. I can go to this meeting."

"Are you sure? Because it won't be a problem if you miss one of them."

"I'm sure. And please, stop treating me like a child. Talk to me, especially if you have doubts. You don't need to walk on eggshells around me. Yes, I was in love, and yes, I lost that love. I'm fine, though."

Neither of Chris's parents looked convinced, so he left them in the kitchen to get ready. He didn't have much to do, so he just washed his hands and face, then stared at himself in the mirror.

He wished he could stay home and that he didn't have to do any of this. He wished Nico had been born first.

But Chris was the oldest son. His older sisters couldn't be alpha. That meant the role was on his shoulders, and he had to learn to deal with it. He'd dealt with it for years, ever since he was a teenager. Nothing had changed.

Except for Chris.

He knew what love was like now. He knew what he was missing in his life. He knew what he would never have with Jacob.

And he really had to stop thinking about that kind of thing. The situation was what it was. Neither he nor Jacob had been ready to compromise, which meant they had to deal with this.

When he left the bathroom, his father was waiting for him in the entrance. He looked hesitant. "Are you sure you want to come? Even though Jacob isn't supposed to be there, there's a chance you'll see him."

"I'm sure. Stop worrying about it, Dad. I knew what I was doing when I made this decision."

"But you *weren't* the one who had to make the decision, were you? You always had to come home. Jacob could have come with you, but he decided not to. I know you're angry because of that."

"You're right. I am. He chose his life as he knew it instead of me. I'm angry, but I also do understand. He would have lost everything if he'd agreed to come back home with me. I shouldn't have asked that of him."

"Yet you did."

"Because I love him. Because I wanted him with me."

"And you don't anymore?"

"I do. But I know that it's useless to hope. I have to focus on what I *can* do, and that's staying here and learning from you. You're ready to go?"

"Whenever you are." But before they could get outside, he

stopped, his hand on the door handle. "But if this gets to be too hard for you, tell me, and go sit in the car. I'll understand. I'm sure Thomas will, too."

It was tempting to go to the car right now, but Chris shook his head. "I'll be fine. I have to learn to live with this."

He didn't want to, but he knew how true it was.

His father nodded. "All right. Let's go."

Chris dragged his feet, but he followed his father to the car. He might as well get this over with. Eventually, he would have to face Jacob, and today was as good as any day for that to happen.

"I just feel we need as many people as possible," Thomas said.

Jacob wasn't angry about Thomas putting someone to work with him. He was head of security, but cete territory was huge. He wouldn't mind working with Bart. "I understand."

Thomas stared at him for a moment. "You've been doing a great job. The only reason I want someone to work with you is that I want to be sure there's someone who knows how to do your job in case something happens."

Jacob frowned. "Do you mean if I get sick or something?"

Thomas hesitated, then nodded. "Exactly. The forest is at peace right now, but we both know some groups of shifters aren't happy with how things are going. I don't want to risk it. I want someone to be available twenty-four seven for security, and you can't do that on your own. Please, don't take this as me telling you I'm not happy with your work, because I am."

Jacob waved Thomas's words away. "I know that. I already told you I don't have a problem working with Bart."

"If you're sure."

Jacob chuckled. "You'll send me away if I'm not?"

"I can't do that. We need you—and Bart. Having him

working with you will take some pressure off your shoulders, which can only be a good thing. You've been overworking yourself."

That much was true. In the beginning, Jacob had only overseen the Bishop house security. Then the head of security of the entire cete had retired. It had been terrible timing, but no one had managed to make him change his mind. That meant that Jacob had to do everything on his own, and he was kind of relieved he'd have help from now on. "How is it going to work, though? Are we coworkers, or is one of us on top of the other?"

"Well, I'd like you to be coworkers, but he still needs to learn the ropes. You'll be more teacher and student in the beginning, although he does know what he's doing. He'd been working with the former head of security for a while."

"That's fine with me. I just need to know what you want." Thomas was Jacob's alpha, after all.

"I already told you. Start working with Bart. Unload some of your responsibilities on him. Keep me up to date so I can make sure everything runs smoothly. I hope you and Bart will be able to work together."

"I have no doubt."

Thomas looked at the planner on his desk. He grimaced. "Well, I have another meeting."

Jacob knew when he was dismissed. "I'll go." He rose from his chair. "Thanks for letting me know about Bart."

"You deserve to have more free time. And please, let me know if something happens. I want to know if the two of you don't work well together."

Jacob understood that, but he would do his best to work with Bart. He had to. He'd been overseeing everything — the Bishop house security, the cete's security, meetings with Eden and the bears, recruiting and training new guards, planning the shifts, talking with the guards, and making sure they did their job. It was a lot for one man.

He headed out of the office, but Levi popped out of the kitchen before he could get to the front door. He saw Jacob and grinned, and Jacob knew he wouldn't be getting away easily.

"Come get something to drink," Levi said.

Jacob was slightly wary. He and Levi weren't friends, but Levi was his alpha's son. He would have been the next alpha if he hadn't had an older brother. "I'm fine," he said.

"You can still get something to drink, can't you? I know you've been talking with my father for a bit."

Jacob sighed. He had a lot of work to do, but he couldn't say no. "All right."

He followed Levi into the kitchen. He wasn't surprised to see Dimitri and their son were there. He relaxed, smiling at the baby. Well, he was more like a toddler now.

"He's cute, isn't he?" Levi asked as he opened the fridge. "What do you want to drink?"

"Whatever you have on hand."

Levi turned and glared at Jacob. "You can choose. I wouldn't be asking you otherwise."

"Soda. Something lemony if you have it."

Levi nodded and put his head back into the fridge. Jacob turned his attention back to Dimitri. He was a bear shifter, and it was thanks to him and Levi that the cete and the sleuth were united. They'd gotten married, even though Levi hadn't wanted to in the beginning, and they had a child. The child would eventually become alpha after his father and his grandfather, and Jacob knew that the bears and the badgers would be friends until then at the very least.

It was a soothing thought. Life in the forest was hard, especially when you didn't have friends. The badgers had always had a wide territory but very few members in the cete. Uniting with the bears had solved that problem. They'd been mixing, with some bears starting to live in the cete and a few badgers moving with the sleuth, and it felt good. It felt like finally things were going well in the forest.

Well, that was without considering the fact that a human team was nosing around, looking at everything, and possibly deciding the fate of the shifters who lived in the forest.

But that wasn't Jacob's problem to worry about. He already had his orders, and that was what he should focus on.

"Here you go," Levi said as he put a glass and a can of soda on the table.

Jacob smiled at him and took the can. He cracked it open and took a sip, enjoying the bubbles on his tongue.

He took a deep breath. Thomas hadn't been wrong when he said Jacob was overworked. He'd been trying to do everything, but he couldn't deny he'd been more focused on the Bishop house than everything else. He shouldn't have, but he couldn't help it. The people who lived at the Bishop house had become his friends, his family, and he had to keep them safe.

And he was. Very few people knew about the Bishop house. Those who did would keep its location a secret, because they might need it again. It was the safest place for carriers, even though for now, most had gone back home.

Not all of them, though.

"How are you doing?" Levi asked.

Jacob frowned. "I'm fine. Why?"

Levi and Dimitri exchanged a glance. "I was just asking," Levi said. "You know, now that the carriers mostly went home, it has to be strange for you."

Jacob groaned. "You're talking about Chris."

Levi didn't even look sorry. "We're all worried about you. We know how much you cared about him."

Jacob was both annoyed and touched. "I did care about him. I still do. Things went the way they should have gone, though, so you shouldn't worry about me."

Levi wrinkled his nose. "I don't think I agree with that. The fact that you come from two different shifter species doesn't mean you can't be together. Look at Dimitri and me."

Jacob took another sip of soda. "That's not why we broke up. I didn't want to be alpha mate, and he'll be the next bobcat alpha."

Levi grimaced. "I can see why that's a daunting thought. I have to admit I'm not looking forward to taking the place of Dimitri's mom, and I've been raised in an alpha family. I can't imagine how hard it would be for you."

Jacob found that he didn't mind talking to Levi about it. He was probably one of the few people who could understand what Jacob had been going through. "I'm head of security, not an alpha mate. I wouldn't know how to behave."

"It's a pity, though. It was nice seeing you happy for a while."

"I *am* happy."

Levi's gaze told Jacob that he didn't believe him, but then, Jacob didn't believe himself, either.

"Come in, come in," Thomas said.

If he were any other alpha, Chris wouldn't be smiling, but this was Thomas. He'd helped Chris and Nico and all the other carriers when they'd needed him, and it was almost like being back home. Hell, the cete *had* been home for a while. Chris regretted leaving, even though he hadn't had a choice.

They followed him to his office. Chris could hear voices coming from the kitchen, but they didn't stop to see who it was. Probably one of Thomas's children. Chris wondered how Seamus was doing with his new baby girl, and it was a pity he couldn't stop and visit.

They stepped into Thomas's office, and he closed the door.

Chris and his father sat on the other side of his desk, and the meeting started.

It was about the human team being present in the forest and the relationship between the clowder and the cete. It was nothing new, and Chris didn't understand why his father and Thomas wanted to talk about it. They were probably strengthening the bond between the clowder and the cete by doing so, which was a good thing, but slightly boring.

Chris had trouble focusing. He couldn't deny that. Being back made him think about Jacob, and that was the worst thing that could happen. He didn't *want* to think about Jacob.

That was a lie. He was always thinking about Jacob, even though he knew he shouldn't be. But he still loved Jacob, and there was no denying that. If things had been different, they would still be together right now, and Chris couldn't ignore that. He couldn't ignore the feeling that he'd lost something huge, something life changing. He couldn't ignore the fact that he'd lost it because of his own behavior, even though he was still convinced he'd done the right thing.

"Chris?" Chris's father snapped. He sounded like he'd tried getting Chris his attention a few times already.

Chris blinked at him. "Yes?"

"Weren't you listening? I asked you a question."

Chris's father was annoyed with him. Chris didn't care much, though. His dad known things would be hard for him when he'd decided to take him to this meeting, and this was the result. "I apologize. I wasn't listening."

Chris's father huffed, but Thomas smiled at him. "It's entirely understandable. Why don't you go to the kitchen? Levi and Dimitri were there. I'm sure they can keep you company while your father and I talk."

Chris looked at his father, then back at Thomas. "I'm supposed to sit in this meeting. I have to learn what being an alpha means."

Thomas's eyes twinkled. "Mostly, it means having to sit through boring meetings. I understand why you're distracted. It's not a problem. You can leave the office, as long as your father approves."

They both turned their attention to Chris's father, and Chris knew what his decision would be. He couldn't exactly say no, not when Thomas had agreed to it. "Fine. You can leave the office. There's nothing you don't know happening right now here anyway. But don't go too far. I'll be ready to go home soon."

Chris was on his feet before his father could finish speaking. It made Thomas smile, and the corner of Chris's father's lips curled up. They were both amused, even though Chris could tell his father was trying not to show it.

"Thank you," Chris said before rushing out the door. He closed it behind himself and took a deep breath, closing his eyes.

He was free, at least for the moment. He knew it was only temporary. He'd been lucky because he was in Thomas's home. Thomas was kind of Chris's second alpha. Chris wouldn't be this lucky if they were meeting with any other alpha, but they weren't, and he was going to take advantage of that.

He headed to the bathroom to splash his face with water. He felt like he needed it. The office had been warm, and now he felt *too* warm. His cheeks were red, probably a mix between the temperature and embarrassment at being caught day-dreaming. He gripped the sink with both hands and stared at himself in the mirror.

He could do this. So far, he hadn't seen a peek of Jacob, and he hoped things would continue that way. Maybe he should go back to the meeting. It would be a sure way not to meet Jacob, unless he came to knock on the door. He probably wouldn't, though.

But Chris didn't want that. He didn't want to have to listen to his father drone on and on about the relationship between the cete and the clowder. It was a good one, especially after Thomas had taken care of Chris and Nico—and Redley. Redley hadn't come home with them, and Chris understood why. He wished he could have done the same.

He loved the clowder, and he loved his family, but he hated the responsibilities weighing on his shoulders. Being the next alpha hadn't been his choice. It had been decided for him when he was born because he was born a few minutes earlier than his brother. It had made him the future alpha.

He tightened his hands around the cold ceramic. He couldn't come back to the cete. This was his life now, and he had to accept it.

He pushed away from the sink and opened the bathroom door. He stepped outside, colliding with someone who was coming down the hallway. The man's hands shot out and grabbed Chris's forearms to steady him, and he looked up into Jacob's eyes.

Chris's throat closed. He couldn't do anything but stare at Jacob.

He looked good., although tired, with shadows under his eyes that Chris wished weren't there. He couldn't help but wonder if Jacob was sleeping enough, and if he wasn't, if it was Chris's fault.

Jacob was still holding onto Chris, and Chris never wanted him to let go. But he did, and he took a step back, looking away and breaking the moment.

Chris cleared his throat. "Hi," he said. It felt awkward, but he and Jacob shouldn't ignore each other.

Jacob rubbed the back of his neck. "Hi. I apologize for barreling into you."

"Don't worry about it. I should have looked where I was going."

"I didn't know you were in the house."

"My father had a meeting with Thomas."

"And you're not sitting with them? Isn't that what a future alpha should be doing?"

Chris bristled, but he didn't say anything about that. "I just needed a moment."

Jacob looked at the bathroom door, and his cheeks pinked. "Of course. Sorry."

Chris forced himself to smile. He wanted Jacob to think he was happy. He wanted Jacob to believe that he hadn't made the biggest mistake of his life and that he didn't regret it. "It's fine. Everyone has to use the bathroom every so often. What are you doing here?"

"I had a meeting with Thomas. I spent some time in the kitchen with Levi and Dimitri, but I'm headed home now."

Chris nodded. "Will you be getting some sleep? You look tired."

Jacob straightened his back. "That's because I am. You shouldn't worry about it, though."

Because it wasn't Chris's problem anymore. It wasn't something Chris should worry about because he wasn't in Jacob's life anymore.

He still loved Jacob, though. He didn't think he would ever forget him, and he didn't know how he would live his life this way. He *wanted* to forget Jacob, but it was impossible, even if he stopped coming around cete territory. Jacob had burrowed his way under Chris's skin, into his heart, and he'd dug his claws in. Chris had loved it when they were together, but now he hated it.

He wished Jacob hadn't been so important to him. He wished Jacob hadn't been his first love, his *only* love.

But he had, and Chris needed to learn how to deal with it. He had to learn to accept that things wouldn't change and that Jacob hadn't chosen him.

Jacob might have looked tired, but he wasn't the only one. Chris looked like he hadn't been sleeping enough, and Jacob wanted to do something about it. He wanted to drag Chris off and put him to bed, to make sure he got enough sleep. He wanted to make sure he ate, that he was taking care of himself.

He couldn't.

It wasn't his role anymore. He'd given it up when he'd decided to break up with Chris, and he had to stay away. It was better that way. He could never be what Chris needed him to be, and the best thing he'd done was to break up with him. He couldn't show Chris that he still cared. It would only give Chris false hope, and Jacob didn't want that.

He took another step back. "Well, it was a pleasure meeting you, but I should go."

Chris stared at him for a moment. "Of course. I'm sure you have better things to do than talking to me."

Jacob didn't. Yes, he had work to do, but he would rather talk to Chris for the rest of the day. Again, though, it wasn't something he could do. "Take care of yourself," he murmured.

Chris grimaced. "I'm trying. It was better when you were taking care of me, though."

Those words threatened to make Jacob's knees buckle. Even though he'd broken up with Chris, he still loved him, and he wanted nothing more than to help him, cherish him, and take care of him. He couldn't, and it broke his heart.

The office door opened down the hallway, and both he and Chris turned to see Chris's father and Thomas come out of it. They were still talking and hadn't noticed them, and Jacob wondered if he would be able to sneak out before they did.

He couldn't. Thomas looked up, and his smile widened. "Jacob. I thought for sure you'd left."

"I was going to, but Levi cornered me and forced me to have a drink with him and Dimitri."

Thomas laughed. "I see. Well, you know my son."

"It wasn't a problem. I do have to go, though. Unless you need anything?"

Thomas shook his head. He and Chris's father reached Jacob, and Jacob was doing his best not to look at Chris's father. He was sure the man knew what had happened between him and his son, and he didn't know what he thought about it.

Maybe he was angry because Chris had dated a nobody. Chris was a future alpha, and his relationships needed to be carefully chosen. He couldn't just be with anyone, especially not with someone who wasn't a bobcat, or who wouldn't be useful to help the clowder. That was who Jacob was, though. He wasn't useful. He was nothing, which was one of the reasons he'd broken up with Chris.

"Jacob," Dan said, nodding at him.

"Alpha Wiley."

He grimaced. "Call me Dan. I think we're too close for you to be calling me Alpha Wiley." His gaze drifted to his son.

Chris was looking away. He was stubborn, and what he was doing was obvious to everyone, but no one called him out on it.

"How have you been doing?" Dan asked.

Jacob wasn't sure *why* he was asking. "I'm fine. Settling into my new role now that the Bishop house is mostly empty."

"It's a good thing. A lot of men went back to their families."

"They did, but not all of them. Some didn't want to, and some couldn't."

Dan grimaced. "I'm aware. I'm sorry Redley is imposing on you."

"He isn't," Thomas intervened. "We're more than happy to have him with us if that's what makes him comfortable."

"I don't understand why he didn't want to come home. His

family has been asking about him."

Jacob could answer that question, but it wasn't his place to do so. He and Chris looked at each other, though, and he realized Chris knew why Redley had wanted to stay.

"Well, he's happy here," Jacob said. "He made friends, and I'm sure he doesn't want to leave them."

"As long as he's not a problem."

"He's not. He's a good man."

Dan nodded. "That's why I was sorry to lose him. But if he's happy here, then I'm glad." He turned back to Thomas. "I'll talk to you soon about that thing," he said.

Jacob could have sworn there was a twinkle of mischief in Thomas's eyes, and he didn't like it. That meant Thomas was planning something, and usually, people didn't like it when he did, not when they ended up involved. Hopefully, it was about Thomas's sons.

"I will. Have a safe trip home."

"Always." Dan turned to Chris. "Ready to go? Or did do you want to stick around for a bit longer?"

Chris peered at Jacob, then shook his head and looked away. "I'm ready to go."

Jacob's heart shouldn't have broken at the words, but it did. Jacob only had himself to blame for what was happening, though. He'd been the one who hadn't wanted to try. He still thought he'd done the right thing, though, and he watched as Chris and his father walked to the front door.

He missed Chris like he would miss a limb. Sometimes it was hard to breathe without him. Jacob knew he'd broken up with the love of his life, and there was nothing he could do to get him back except agreeing to become the alpha mate, and that wasn't something he was willing or could do.

He wasn't an alpha mate. He would never be anything more than head of security, and even that wasn't enough anymore, since Thomas asked him to work with Bart. Jacob understood why, but he didn't have to like it. It felt like Thomas didn't fully trust him, and it hurt.

Nothing hurt more than not being with Chris, though.

"I don't know what to tell you except that I'm sorry," Thomas murmured.

The front door slammed closed, making Jacob jump. "You don't have anything to be sorry about," Jacob told his alpha.

"I wish things were different. They *should* be different."

"But they aren't. I can never be an alpha mate, and Chris won't step down as the heir to the clowder. He thinks it's his duty." And it was. He was the firstborn son.

"But it's not fair. People should be able to decide whether or not they want to be an alpha."

Jacob snorted. "Like Josiah was able to decide?"

Thomas grimaced. "I wish he could have. I never wanted to force him to take his father's place, but you know things would have unraveled if he hadn't. The humans wanted the coyotes to have an alpha, and now they do. It gives the humans one less reason to go against us and find trouble where there isn't any."

Jacob regretted his words, because he knew Thomas was right. No one had wanted to force Josiah to do anything, but he'd been the only logical choice when it came to the coyotes. Josiah might hate it, but he'd been born to it, and he would do a good job. It would be hard to do worse than his father and his brother had.

"Maybe he can stop being the alpha in a few years."

Thomas nodded, even though he didn't look convinced. "Maybe. I don't like what we did, even though we did it to save the forest." He peered at Jacob. "But Chris's position is different. His brother could take his place, and I don't like that this hasn't been allowed."

"Dan isn't a bad man." Jacob believed that, even though he was one of the reasons he and Chris couldn't be together.

"He isn't, no. He should see his son more, though, rather than only seeing his heir."

Jacob couldn't protest that because he agreed. Dan saw the future when he looked at his son, not Chris — not the *Chris* Jacob knew.

CHAPTER THREE

Seeing Jacob had shaken Chris, so much so that even a few days later, he couldn't stop thinking about him. He didn't know *how* to stop.

He knew he'd done the right thing by coming back. He couldn't think just of himself, not the way he had while he'd been away. The more important thing in his life had to be the clowder and his future role as the alpha. It had always been that way. He wasn't just a man or a carrier. All of that came second next to the fact that he was a future alpha. He couldn't run away from it, even though he had, for a bit.

Staying at the Bishop house had made him happy because he hadn't had responsibilities there. He'd been able to be a normal nineteen-year-old man, a man who could fall in love, enjoy his youth, and have hopes and dreams.

All of that had been crushed once he'd come home. He'd known it would, but he'd still hoped. He'd prayed that Jacob would agree to come with him, that they could be together and one day, step into the alpha and the alpha mate's positions.

Jacob hadn't wanted that. He didn't want to be alpha mate, and Chris couldn't blame him, even though he hadn't tried. It had been easier to put everything on Jacob rather than on what Chris's life was.

If Chris had a choice, he would never be alpha. He wanted a quiet life, Jacob, and maybe children one day. He didn't want responsibilities. He knew that made him selfish, and that there was no way out of the situation, but he could dream, even though it hurt.

Jacob had made the right choice. Maybe it was better this way for Chris, too. He didn't have Jacob next to him, distracting him. Things wouldn't have worked between them anyway.

He and Jacob had fallen in love because they'd both been stuck at the Bishop house—Jacob less so, but still. He'd been hanging around every day. Things would probably have crumbled as soon as they spent time together as a couple outside of the house. Chris *had* to believe that, because if he couldn't, his heart would break a little more.

There was a knock on his bedroom door, but it opened before he could call out. Nico peeked in, grimacing when he saw Chris sitting at the window seat staring outside. He stepped in, closing the door behind himself. "You're still moping around."

"And you're still annoying."

Nico grinned. He was used to Chris's sharp tongue, and he didn't mind, or at least, Chris didn't think he did. "Come on. We have to head out."

"We don't have to do anything. You're free to do whatever you want, but I have to stay here." There was bitterness in Chris's tone, and he knew Nico could hear it.

Nico sighed. "If I could do anything to help you, I would. You know that. I want you to be happy. I want you to be with Jacob."

Chris snorted. "Even Jacob doesn't want me to be with him. What do you care?"

"I care because you're my brother. You're the most important person in my life, and while I know that'll probably change if I fall in love, it hasn't for now. You're my twin brother, Chris. We've been together since we were conceived, and I want you to be happy. It's obvious you're not."

Chris couldn't hide it from Nico, not the way he had been

with his parents and his sisters. He'd put up a good front when it came to them. He didn't want his father to see how miserable he was taking his rightful place by his side. It wouldn't change anything anyway, and it would make his father unhappy. Nico was different, though. He was Chris's twin, and as he'd said, they'd been each other's pockets all their lives. He could read Chris better than anyone, probably even better than Jacob.

"What do you want me to say?" Chris asked.

"We could try talking to Dad. Show him how unhappy you are. He wants you to be the next alpha, but he also wants you to be happy."

"Those things don't go together, Nico. You don't know because you haven't been in my position, but I can't be the alpha and be happy at the same time."

"So be happy and that's it."

Chris shook his head and looked out the window again. "I can't. I'm the heir. That's what I have to focus on. Things with Jacob would have ended anyway eventually."

"That's bullshit. Come on. I'm taking you away."

Chris wanted to resist, but he couldn't deny he'd had enough of his bedroom. Yes, he was moping, but it was starting to be a bit much, even for him. "Where are you taking me?"

"We're visiting Josiah."

Chris blinked. "I didn't know the two of you were friends." As far as he remembered, Josiah had mostly kept to himself while they'd been at the Bishop house. It was understandable, considering everything he'd gone through, and Chris was in awe at his strength. He hadn't wanted to bother him, so he'd stayed away, but Nico obviously hadn't.

"You would know if you hadn't been up Jacob's ass all the time," Nico teased.

It still hurt to hear Jacob's name, but it helped that it came from Nico's lips. "I wasn't in his ass."

"Was he up yours, then?"

Chris bit his lower lip. "No. We've never done that."

Nico's eyes went wide. "You haven't? Why not?"

Chris shrugged and looked away from his brother. "I wasn't ready. We did plenty of other things, though. I'm not a virgin." Not in all the ways, but in one, he still was.

"I'm surprised. I thought for sure the two of you were banging all over the Bishop house."

Chris grimaced. "Can you not talk about that? You're my brother."

"I know." Nico hesitated. "But I want you to know that I'm here if you want to talk about anything. Even if it makes us uncomfortable. You can tell me about how good Jacob was in bed, about how angry he makes you, and about how much you hate your life. You don't have to keep up the pretense with me."

Chris sighed. He shouldn't have pushed Nico as much as he recently had, but he'd wanted to be alone. He still did most of the time, but he knew he couldn't behave like an island. "Thank you. I think that eventually I'll be strong enough to talk about him. Not yet, though."

Nico stared for a second. Then he nodded. "I understand. I've never been in love, but I know how happy you were while we were staying at the Bishop house, and I wish you could have that back. I'm not going to push, though. If this is what you want, then I'll go along with it."

It *wasn't* what Chris wanted, but he was grateful his brother wasn't pushing. "Thank you. We're visiting Josiah, then?"

Nico beamed. "We are. Let's go."

"Was there something going on between the two of you that you look so excited to see him again?" Chris asked.

Nico looked horrified. "Of course not. I told you we were

friends."

"You were nothing more than friends, then?"

Nico shook his head. "You know two carriers shouldn't be together."

"That's bullshit," Chris threw Nico's words back at him. "It happened before. Besides, I don't think of us as carriers."

Nico cocked his head. "What do you think of us as, then?"

"We're men. We're allowed to fall in love with anyone we want." Even if it ended badly.

"You're right. But no, there was nothing between Josiah and me. We're just friends. Come on. I told him I was dragging you along, and he'll be relieved to see us. He's been trying to get used to being the alpha, but it hasn't been easy for him, and I think you might be able to help him."

Chris wasn't looking forward to talking about what being an alpha was like, but it was the right thing to do. He had all this training, and for now, he was doing nothing with it. He could help Josiah. It was important to Nico, and hopefully it would help distract Chris so he could stop thinking about Jacob.

Jacob raised his arm to block the punch, then moved down and kicked the trainee on the legs. The guy tumbled down and stayed there, looking up at Jacob with wide eyes. "You're making it too easy," Jacob snapped.

The trainee swallowed heavily and nodded. "I'm sorry. I'm not trying to."

Jacob snorted. "You're not trying to do anything. You're letting me beat you up, and that's not the way to go if you're going to be part of security. If you want the job, you need to try harder."

The training nodded again.

"Jacob?" a voice asked.

Jacob looked around until he located Raven. He was leaning against the wall of the gym, staring at Jacob with an arched a brow.

Jacob huffed. He left the trainee on the ground where he belonged, grabbed a towel, then headed toward his friend. "What do you want?" he asked.

Raven's other eyebrow shot up. "Well, I'd like to know why you're so angry with everyone."

"I'm not angry." Maybe a bit brusque, but who could blame him?

"You beat that trainee into the ground."

"I didn't. He's still breathing."

Raven sighed and shook his head. "You're biting everyone's head off. Something is going on with you, and we both know what it is."

Jacob didn't want to talk about it. He couldn't deny Raven was right, though. His anger and sadness were impacting the way he did his job, and it had to stop.

"Leave the trainees alone. They can train without you for one day. Come on," Raven said, pushing away from the wall.

Jacob looked around. Raven wasn't wrong. The trainee was still on the ground, staring at Jacob and looking like a kicked puppy. The others were lined against the wall, and they looked like they wanted to run away.

Maybe Jacob *had* been a bit harsh on them. And maybe he'd been taking out his anger and sadness on them, too. He shouldn't be doing that, so even though there was nothing he wanted less, he followed Raven outside.

He took a deep breath and closed his eyes, trying to drain the anger from his body. It wasn't easy, though, not after he'd seen Chris. He wanted to go back to Chris and shake him, to make him see that he didn't have to be the alpha if he didn't want to.

Because Chris didn't. It wasn't something they'd talked

about, but Jacob knew him well enough to be aware of that. Chris had never wanted to be the alpha, and Jacob had thought that he'd leave the clowder behind and move in with the cete permanently. He'd thought he was more important than being the alpha heir, but he'd been wrong.

Chris wanted to make his father happy. That was why he'd gone back and why he was once again learning how to be the alpha. Chris loved Jacob—Jacob didn't doubt that—but it hadn't been enough. *Jacob* hadn't been enough.

"Talk," Raven said.

Jacob opened his eyes and glared at him. "What do you want me to say? You already know what happened."

"Maybe I do, maybe I don't. Act like I don't and tell me why you're so angry."

Jacob shook his head and started pacing in front of Raven. "I miss him. I still love him. No amount of telling myself that it was the right thing to do and that things couldn't have worked between us is helping. I saw him the other day, and he looked miserable. He still went back with his father, though."

"Why do you think it wouldn't have worked?"

"Because look at him and look at me. He's nineteen. He's a future alpha. He'll have an entire clowder to lead once his father retires. And me? I'm just the head of security here. Hell, I haven't been that for long, and I'm thirty-four. We're too different. He's too young for me, and he should have someone else in his life. I was crazy to agree to be in a relationship with him. I should have said no."

"But you didn't."

"I didn't. I feel guilty about it. He's only *nineteen*, and he has his entire life in front of him."

Raven snorted. "It's not like you have a foot in the grave. You're only thirty-four."

Jacob stopped moving and looked at his friend. "And

again, he's nineteen. That's a fifteen-year difference. It's huge."

"Not as big as you think."

"Okay, maybe it's not. Maybe it wouldn't be if he were twenty-five and I were forty. But he's not. He's barely legal." That was something Jacob had grappled with in the beginning. He'd wanted Chris, but he thought Chris was too young, and he still did. He'd eventually given in when Chris had pointed out that he might be nineteen, but he was an adult, and if something happened to his father, he would become the alpha. His age didn't matter.

And maybe it didn't. That wasn't the reason they'd broken up anyway.

Jacob started pacing again. "Okay, maybe his age doesn't matter. The fact that he's the alpha heir does, though."

"Maybe you could be the alpha mate. I think you'd be good at it."

"I wouldn't. Come on, Raven. You saw. I just took my anger on the trainees. Do you really want me to be at the head of the clowder?"

Raven grimaced. "Okay, maybe that wasn't a good idea. But you said Chris didn't want to be the alpha."

"That's not going to stop him from doing just that, though. He won't step back. He thinks it's his duty, and while I understand where he's coming from, I disagree."

"He is the firstborn son," Ryan pointed out.

"So what? He's also a carrier, and they shouldn't be alphas."

"So you're saying he shouldn't be the alpha because he's a carrier?"

Jacob stopped in front of his friend and raked a hand through his hair. He was frustrated, and he wanted to strangle Raven. "That is *not* what I said. I'm just pointing out that there are rules that can be broken. The fact that a carrier can't be alpha is one of them. The fact that the firstborn son should be the alpha should be one, too." Chris would be miserable as the alpha, and both he and Jacob knew it.

"I don't know what to tell you," Raven said.

"Because there's nothing you can tell me. Chris made his choice, and so did I. He needs someone better, someone who will be by his side, and it's not something I can do."

"Because you don't want to."

"Because I'm not good enough," Jacob yelled. He regretted raising his voice right away, but Raven had pushed him to it.

"I see. I think it's a pity, but since neither of you will compromise, I doubt there's a solution," Raven said gently instead of yelling back at Jacob.

"It's what I've been telling you from the beginning. Yes, Chris and I love each other, but sometimes, love isn't enough."

"I don't think that should be the case."

"But we don't live in one of those romance novels you like to read, Raven. This is not a book. It's true life, and Chris made the choice he wanted to make. I wasn't good enough for him to choose me. I don't blame him for that." If anything, Jacob blamed himself.

Yes, he was head of security, but that wasn't a lot, was it? He would never be an alpha, or an alpha mate. He and Chris had both made the only right choice, and they had to deal with it. Jacob had to stop taking out his anger on other people and focus on the fact that he still had a home and a family. He had his entire life in front of him. He was only thirty-four, and he would meet someone else. He would fall in love with someone else.

The thought filled him with dread.

Chris didn't know what he'd expected when he arrived in

coyote territory, but it wasn't what he saw. There was still a lot of work to do, but it was obvious that Josiah was a good alpha, no matter what people thought about it.

Everywhere Chris looked, he saw houses being rebuilt and fixed, kids playing, and people talking to each other. They were cautious when they heard the car and didn't recognize Chris and Nico, but they didn't run away. Chris had never been here before, but he'd heard stories, so he knew things hadn't always been this way. Josiah might not have wanted to be the alpha, but he was doing a good job. That made Chris think about how he didn't want to be the alpha, either, yet he was going to be. Their situations weren't even remotely similar, but Chris felt a kind of kinship with Josiah, and now that he was here, he couldn't wait to see him.

Nico parked in front of a slightly larger house than the others. It wasn't the alpha's house — Chris could see that one a bit in the distance, and it looked like no one lived there — and Chris wondered why Josiah wasn't there. It might be that the alpha's house wasn't to his taste. It wasn't to Chris's taste, either. It was too modern, all glass and metal, and it looked out of place.

"He's not living in the alpha's house?" he asked Nico.

"He hates it, so no."

"Well, I won't deny it's a bit gaudy."

Nico snorted. "A bit? Josiah's father built it, and that man had horrible taste."

"He was also a horrible man."

"True."

Nico climbed the porch steps and knocked on the door. The man who opened wasn't Josiah, and he stared at Nico for a second, obviously trying to understand who he was and why he was there. Nico beamed at him. "I'm here to see your alpha."

"Does he know you're here?" the man asked.

"He does. We talked on the phone a little while ago. Can we come in?"

The man looked like he wanted to say no, but he stepped to the side. Nico strode inside the house as if he belonged there, but Chris was slower. He looked around, surprised at the state of the place. It had looked small from outside, but it was even tinier inside. There was too much furniture, and it looked stuffy. The room they were in was both a living room and kitchen, and there was barely space for three adults to move around.

"Is *this* the style Josiah likes?" Chris asked.

"God, no. I hate it," Josiah said as he walked into the room.

Josiah looked at the man who had opened the door. "You can go."

"Are you sure?"

Josiah rolled his eyes. "They're friends. I promise I'm safe with them. Don't worry."

The man hesitated, but he nodded and left the house, gently closing the door behind himself. Josiah stared at the door for a moment. Then, he sighed and turned toward Nico. "I didn't expect you to drag your brother here."

Chris crossed his arms over his chest. "I'm here, you know. You don't have to talk about me as if I'm not in the room."

"Sorry. I'm just surprised to see you. I thought you'd be too busy working with your father."

Chris smiled. "I *am* swamped, but I needed a change of scenery."

Josiah gestured at the couches. "Why don't you sit down? Can I get you something to drink?"

Chris shook his head, but Nico asked for a glass of water. Once the three of them had settled down, things were slightly awkward.

Chris wasn't Josiah's friend. They'd shared a home for a while, but Chris had been so busy with Jacob that he hadn't actually made that many friends. He was friendly with every-one in the Bishop house, but that was where things stopped, and he found himself regretting that. Yes, he'd been focused on Jacob, but that didn't mean he had to neglect everyone else.

"How are things going?" Nico asked, leaning toward Josiah.

"Weird. I'm not used to being in charge, and a lot of band members don't like me doing so. They're going to have to get used to it, though."

"Wouldn't this be the perfect opportunity for you to step down from the position?" Chris asked. "I know you never wanted to be alpha." And he shouldn't have been. He'd had an older brother. If the man hadn't been a cruel asshole, Josiah wouldn't be here right now.

Josiah sighed. "You're right. I never wanted to do this, but I don't have a choice. There's no one else who can take my place, and with the human team still going around and trying to find problems, I couldn't say no. Maybe I'll be able to step down once they leave, though."

Chris suspected all three of them knew that wouldn't happen. Josiah was the alpha, for better or worse. There was nothing he could do about it. He didn't have an heir, not yet. *He* was the first alpha carrier, and as far as Chris knew, while there had been a few grumbles about it, no one had said anything against him.

They couldn't. The future of the forest and of the coyote band depended on Josiah. He had to be the alpha, because if he wasn't, things would go to shit.

"What about you?" Josiah asked. "I know you weren't happy to go back home."

This was the last thing Chris wanted to talk about. "I might not have wanted to go home, but I had to. Just like you, I don't have a way out of this."

Josiah stared at Chris for a moment. "You do realize that's

bullshit, right?"

Chris blinked. "I'm sorry?"

"You say you don't have a way out of this. That's bullshit. Is that why you and Jacob broke up?"

"I thought everyone knew why Jacob and I broke up."

Josiah waved. "I know about it, but I wasn't exactly listening to gossip. Tell me."

He sounded in charge, which surprised Chris into speaking. "I had to go home because I'm my father's heir, while Jacob didn't want to be alpha mate. That's all there is to it."

"And that's bullshit again. One of you could have stayed with the other. You just said you didn't want to be alpha. Why didn't you just tell your father that?"

"You should know better than to think you can get out of being an alpha. I'm the firstborn son. It's my duty to take my father's place once he retires, and that's why I had to go home. Jacob could have come with me, but he didn't want to be alpha mate. He didn't even try."

Josiah stared at Chris for a bit. Chris wasn't sure what he expected from him, but it wasn't what came next. "So neither of you was willing to compromise."

"I *couldn't* compromise. He was the only one who could, and he wasn't willing to."

"You're an idiot."

Chris jerked back. "I'm sorry?" He and Josiah weren't friends, and he certainly hadn't expected Josiah to say that kind of thing to him.

"You could have said no to your father. We both know Thomas wouldn't have minded. Hell, he would have welcomed you as a permanent cete member. You could have stayed there with Jacob and been happy. Instead, what do you have? You went home, and from what Nico told me, you've been moping around."

"How can you say that I could have said no to my father?

You're the alpha now because you're your father's son."

"Not because I wanted to. I told the council no, but they insisted, and I had to agree. The way I see things, I understand why Jacob decided to break up with you. You asked him to change his life entirely, while you weren't even willing to think about changing yours. Jacob just wasn't that important to you, was he?"

"Of course he was important to me," Chris snapped.

"Yet you never even thought about telling your father you didn't want to be the next alpha."

"I did! I've been thinking about that for years. Don't you think I would already have told my father if it was at all possible?" Chris got to his feet. He couldn't stay in this room. He couldn't listen to what Josiah had to say, not anymore.

"Chris!" Nico yelled, but Chris didn't want to listen.

He rushed through the door and slammed it behind himself. He didn't know where to go, though, so he went to the car, slipping into the passenger seat.

He couldn't believe what Josiah had said to him. Did he really think Chris had a choice? Didn't he understand that wasn't true?

Chris buried his face in his hands. Josiah's words kept twirling into his head, and he couldn't stop thinking about them.

Had he had a choice? Had he given up Jacob and shown him he wasn't as important as being an alpha?

CHAPTER FOUR

"Now that the problem with the coyotes has been resolved, the human team wants to be shown around all of the territories in the forest," Thomas explained.

Jacob blinked. "You told them how impossible it is?" While they could visit coyote territory, and even most of the other territories, at least a few of the alphas would say no. It was going to be a fight, and it was a fight no one wanted.

Thomas winced. "I tried telling them. I'm pretty sure Luther would have listened, but he's not the one in charge, not really. He can't make that kind of decision. If his boss wants him to explore all the territories, then he has to do it."

Jacob crossed his arms over his chest. "So he's not actually a leader."

"He leads his team, but that's it. I don't think we understand how the humans work very well, but I suppose it's a bit like he has an alpha, and he has to follow their orders."

"That's going to be a problem."

"I know. We're all aware of it, but we can't say no."

"Well, I hope you'll find a way to make all the alphas open their territory." Jacob was sympathetic to Thomas's problem, but he didn't understand what it had to do with him. "I don't have a problem with them coming in cete territory, as long as you're okay with it. Is that why you're telling me this?"

Thomas grimaced. "It is, but I have another favor to ask from you."

"I'm not going to like this, am I?"

"I'm sorry. I thought you were the best man to do this,

though."

Jacob sighed. "Just tell me." The sooner he knew what was going on, the sooner he could deal with it.

"I talked with most of the alphas, and with the council. We've decided to assign two people to the human team. They're going to be two people who belong to different shifter groups, so the humans can see we *can* collaborate. You'll have to drive the human team around, talk with the various alphas, and show the humans the territories."

"So I take it that I'm one of those people?"

"You are."

"Who's the other one?" Jacob had a sneaking suspicion he knew who it was going to be, and that Thomas wasn't as innocent as he was trying to look.

"Chris Wiley. Alpha Wiley's son."

Jacob briefly closed his eyes. He couldn't yell at his alpha, no matter how much Thomas liked him. Most of the time, they were more like coworkers than boss and employee, but that didn't change the real situation. Thomas wasn't Jacob's boss. He was his alpha. "I know who Chris is, and you know it." He opened his eyes. "That's why you chose him."

"I don't know what you're talking about."

"You're trying to get me and Chris to get back together, but it's not going to work. He made his choice, and I made mine."

"Again, I have no idea what you're talking about."

"Why did you choose us, then? You could have chosen anyone else. Maybe Levi, since he has a foot in both the cete and the sleuth. Anyone else would have been better than me." And Chris. Jacob didn't want to spend any length of time with his ex.

Thomas stared at Jacob for a second. "Are you saying no?"

Jacob knew he could. Thomas wouldn't yell at him, and he wouldn't threaten him. That wasn't the kind of alpha he was. He wouldn't be happy, but Jacob suspected that he knew what he was doing, putting Jacob and Chris together.

Still, Thomas was Jacob's alpha. Could he really say no? Thomas wanted Jacob to be happy, and he knew Jacob was in love with Chris. He was playing matchmaker, and the thought made Jacob smile, even though it shouldn't have. "I'm not saying no," he began.

Thomas beamed. "Good. You can start as soon as possible."

"I wasn't finished."

Thomas arched a brow. "No? What else do you want to say?"

"That you shouldn't have too much hope for this. Yes, I'm still in love with Chris, and I suspect he loves me, too. Forcing us together isn't going to fix our relationship, though. Love wasn't enough, and that's because there are more important things than love."

Thomas's expression softened. "I'm not sure about that. Are there?"

"When you live in the forest, yes. You know that as well as I do. I'll work with Chris, but that's all that will happen. He went back home because he'll be the next alpha, and I couldn't leave my home."

"Why not? You never explained why you decided to stay here instead of going with him. I thought for sure you were going to leave me."

"I thought about it." God, how Jacob had thought about it. He'd spent countless nights away, wondering what he was supposed to do once Chris went home. He'd thought about it so many times that he'd lost count. Chris had never even thought about staying. He'd always believed Jacob would follow him, and Jacob had wanted to give him that. He couldn't, though.

"But you didn't go."

Jacob shook his head. "I couldn't. This is my home."

"And you weren't willing to leave it. You wanted Chris to leave *his* home, though."

"It's not that I wasn't willing to leave the cete. It's that I can't be an alpha mate."

"You don't exactly have the patience, but it can be learned."

"You don't understand. You've always known you were going to be an alpha, and you were raised that way. I'm no one. I'm pretty sure Chris's father wouldn't have been happy if I tried to become alpha mate. I'm surprised he was civil to me the other day."

"I think you're wrong about Dan. He might seem like a hard man, but he's not. He wants his sons to be happy."

"Yet he doesn't realize how unhappy Chris is." Jacob shouldn't have said it, but he knew Thomas wouldn't tell anyone, not even Dan.

"That bad, huh?"

"He talked to me about it a lot. Chris feels like he's only the alpha heir, nothing else. He doesn't like how his father can't see the son, the man, or even the carrier. He ignores all of that in his focus on getting Chris up to date and able to take his place once he retires."

Thomas grimaced. "I hope I didn't do the same thing with Alex."

"You didn't. I think the biggest difference here is that Alex *wants* to be the alpha. He wants to follow in your footsteps, to do as good a job as you do. Chris doesn't. He's been told he would be the alpha since he was a child, and he truly believes he doesn't have an alternative. That's why he didn't even mention that he might want to stay here to his father."

"You think Dan would have said no?"

"I don't know him well enough to guess what his reaction might be if Chris brought it up. Chris isn't going to risk it, though. He's wanted to make his father happy and to make him proud of him for most of his life. Leaving the clowder behind would mean that his father won't be proud of him, and he can't deal with that."

"I'm pretty sure Dan would be proud, whatever Chris does."

"We both know that's not true. Well, he might be proud of his son eventually, but in the beginning, he'd be angry. He'd make sure Chris knows it, and he'll try to change his mind."

"I'm sorry."

Jacob shook his head. "Don't be. You have nothing to do with this. If anything, you showed me and a lot of other people that your children's happiness comes before the alpha position or anything else. Alpha Wiley should be more like you, but unfortunately, he's not."

"Are you still okay with working with Chris? Because I can send someone else."

"I'll be fine." Jacob couldn't deny he was looking forward to spending time with Chris as much as he dreaded it. He still loved the man, even though he knew he would never have him. Those were complicated feelings to deal with, but he was going to have to learn.

"Chris? Can you come to my office?" Chris's father called out.

Chris had been lounging on the couch. His mother had asked him to spend more time in the rest of the house rather than being in his bedroom all the time — and he was wary. He didn't know what his father wanted, but he was sure it had to do with alpha business. That was the only reason his father talked to him these days.

He didn't want anything to do with his dad. He'd been thinking about what Josiah had told him the other day, and he still couldn't wrap his mind around those words. He didn't know whether or not Josiah was right. He wanted to think that wasn't the case, but maybe it was. Was the alpha position really more important to Chris than Jacob was?

No. It wasn't. Chris loved Jacob with all his heart, and he desperately wanted to go back to him. The fact that he couldn't didn't have anything to do with the alpha position, not in the way Josiah seemed to think. Chris had never wanted to be alpha, but it was his duty. He couldn't disappoint his father that way. He wanted his father to be proud, and that would only happen if he took his place once he retired. It would only happen if he became a good alpha like his father was right now.

That didn't mean Chris wasn't sad, worried, or angry. He wished things were different, but they weren't, no matter what Josiah thought. If Chris had a choice, he would leave the clowder today and head back to Jacob and beg him to take him back. That was never going to happen, though, and he had to accept it. Everyone had to. Chris was getting tired of people trying to push him and Jacob together. He understood why they did it, but they were wrong. Doing this was only going to hurt Chris and Jacob even more than they already were, and Chris didn't want that for Jacob.

Jacob deserved to be happy, even if it wasn't with Chris. Chris knew how much it would hurt to see Jacob with someone else, but eventually, he would have to deal with it.

He would once it was time to, and not one second sooner.

He pushed away from the couch. Even though he didn't want to know what his father wanted, he had to. If he didn't go, his father would try to find him, and that wouldn't end well.

Chris's father had never been violent, and Chris didn't think he was going to start now. Still, he was uncomfortable. His father knew what he'd left behind, what he'd sacrificed to come back home, yet he hadn't said much about it. He hadn't told Chris he understood how hard it was, how sad Chris was. He'd ignored all of that because he'd had what he wanted — Chris back home, working with him and training to be the next alpha.

Chris headed toward the office. His father was sitting behind his desk, but the door was open, and Chris stepped in. He briefly knocked on the door, making his father look up. "There you are. I'd like to talk to you. Close the door."

That wasn't going to be good. Whatever it was, he didn't want anyone else to hear, and Chris's stomach churned with nervousness.

He closed the door and moved toward the desk. He sat on the edge of one of the chairs on his side of it, leaning forward to. "Yes?"

"I have a job for you."

Chris blinked. This would be the first time his father trusted him to do any kind of work related to the alpha position. "You do?" Before, it would have made Chris happy. He would have loved that his father had faith in him. Now, though, he dreaded whatever was going to happen next.

"I talked to the other alphas and the council, and we've made a decision."

Chris blinked. "About what?"

His father frowned. "I told you yesterday that the human team wants to explore all the territories in the forest."

Right. "I didn't realize that was what you were talking about, but please, go on."

"As I said, the human team wants to meet every alpha and explore their territory. As far as I understood, they're not planning on invading private homes or anything like that. They just want to see how we live, and if we can effectively be peaceful."

"And the council agreed to this?"

"They don't have a choice. It's either that or the human team goes back home and tells their boss that we're not obeying orders. We have no way to know what will happen if they do that, so yes, we do have to obey."

"I see. Some of the alphas aren't going to be happy."

"We're all aware of that, which is why the council decided to send two shifters with them."

"What kind of shifters? I can think of at least a few territories, like the rodents and the skunks, who won't want *anyone* inside."

"But we're going to try. We can't allow anyone to go against the council's orders. That's why the council was created in the first place. We knew that we eventually would have to deal with humans, and we needed someone to do that for us. I'm sure those few alphas will understand that it's best for everyone if they just go along with it."

"And at the same time, the human team won't be allowed to go around on their own."

Chris's father beamed. "Exactly. I'm glad you understand." He got up from his chair. "Come on. Let's go."

Chris blinked. "Where are we going?"

"To cete territory."

Chris had no idea what was going on. "Why should we go there?"

"Because I didn't make this decision on my own. The council and all the alphas, or at least, all the ones who are working with us, were involved."

"I don't understand." Chris followed his father down the hallway.

"You'll understand once we get there."

Chris narrowed his eyes. "You're hiding something. Why? What's going on?"

"Chris." Chris's father stopped in the middle of the hallway and turned to look at him. "Do you trust me?"

Chris had no idea how to answer that. "Of course." And he did, more as an alpha than as a father, though.

His father nodded. "Then come with me. You'll understand soon enough. And before you continue protesting, I know what I'm doing. I didn't make this decision lightly."

"What decision?" Chris asked.

But his father was already walking away, and Chris's only choice was to follow him.

So he did.

They climbed into the car, and Chris's father headed out. Chris's stomach was churning, and he wanted to ask more questions. He knew his father wouldn't answer, though. Whatever he'd planned, he wanted Chris to stay in the dark until he revealed it.

His father had always believed that an alpha should be patient, and he was trying to teach Chris that. Most days, he was successful, but not always. Chris could already tell he wouldn't like whatever was going on, and he suspected that was one of the reasons his father didn't want to explain while they were alone. If there were other people around, especially another alpha, Chris would have to keep his anger in check. He couldn't be disrespectful, not to his father, and not to his alpha. Whatever his father was planning, Chris would have to go along with it.

Even if he didn't want to.

Jacob was *not* happy.

After telling him that he was going to have to work with Chris, Thomas had asked him to stick around. Apparently, Chris and his father were coming, and Jacob and Chris would have to see each other today. Well, they would have to see each other every day from now on if Thomas had his way, and apparently, he did.

Jacob had thought about arguing some more, but he knew it was pointless. Thomas was his alpha, even though he would have accepted a no from Jacob.

But Jacob didn't really want to say no, did he? A part of him never wanted to see Chris again, but another part, apparently, the bigger one, wanted to see him and never let him go. That second part had won for now, and Jacob didn't know what to do about it.

Seeing Chris again, and worse, working with him, would hurt. Chris wasn't going to change his mind and choose Jacob over his father suddenly. That would never happen, and Jacob was aware of that. It was one of the reasons he'd refused to go with Chris.

Yes, he could have gone and become an alpha mate, but he was thirty-four. He was an adult, and he wouldn't let Chris's father jerk him around the way he was doing with his son. Dan might be an alpha, but Jacob would have stood up to him, especially if it was for Chris. That wouldn't have gone down well with Dan, and eventually, Chris would have had to choose anyway.

He would have chosen his father even then. Jacob was convinced of that.

Chris was only a kid. Even though Jacob didn't fully understand the relationship between Chris and his father, he knew why Chris hadn't told his dad that he didn't want to be the alpha. He wanted to make his father proud, and it made sense. He was nineteen. His parents were still the most important people in his life. For a while, Jacob had thought he would take that place, but he'd been wrong. Now he had to deal with the consequences.

"You look like you're going to kill someone," Thomas said.

Jacob stared at him. "I'm tempted."

Of course, that made Thomas smile. "Were you thinking about killing *me*?"

Jacob shook his head. With any other alpha, he would have been afraid to answer. With Thomas, though, he didn't care.

He already knew Thomas wouldn't do anything. "In part."

"And the other part?"

"Dan," Jacob confessed.

Thomas grimaced. "I promise, he's not a bad man. I've been working with him for decades. We didn't grow up together, but we're around the same age, and when we followed our fathers to meetings and things like that, we spent time together. He only wants the best for the clowder and his sons."

"If that were the truth, Chris would be on his way right now."

"He's not a bad man, but it doesn't mean he's not blind to what's going on around him. I think that he's so used to everyone doing what he wants, especially when it comes to Chris, that he can't conceive that Chris doesn't want the same thing he does."

"He should open his eyes, then."

"Maybe if Chris steps forward and explains, things will be easier."

But Chris was never going to do that. He wanted to make his father proud, and that was the only thing that mattered to him.

They both heard the car stop in front of the house at the same time. They stared at each other, and Jacob swallowed. He was going to see Chris again today, and he would have to work with him daily for who knew how long. He needed to get hold of his feelings. He couldn't be this angry, not when it came to Chris or his father. Chris already knew that Jacob was still in love with him. He already knew what Jacob thought about this entire situation.

Nothing would change anyway.

Thomas got to his feet. "Stay here," he said before heading out.

Jacob was more than happy not to get up from his chair. He wasn't looking forward to facing Chris, especially after

Chris found out what Thomas and his father had been planning. Jacob didn't understand why Dan was going along with this. He knew Chris and Jacob were still in love with each other and that putting them together wasn't going to make things better. Thomas's decision made sense since he wanted Jacob and Chris to get back together. What was Dan getting from the situation, though? Why had he agreed to this?

Jacob supposed he was going to find out.

He heard the voices before he saw Chris and Dan. Chris wasn't speaking when they stepped into the office, but Dan and Thomas were close together, looking almost like two friends sharing a secret. That confused Jacob, but he didn't ask what was going on and instead stayed right where he was.

He saw the exact moment Chris noticed him. His eyes went wide, then they narrowed. He turned to his father, but he didn't ask the questions he obviously wanted to ask.

"Sit down," Dan told Chris.

Chris obeyed. He sat on the chair next to Jacob's, but he tried to put as much distance between them as he could. It was childish, but again, Chris was only nineteen.

Jacob had loved that, but not always. He enjoyed Chris's eagerness, the way he had of throwing himself into their relationship without pausing to think. He loved how spontaneous Chris was.

He didn't love it when Chris didn't think about what he was doing and made stupid decisions.

"Why are we here?" Chris asked.

His father turned to look at him. He sat on the edge of Thomas's desk, while Thomas went to sit behind it again. "I already told you about the two shifters we're going to have shadow the human team around," he started.

"What does it have to do with Jacob? Because it *has* something to do with him, doesn't it?"

Dan nodded. "It's why we're here. Thomas and I both

thought it would be a good idea for you and Jacob to work together with the human team."

Jacob held his breath and waited for the explosion.

"What the fuck?" Chris snapped.

His father's eyes narrowed. "Are you sure this is how you want to talk to Thomas and me?"

To Jacob's surprise, Chris paused. He took a deep breath, and his tone was calmer when he spoke again. "You can't be serious."

"We're extremely serious. You and Jacob will work together. We don't know for how long, but it's going to be a while before the human team can visit all the territories. You'll go with them, talk to the alphas, and explain what's going on, even though they already know. You'll keep an eye on the humans and make sure they don't stick their nose where they shouldn't."

"You could have chosen anyone. Why not Nico? Why does it have to be a bobcat and a badger?"

"This is the way things are going to go, Chris. It's not only a good opportunity to show the humans that we can work together without fighting, but it's also a chance to keep an eye on them, and more importantly, to see the territories we haven't been able to see yet. We still don't know if the skunks and the rodents have more carriers in their territories. We hope we found them all, but that's a possibility we have to accept. We also don't know what's going on in those territories. The skunks and the rodents could be abused, and if that's the case, the council will have to intervene. The only way for us to know about this is for some of us to see it with their own two eyes."

"And what's the human team going to think if that's what we find?"

"Hopefully, they'll see that the council is ready to step in and intervene to save the shifters who live in the forest. They already know that we take care of our own, even if it means going against some of the alphas."

"I still think someone else would have been better."

Chris wasn't going to back down, was he? Jacob wasn't surprised, but now, he realized why Thomas had told him before Dan and Chris arrived. He wanted Jacob to make things easier for both him and Chris, which meant that Jacob was going to have to intervene.

Dammit.

Chris needed his father to change his mind. He couldn't work with Jacob. This sounded like it was going to be a long project, and Chris couldn't do it.

His father was aware of that, though. That had to be a reason he chose Chris of all people to work with Jacob. There had to be a reason for Thomas to choose Jacob, too. If what Thomas and Chris's father had said was true, the entire council and most of the alphas had met and made this decision together. Why a bobcat and a badger?

Chris didn't understand. Surely his father didn't want him and Jacob to get back together. Why would he want that? He knew Chris was miserable without Jacob, but he also knew that Jacob would be a distraction. Hell, the entire situation would be distracting.

"I'm supposed to shadow you and learn how to be an alpha," he told his father, still hoping to make him change his mind.

"And like I just said, this will be a good opportunity for you to start working on your own. You've been shadowing me for almost five years. I'm pretty sure you already know everything there is to know about being an alpha. Now, it's time you start putting it into practice. This is an important job. We need to know what's going on in skunk and rodent territories. It's imperative. We also have to keep the human team happy, unless you want them to run to their boss and tell them to burn the forest to the ground. Is that what you want?"

Chris looked away. "Of course not. I don't think I'm the best person to do this job, though."

"And I think you are. It's time you have responsibilities and for you to learn to deal with the humans. I doubt this is the only time they'll be sent to the forest. They need to reassert their power over us, and this is how they do it, at least for now."

It was a terrible idea, even though Chris understood everything his father was saying. In any other situation, Chris would have been eager to please his father and show him he could do this. Working with Jacob was going to be hell, though.

Chris was still in love with him, but he was also still angry. He didn't want to spend time with him. It was too soon.

Chris's father sighed. "I don't know what you're thinking, Chris, but I'm sure you understand why this is so important, and why I chose you. Still, if you're actually against it so much that you're not going to do a good job, I'll assign your brother to it. It wouldn't be a bad thing for him to learn to deal with all of this anyway."

Chris was surprised by the suggestion. He was also torn. He wanted to say yes, but he also wanted to make his father proud. Doing this successfully would be the best way to make that happen. It would be a way to show his father that he could become the alpha, and that he was ready.

He wasn't, and his father was aware of that, but still. This would be a good experience.

Chris sucked in a breath. "I'll do it."

His father smiled, obviously pleased. "Good. I knew I could count on you."

And that was all that mattered, wasn't it? Chris's father had gotten what he wanted. His son was obeying his orders, and he'd put up only a minimal amount of fuss. "You always can."

Chris's father turned to Thomas. "What now?"

Thomas straightened in his chair. "Everyone here already knows what they have to do. Chris, Jacob, you'll meet the human team in two days. I'll call them today and explain what's going to happen. They already know some territories will be harder to deal with than others, so they expect it. I'll also try to contact the rodents and skunk alphas, but we all know that's not going to be good. They'll push back, and it'll take a lot for them to agree to let the humans in."

"So you think it's possible?" Jacob asked.

"I hope it is. It's the only way for us to get rid of the humans. We can't fight them. Even if we got rid of this team, they would send someone else, and next time, it wouldn't be to talk. We can't afford the humans to start a war against us. There are a lot more of them than there are of us."

And they would massacre the shifters in the forest if they decided it was a good idea.

Chris swallowed. He hoped Thomas and the rest of the alphas would be able to convince the two alphas who didn't want to obey, but he wasn't holding his breath. Still, in the meantime, they had enough territories to explore to last them several weeks. Hopefully, that would make the humans happy. They were obviously aware that something was going on with the skunks and rodents, but as long as they didn't ask, Chris wouldn't volunteer any information.

"The two of you should talk about how you're going to work together," Thomas said as he rose from his chair. "Want something to drink?" he asked Chris's father.

"That would be great, yes." Chris's father looked at him. "Will everything be okay here?"

"Of course. We're going to work together, so why not start today, right?"

Both Chris and Jacob watched as the two men left the office. Then Chris turned to Jacob. "How could you allow this to happen?"

Jacob blinked, then, his expression turned angry. "What do you mean? Do you think I had a say in it?"

"I know you did. Thomas wouldn't have forced you to do this if you didn't want to."

"That doesn't mean I could say no when he asked me. He's still my alpha, Chris. You of all people should understand that, considering the way you always say yes to your father."

Chris jerked back. Jacob couldn't have hurt him more if he had hit him. "I do *not* always do what my father wants me to do."

Jacob snorted. "Could have fooled me."

Chris twisted in his chair. "What do you want from me?"

Jacob stared at him for a moment. Then, he shook his head. "I don't know. What I do know is that I don't want to work with you."

"Well, the feeling is mutual. There's not much we can do about it, though, is there?"

"Your father offered to have your brother do this instead of you. You could have said yes to that."

"And you could tell Thomas you don't want to do this. He'll assign someone else to the task."

They stared at each other. Neither of them was willing to compromise, and Chris knew it was going to be a problem. It had already been. It was the reason they'd broken up.

But as it was, they were going to work together for weeks. Chris wasn't sure whether they'd both be alive at the end of it, or if one of them would kill the other. He already felt the urge to strangle Jacob right now.

CHAPTER FIVE

Today was the day for Jacob and Chris to start working together. They were meeting the human team for the first time in a few hours, but they'd agreed to meet together ahead of time. Jacob had insisted because he knew they needed to talk. They couldn't afford to fight when they shouldn't, and that included in front of the human team. One of the reasons he and Chris were supposed to work together was to show the humans that shifters, even different species, could live peacefully. It wouldn't work if they were at each other's throats the entire time.

He wasn't looking forward to any of this. There wasn't a lot he could do, though. He'd already agreed, and so had Chris.

Jacob had been sure Chris would say no to his father, especially when Dan had offered to ask Nico to do it instead of him. But instead of saying yes to that, Chris had agreed to work with Jacob, and Jacob hoped it wouldn't be a disaster. Their relationship had been. They couldn't compromise, and working together, just like relationships, included compromises.

"You're moping," Raven said.

Jacob glared at him. "Why are you here so early in the morning? Don't you have things to do?"

Raven grinned and wrapped his fingers around a steaming mug of coffee. "Nothing better than to annoy you."

Jacob sighed. He hadn't planned on becoming Raven's friend, but Raven had pushed his way into his life. Raven was a secretive man, and Jacob hadn't expected him to latch onto him. He had, though, and Jacob wasn't sorry—most of the time.

"So why are you moping?" Raven asked.

"I'm surprised you don't already know."

"Maybe I do, and I just want you to tell me anyway."

"Chris and I have to work together. We're meeting with the human team later today, and we have to show them around the forest."

"I don't know what you're most worried about, though. Is it about working with Chris, or about the territories who won't welcome the humans?"

Jacob wasn't sure. He wanted to say the second one, and he *was* worried about that, but all his thoughts were focused on Chris. He wanted Chris so badly, and working with him would make things even harder on both of them.

Jacob knew Chris still loved him. They hadn't broken up because they weren't in love. They'd broken up because they couldn't compromise, because they couldn't find a way to be together that would keep both of them happy. Jacob still hoped they could have a second chance and that working with Chris would make him desire more. But he wasn't convinced. Neither of them would go back on their decision, which meant that this was it. It was what the future would be like, without Chris, yet here Chris was again, barging into Jacob's life.

There was no getting rid of it him, was there?

"I'm worried about both," Jacob finally admitted.

"Well, at least you know you can talk to me."

"If you're not going to help me, maybe I should stop. What did you want again?"

Raven raised his mug. "Coffee. What else?"

"I guess that answers the question of why you're here. You need anything else?"

Raven stared at Jacob for a bit. "You know, I still don't understand why you and Chris can't be together."

Jacob huffed. He didn't want to talk about this again. He'd already talked about it too many times, and if he had his way, he would forget all about Chris. "I don't want to leave the cete, and he can't leave the clowder. What's so complicated to understand?"

"What I understand is that both of you have issues. He wants to make his father proud, and he thinks that the only way to make that happen is to become the alpha. I don't understand you, though. You're convinced that you're not good enough to be alpha mate. It's true you don't have that much patience, but that can be learned. You *could* be an alpha mate if you truly wanted to be with Chris."

Jacob tightened his hand over the porch railing and looked out at the forest. He knew Raven wasn't entirely wrong. If he tried, he could become the alpha mate. He could do it, for the love of Chris.

But things were more complicated than that. "Do you know my parents?" he asked.

Raven blinked. "What do they have to do with the situation?"

"Do you know them?"

"Of course. They live around here, right?"

Jacob nodded. "They live in badger territory."

"But you don't see them often. I'm pretty sure you spend more time at the Bishop house than with your parents."

"I see them once or twice a year if even that."

Raven's expression shifted. "Are they the reason you think you're not good enough to be an alpha mate?"

Jacob had to look away again. He didn't want to look Raven in the eyes when he explained why he *knew* he wasn't good enough. "My father isn't an easy man to get along with. He's hard, doesn't show affection. I don't think he's ever hugged me."

"And your mother?"

Jacob turned to glare at Raven. "I was talking about my father. Do you want to hear the story or not?"

Raven made a show of zipping his lips and throwing away the key. Jacob shook his head, but he was amused.

He turned around to face the forest. "Like I said, my father doesn't show affection. I'm not sure he's ever loved me, and I'm not saying that only because he doesn't hug me. He's very demanding. He didn't do much with his life, staying a guard for the cete until he retired, and he wants me to do better. The problem is that he went about it the wrong way. He kept berating me for not being good enough. He wanted me to work harder, to climb higher in the cete hierarchy."

"You're head of security. Isn't that good enough for him?"

"Apparently not, since the last time I went to see my parents, he told me I need to work harder."

"So your belief that you're not good enough comes from that. Didn't your mother ever say anything?"

Jacob shook his head. "She never wanted to make my father unhappy, and talking back to him would have done just that. She never defended me."

There was a pause before Raven asked, "Is your father abusive?"

"He's never been violent, if that's what you're asking."

"It doesn't mean he's not abusive. There's emotional abuse, too, and if at thirty-four, you're convinced you're not good enough to be with Chris, then maybe that's what happened."

Jacob heard Raven move behind him, but he didn't turn around. He wasn't surprised to see Raven lean against the railing right next to him. Raven didn't look at Jacob, staring at the forest instead.

"I don't know that he was abusive," Jacob said. "Maybe he was. Maybe I'm overreacting. The point is that no matter what happened, I still feel like I can't be the man Chris deserves. And I know it's true. You might be right when you say it's because of my father, but come on. Chris is going to be an alpha one day. Can you imagine me as an alpha mate? I'd tear someone's head off if they looked at him the wrong way. That's not what an alpha mate has to do."

Raven finally looked at Jacob. "Patience can be learned. You'll never be the most patient man in the world, but it doesn't mean you have to stay away from Chris."

"I have to. He deserves better." He deserved better when it came to Jacob's age, to the kind of person he was, to what he could do with his life. Jacob was content with what he was doing, no matter what his father thought. He didn't want to be more. Besides, he didn't know what more he *could* be. He was head of security at only thirty-four. What more did his father want?

Jacob didn't know because he'd never asked. He knew that by now, his father liked to rant about how he wasn't good enough only because it was a habit. That habit had destroyed Jacob's self-esteem, even though he'd been doing his best to rebuild it.

He obviously hadn't done as good a job as he thought.

Chris looked at himself in the mirror. He looked okay, but he wanted to look incredible for Jacob. He wanted to show Jacob that he didn't need him in his life, that he was doing good even without him.

It was a lie.

No matter how many times he told himself things had gone the only way they could go, he couldn't stop thinking about Jacob. The fact that they were going to work together wasn't going to help. Chris would have to keep his feelings in check and make sure Jacob didn't understand how much he missed him, and how much he still loved him.

It was going to be hell, but Chris could do this. He had to show his father that he could. His dad counted on him to keep the situation in check, to make sure that the human team didn't stick their noses where they shouldn't, and to explore to territories the council didn't have a hold on yet. It was a daunting task, but it was one Chris knew he could do.

A knock on the door made him jerk. He stared for a moment, wondering who was behind it. It could be any of his sisters, his mother, or his brother. He doubted it would be his father, since he knew Chris was leaving the house soon to head to cete territory. Chris doubted he would want to talk to anyone who was there, but he had to leave his bedroom through the door, so he couldn't avoid them.

"Yes?" he called out.

The door creaked open, and Nico slipped in. He closed it behind himself, then he turned around and pressed his back against it. He looked Chris up and down and frowned. "This wasn't what I thought you would wear for your reunion with Jacob."

And *this* was one of the reasons Chris hadn't wanted to talk to his brother or any other family member. "It's not a reunion. We're working together." Chris looked at his reflection. He was wearing a button-down shirt and a pair of dress pants. He hoped it would be enough to impress the human team, even though every time he'd seen them, they'd been in comfortable clothes. They usually wore fatigues or some kind of uniform. Chris, on the other hand, would have to stick with dress pants. His father would pitch a fit otherwise.

"I'm sure things will work out between the two of you eventually," Nico said.

Chris didn't want his brother to keep his hopes up. He also didn't want himself to keep his hopes up. "Will you please stop thinking I can get back with Jacob? And please, stop mentioning him. We're never getting back together."

"There's no reason you can't."

"There's every reason we can't!" Chris snapped. "Will you stop talking about him? I don't want to hear about Jacob. I never want to hear his name again, and if I had a choice, I wouldn't be working with him."

Nico lowered his head. Chris had been able to see his brows were furrowed and his eyes narrowed, though. He'd hurt his brother, and he wished he hadn't.

If this was the kind of alpha he was going to be, then maybe he should step back. He couldn't lash out when someone told him what they were thinking. He knew Nico only wanted the best for him, which was why he was trying to push him back toward Jacob. He wanted Chris to be happy, just as much as Chris wanted himself to be happy. It wasn't going to work, though, and while it was frustrating to have everyone asking him about Jacob, he needed to keep his temper in check.

He took a deep breath. "I apologize for snapping at you."

Nico looked up, one brow arched. "You don't have to talk that way to me. I'm your brother, not just a clowder member."

"I know. I still shouldn't have talked to you like that."

"You're right. You shouldn't have. I was only trying to help."

Chris rubbed his face with his hands. "I'm going to be a bad alpha, aren't I? If I snap at you the way I did just because you're concerned, I'm going to be shit at this." He was starting to suspect that eventually, if nothing changed, he would resent the clowder for not being able to live his life the way he wanted to. That was the worst thing that could happen, but he didn't know what to do about it.

He was in love with Jacob, and he grieved the loss of the life he could have had with him. Hopefully, that would change in time, but it wasn't changing fast enough. Chris had to focus on working with his father, and now, with the human team. He couldn't start thinking about Jacob and what they could have had together.

"You're not going to be shit at it," Nico said. He touched Chris's elbow.

Chris lowered his hands to look at him. "I'm starting to think I will be. We both know I don't want to do this. Is there anything worse than an alpha who resents the shifters he's supposed to guide and take care of?"

"You're not wrong there, but that doesn't have to be the kind of alpha you'll be. I know this is hard. I'd never seen you so happy as you were when we were at the Bishop house with Jacob, and I think it's a pity you won't try to fix things with him."

Chris hesitated. He hadn't told anyone about this, but Nico was his brother. He wouldn't tell anyone. "It's not just that."

"What else is it, then?"

"I don't want to take Dad's place. I don't want to be in charge of the clowder. The thought is terrifying, and I've never wanted it. That's why I was so happy at the Bishop house. I didn't have any responsibilities. I was free to be a normal nineteen-year-old guy, and I want that feeling back. I'm not even twenty, Nico, yet I have so many responsibilities on my shoulders that I feel I'm going to break."

Nico grimaced. "I wish I could take that away from you. I wish I could take your place."

Chris shook his head. "You don't wish that. Trust me. You wouldn't be happy being the future alpha, just like I'm not. It's too much." Too much for Chris, anyway. He wasn't entirely sure Nico wouldn't do a better job, but it was a moot point. Chris was the eldest son, and as such, it was his duty to become alpha.

"You could tell Dad you don't want to be the next alpha. I would take your place."

"I can't. Dad has put all his hopes in me, and I won't

disappoint him."

"He wouldn't be disappointed if you could live your life happier. That's what he wants, Chris. He wants you and I to be happy, and he would say something if he knew you weren't."

Chris knew that wasn't the case. Nico didn't spend as much time with her father as Chris did. "Dad is only interested in me because I'm the future alpha. He wants me to be perfect, which is what he's been working on since I was a teen." And Chris knew he'd been lucky his father had waited that long. He'd wanted to start when Chris was a child, but Chris's mom had told him no. She wanted Chris to be able to be a teenager, but even that hadn't lasted long.

At fifteen, he'd stopped having friends. Between the classes at the tiny clowder school and the lessons he got from his father, he just hadn't had the time. He and Nico had become even closer once that happened, but Nico still had an outside life.

Chris didn't. Becoming alpha was his entire life, or at least it had been until he got to the Bishop house. That had been both the best and the worst thing in his life. He'd known what having a normal life was like, but he'd had to leave it behind, and now, that knowledge tortured him.

He swallowed. There was no point whining about it. Things were the way they were, and there was no changing them. Chris had to focus on that instead of what he could have had because he would never get it.

Jacob looked up when he heard the sound of a car. He'd never seen Chris drive, but he knew he could. He wasn't surprised to see Chris was alone this time. It wouldn't have made sense for Dan to be there, too, and Jacob was relieved.

He didn't hate Dan, but he didn't like him. He thought that

the man was too focused on having an heir — on making Chris a perfect alpha — to see that his son wasn't happy. Knowing that wasn't going to change anything, and he was trying not to hold it against Dan every time he saw him, but it wasn't easy. He could see how unhappy Chris was, and if he could see it even though he hadn't known Chris long, so should his father. That wasn't the case, but Jacob had to forget about it.

Chris parked his car in front of Thomas's house. This was where they'd agreed to meet, because Jacob didn't want Chris at his home. Well, he didn't want him there in this situation. Any other time, he would have been over the moon to have Chris in his personal space. They could have shared the house if Chris had decided to stay with the cete, but instead, he'd gone home, and both their hearts had been broken. It would be too hard to see him in the house as if he belonged there, and Jacob wasn't ready for that.

He waited on the porch, staring at Chris as he got out of the car and slammed the door shut. Chris looked around, and his gaze landed on Jacob. Jacob couldn't tell what he was thinking, and he kept his expression neutral. He didn't want Chris to think he was happy to see him, even though in part, he was.

The other part was torture, though. Seeing Chris and working with him wasn't going to be easy, but they'd get through it.

Chris climbed the porch steps and nodded at Jacob. "Good morning."

"Good morning."

Chris looked around again. "You wanted me here early. Why?"

"I thought we should talk."

They stared at each other for a bit. It looked like neither one of them wanted to take the first step, but Jacob was the one who'd asked for this. "We need to talk about us," he said.

At the same moment, Chris asked, "What did you want to talk about?"

Jacob huffed. "Us."

Chris finally looked away. "There's no us."

"You're right. There isn't, not anymore, but we're being forced to work together. I don't want it to be a disaster, which means that we have to come to an understanding. You know how we are. When one of us gets angry, we start yelling at each other. That wouldn't make the best impression on the human team, and we can't afford that."

"I promise not to yell, if that's what you're asking. I know it was always my fault."

"That's a good start, but we both know it's not going to be easy. You'll get frustrated and probably angry at me."

Chris straightened. "Are you saying I can't do this?"

"You can do anything you want." Including leaving the clowder behind, but Jacob didn't add that bit. "I like to think we're friends."

Chris snorted. "I wouldn't call us friends."

"All right. Then we're friendly. That's all there is to it, though, and this is a job. We're going to do it, and then we'll go our separate ways."

They both knew that was a lie. They would probably never be friends. They couldn't be, not when they still loved each other. The only thing Jacob wanted to do right now was to gather Chris into his arms and kiss him. He kept his hands to himself, though. He couldn't afford this to be a disaster.

Their feelings wouldn't disappear anytime soon. They had to deal with them, and with the human team. They had to be professional, and Jacob wasn't sure they could be.

"All right. We can do that," Chris agreed.

"We'll be professional, and that's it. We can't talk about our personal life while we're with the human team."

Chris shrugged. "Why should we? This is work and

nothing more, isn't it?"

Jacob was saved from having to answer by the sound of a car approaching. He and Chris both turned to look at it, and Jacob was both relieved and anxious at the sight of the human team arriving.

They weren't bad people, not from what he'd seen. He hadn't talked to all of them, but he knew what had happened when Seamus had been in labor. Everyone in the forest knew. He was relieved that Luther, the team leader, had agreed to take a step back and listen to Thomas. That meant there was a chance the human team didn't hate shifters, and they were trying to understand. It still wasn't easy, though.

Humans and shifters were different, but not that much. The main thing that put them apart was the fact that humans were free to live where they wanted. The shifters in the forest, on the other hand, were stuck there. They would never be able to leave because humans didn't want them to. It wasn't an easy thing to swallow, which was why most shifters didn't like humans.

Jacob was going to have to deal with them. He hoped these humans were good people, but he couldn't be sure, no matter what he'd seen.

The humans climbed out of the car. There were only four of them left, plus their team leader, after one of them had been kicked out. That was one more reason Jacob had to trust the team leader. As soon as he'd realized what had happened, he'd fired the guy who had tried to sabotage the mission along with Jacqueline. They'd both wanted the forest to burn, although for different reasons, and they'd worked together to make that happen. Luckily for the shifters in the forest, Luther had a brain. He'd understood what had happened, and he'd made the right decision.

Now, he got out of the car, followed by two women and two men. They stood there for a moment, and Jacob decided to make things easier on them. He might not like what was happening, but he knew that the humans hadn't chosen to be here. They had to obey orders, which was why they hadn't left yet. Thomas had told him that Luther was a good man who didn't want to do this since he could tell that to the shifters were best left alone, but he had to answer to his boss, and there was no getting around this.

Jacob climbed down the porch steps. He approached Luther, one hand out. "I'm Jacob. This is Chris, and we've both been assigned to show you around the forest."

Luther nodded. "Luther," he said, shaking Jacob's hand. "I'm pretty sure I've seen you around here."

"You would be right. I'm the head of cete security."

"And they can spare you so you can show us around?"

Jacob shrugged. "I might be head of security, but things mostly run smoothly on their own. Besides, the council wants to know what's happening in the territories, and sometimes, we can't trust the alphas to be honest."

Luther's eyebrows quirked. "I see." He turned around. "These are Miriam and Suzanne, and Dean and Marlowe," he said, pointing at the other four humans.

Jacob nodded at them. They hovered there as if waiting for something to happen.

"So. Where are we starting?" Luther asked.

Jacob opened his arms. "I thought the cete would be perfect since we're already here. I know you've seen a bit of it already, so I'll finish showing you around, and you can ask any questions you have."

Luther smiled. "That sounds good. We can start anytime you're ready."

"You don't want coffee or anything like that?"

"We already had breakfast. Don't worry about us."

Jacob sucked in a breath. "Let's start, then."

Chris was nervous. He didn't know if he and Jacob would be able to stay away from each other and be professional, or if they could trust the humans. It was obvious Jacob already knew them, at the very least from sight, but that wasn't the case for Chris.

Chris's father had told him everything he could about the human team, but it wasn't a lot, and not enough for Chris to know if he could trust them. He *did* trust Jacob, though. That would never change, no matter what happened between them. He decided to follow Jacob's lead, especially since they were in badger territory for the day. Besides, he was curious about it. He'd spent a lot of time in the Bishop house, but he hadn't been allowed to explore. It had been too dangerous. Now was his chance to do so.

It wasn't going to be easy, though. This was the place in which Chris could have lived if he'd decided to stay with Jacob. He felt like he'd lost it, and it hurt. But there was no way out of it, so he straightened his shoulders and listened to Luther and Jacob talk.

"You haven't introduced your co-worker," Luther said.

Chris's cheeks heated. He was right — he hadn't introduced himself. He shouldn't have waited for Jacob to do it, either. "I'm Chris. Chris Wiley, Alpha Wiley's son."

"What kind of shifter are you?" Suzanne asked.

"A bobcat."

She nodded, looking impressed. Chris thought he knew what she was thinking about. He looked like a normal nineteen-year-old guy. He was thin and short, so people didn't expect him to be dangerous. He would be if he shifted, though.

Not that he was going to today.

"Now that everyone's been introduced, let's start," Jacob said.

He walked away from Thomas's house, and everyone

followed him. Chris made sure to keep his distance but also not look like he was angry. He was, but not at Jacob, or at least, not entirely.

"How many people are there in the cete?" Luther asked.

"Do you really need that answer? We usually don't tell people how many members we have," Jacob said.

To Chris's surprise, instead of snapping, Luther smiled. "I guess I don't. Just an estimate will be fine."

"Well, there were only around twenty of us in the beginning."

"What you mean by beginning?"

"Before Levi and Dimitri got married."

"You're going to have to explain who they are. I'm pretty sure I've heard Levi's name, but that's all I know."

"Levi is Thomas's second son. He married Dimitri, who is the next bear alpha."

"They got married even though they're not the same animal?" Marlowe asked.

Jacob barely looked at him. "Of course. It happens often. Once, most marriages were arranged when it came to the alpha family. It was used to create alliances and things like that."

"Is that why Levi and Dimitri got married?" Luther asked. He sounded displeased by that suggestion.

"Not entirely. Levi is a carrier. You know about them, right?"

"We also know about the laws that were in place until recently."

"Well, he was over twenty-six. It was dangerous for him not to be married, which was why Thomas gently pushed him to choose someone. He wouldn't have cared even if Levi had chosen someone else, but he was hoping to make an alliance with the bears. Luckily for us, things worked out, and Dimitri and Levi fell in love."

"How does that work? Where do they live?"

"In bear territory since Dimitri is the future alpha. They visit often, though, and now that the cete and the sleuth are united, bears and badgers can move around both territories freely. That's one of the reasons we have more members now. Some bears have decided to move into badger territory, while a few badgers went to the sleuth. Then there are the other shifters."

"What do you mean?"

"Alex, the future badger alpha, got married. You've met Seamus."

Jacob smiled, and Chris wanted to kiss him. Jacob didn't smile often, and every time he did, it was like a gift. Chris had worked hard to make it happen more often when they were together, but now, Jacob barely smiled at all.

"Right. He's the guy who gave birth that time."

One of the humans snickered, and Luther turned around to glare at them.

"You'll excuse us, but we're still getting used to men being able to get pregnant and giving birth," Luther explained.

Jacob nodded. "I understand. Anyway, Seamus isn't a badger. There are other kinds of shifters living with us, mostly because Thomas is generous and doesn't want anyone to feel like they don't have a home."

"He sounds like a good alpha."

"He is. I'm relieved I don't have to work for anyone else."

Chris could hear the bitterness in those words. He knew what Jacob was referring to. If Jacob had agreed to become alpha mate, he would have had to move away from the cete and in with the clowder. That was one of the reasons he'd broken up with Chris. Chris knew there was more than one, though, and he wanted to prod and poke, but now wasn't the time. He and Jacob had agreed to be professional during this, and they were going to be.

"So the cete doesn't have any problems?" Luther asked.

"It depends on what you mean by *problems*. Every shifter group has problems."

"I mean some of the bigger ones I've heard about. I know the men who get pregnant have been abused in some shifter groups."

"The carriers. Yes, they were."

"But Thomas was one of the people who pushed to help and save them, wasn't he?"

"You're well-informed. He did. Like I said, he's a good alpha. I wouldn't be working for him otherwise. He doesn't want anyone to suffer, especially not for something they can't help. It's one of the reasons he didn't force Levi to get married. He knew it would be dangerous if Levi didn't, but he wanted Levi to be happy."

"I see. Do some of the carriers you rescued live here?"

Chris held his breath. He didn't know how much Jacob was supposed to share with the humans. Jacob might trust Luther, but Chris he wasn't sure how far. Luther was a newcomer, and he wasn't a shifter.

"They do. I won't give you details on that, though. They're here for a reason, and we can't afford for anyone to find them. The council has most of the forest under control, but there are still a few alphas who don't like being under their thumb."

Luther smirked. "Which is one of the reasons you agreed to do this. Because you want to check their territories and make sure they're not abusing anyone else."

"The only reason I agreed to do this was that Thomas insisted."

Luther chuckled. "I see. I know no shifter is happy about my team being here, and I understand why. I can't make any promises, especially not since I'm not the one making decisions, but I'm not trying to sabotage you. I've seen a lot since I arrived, and I don't think you're dangerous, not to the humans outside the forest. I have to obey my orders, though, which is why I'm doing this."

"I understand. I have my orders, too."

"Then you do understand. I don't want to be here. I don't want to disturb anyone's lives. I have to, though, and I'm grateful to the two of you for agreeing to do this."

Chris didn't know what to make of those words. He wanted to trust Luther. He wanted to believe what he was saying and that the humans would eventually leave and never come back.

He knew that wouldn't be the case, though. The humans had remembered they'd locked shifters up in the Allegheny forest, and they were poking at them again. Chris had no clue how the world outside the forest was, not beyond what he'd seen on TV, and he couldn't help but wonder why the humans were suddenly interested in the shifters who lived here.

Chapter Six

"I think it's time to visit skunk territory," Luther said.

Jacob stared at him. He'd expected something like this to happen. Luther was aware of the fact that the rodents and the skunks were the ones creating more problems, and he was curious about them. He also seemed to be the kind of man who would want to make sure no one was abused in those territories, very much like Thomas had. Jacob couldn't blame him, but he wanted him to be aware of how hard that was going to be.

"It's not that easy," he said.

They'd taken a few days to explore cete territory. It was one of the biggest in the forest, although most of it was woods. They'd steered clear of the Bishop house, but Luther and his team had seemed more than happy to be in a relaxed situation. Their little group, along with Chris and Jacob, had talked a lot, and they worked together well. Jacob and Chris weren't part of the team, but it almost felt like they were, and Jacob was relieved.

He'd expected the humans to be argumentative and go against everything Jacob and Chris had to say. They had a lot of questions, but none of them were mean or asked in anger, which was all Jacob cared about. They seemed especially curious about carriers, although that made sense, since apparently no human men could get pregnant. The human team only had a few experiences with pregnant carriers, and none of them had been great. Seamus had been in labor, while Kari, well, was Kari. He would have rather torn their heads off than talk to them about his baby, so it was a good thing they hadn't asked him many questions.

"I understand. I remember what you told me about the skunks and the rodents, and while I enjoyed exploring cete territory very much, it's time we moved to someone else."

"We could go to the bobcats," Chris suggested.

"We could. I'll understand if you need time to contact the skunk alpha. I do need you to remember we have to explore the entire forest, no matter how much some people won't like it."

"We understand," Jacob said. "This is going to need a bit of preparation, though. We need to try to contact the skunks and to explain what's happening. We've been trying to do just that since you decided you wanted to explore the forest, but they're not easy to reach, and neither are the rodents. We also can't barge in. They could attack, and that's the last thing we need."

"That doesn't mean the forest isn't at peace, though," Chris added. "Those two are the last alphas who disagree with the council. They want to cling to the traditions, even if they're horrible ones. We're working to make them change their minds, and eventually, we're hoping to put better alphas and council members in place. In the meantime, though, they're the minority, and it's a good thing."

"I agree," Luther said. "We can wait to visit those territories, but from what you've been saying, I doubt a phone call is going to change their minds."

He wasn't wrong. Jacob knew that Thomas and a few other alphas had tried contacting the skunk and rodent alphas without success. The rodents seemed more inclined, but Jacob knew that the new alpha was having a hard time controlling them. He was only one man, and he had his work cut out for him. He was young, but he was trying. "We might have a better outcome with the rodents," Jacob said.

"Yes?" Luther asked.

"It's complicated, but the old alpha was a mean one. He abused carriers and everyone else. There was a new alpha, but he was killed. There's yet another one now, and he's doing his best, but it's not easy when you have the entire world and mischief against you."

Luther's eyebrows rose. "That does sound like a complicated situation."

"We're handling it, though. We'll send him help if he asks for it, but he's the alpha. He needs to try to stand up to the mischief on his own. Otherwise, they'll never respect him."

"Shifters are more complicated than just humans who can become an animal, aren't they?" Luther asked.

"We are. I don't have much comparison, since you're the only humans I know, but we live following different rules. We're humans, yes, but we're *also* animals. That's why we have alphas and betas and things like that."

"This is so interesting," Miriam said.

Jacob wasn't sure he liked the feeling of being studied and examined, but he didn't say anything about it. He also didn't want to think about how he and Chris had worked together to convince Luther to let go of the skunks for now. He'd never thought much about working with Chris. As soon as he'd realized that choosing him would mean that he would be alpha mate, he'd stopped thinking about them that way. He couldn't help but wonder if this would have happened if he *had* gone with Chris, though.

Spending time with Chris was reminding him of how much they still loved each other. Jacob was a mess, although he was working hard not to show it. He knew Chris was watching him. He was watching Chris, after all. It hurt every time he started reaching for Chris before remembering that he couldn't touch him the way he wanted.

They weren't together, but it almost felt like they were.

They'd been forced to see each other every day for the past few days, and it was only the beginning. They were done with cete territory, and they'd started on sleuth territory. Jacob was pretty sure Luther wouldn't back down and that he'd want to visit the skunks once that was over, which meant that he and Chris were going to have to talk to the skunk alpha and try to convince him.

Jacob wasn't looking forward to it. He would bring it up during the next meeting he had with Thomas. He thought that another alpha, or even better, a council member, would more easily convince the skunk alpha to let them in. As for the rodents, well, no one knew what was happening in that territory. They'd gone through three alphas in a short time. The council hadn't intervened when the second one had been killed because the rodents had insisted it was an accident, even though it hadn't been, since Kari had killed him.

This wasn't any different. Jacob had no clue who the new alpha was, and he was going to have to ask Thomas about it. Hopefully, Thomas would have answers, and things would go the way they should. Jacob didn't know what Luther would do if they weren't allowed into those two territories. He only had four people with him, so it wasn't like they could force their way inside, but still. Luther could create problems for the entire forest if the skunks and the rodents didn't behave, and that wasn't something Jacob wanted to think about.

Luther could ruin everyone's lives. Jacob prayed that what he and Chris were showing him meant that he would think twice about it, but he couldn't be sure. He liked Luther, but he couldn't read him.

He had to hope that this was enough, but when had *he* ever been enough?

Chris trailed behind Luther and Jacob. He couldn't stop

staring, and he hoped the other humans wouldn't notice. They would no doubt have questions if they did—asking questions was all they did after all—and Chris wasn't up to answering those.

He was still in love with Jacob. He'd always known that, but it was the first time he truly realized how much he'd lost by not compromising with him. Now that they were forced to work together, he could see how well they would have done it at the clowder, or maybe at the cete if Chris had agreed to stay. They would have been happy, but now, they weren't.

He sighed. There was nothing he could do. Even though he wanted to, the situation couldn't change.

"Why don't we visit coyote territory?" Luther asked.

Chris blinked at him. "I thought we'd decided to go to the clowder."

Luther smiled. "I'm sure the clowder is interesting, but since the coyotes have a new alpha, I was curious to see how things were going for him."

Chris stared at the human. He was pretty sure there was more to it than what he was saying, but he doubted he would get an answer if he asked. Instead of doing that, he looked at Jacob in question. "What do you think?"

"We can certainly go. I don't know Josiah, but I'm sure he's been informed of this, so he shouldn't have a problem with the human team walking around his territory."

"He won't."

Jacob arched a brow. "How do you know that?"

"He's friends with my brother. I visited him a few days ago. He's doing okay." Chris turned his attention to Luther. "But I have to warn you. Things are still a bit of a mess. He's a new alpha, and he was never meant to be one. It's taking him a bit of time to understand what he has to do and what he *can* do, and the coyotes aren't making it easy on him."

Luther frowned. "I don't expect him to work miracles, but

I'm surprised to hear that the coyotes aren't happy."

Chris bit his lower lip. He hadn't told the humans that he was a carrier, and it was pretty much a secret in most of the forest. Still, more and more people knew about it, and Chris didn't want to hide what he was. He was a future alpha, a man, and a carrier. He shouldn't have to ignore any of those. "As you know, Josiah's father wasn't a good man. Neither was his brother. Josiah was never supposed to be the alpha, both because he had an older brother and because he's a carrier."

Luther nodded. "I'm aware. I still didn't realize it would make his life so much harder."

"It shouldn't have. Most people realize that being a carrier doesn't make you less of a man or anything like that. It's stupid when alphas want their children to be born from carriers. They think that being born from two men means the children will be stronger, and it's ridiculous. Especially if you consider how they actually treat carriers."

"I agree. I find carriers fascinating, but I don't think they're less of men because they can have children. Is that how things went before?"

Chris hadn't expected this to become a lesson about carriers, but the humans seemed interested. They didn't look disgusted or anything like that, which was more than he could say for some shifters. "It was. That's why most carriers were abused. There was a law that if they weren't married before they turned twenty-six, they had to be handed over to the council, who would then use them to create alliances. Everyone worked hard to change that law and make sure the carriers were safe. No one has worked harder than Thomas, actually."

"So the carriers were abused because of tradition?" Marlowe asked. He sounded horrified, and Chris shared that feeling.

"Basically. Well, mostly, it was a few alphas who thought they were all-powerful and could do anything they wanted. They also abused the people they were supposed to take care of and guide. Really, the fact that the men they abused were carriers was just an excuse. We saved all the carriers, though, and they're now free to do what they want." Or at least, Chris hoped so.

"So the coyotes are giving Josiah a hard time because they don't want a carrier to be their alpha?" Luther asked. He looked ready to beat someone into the ground for looking at Josiah funny.

"Mostly. They probably see him as weak and unable to do his job. I wouldn't be surprised if the old alpha and his oldest son hammered that into the coyotes. It's in the way they treated Josiah. They abused him, made sure everyone knew how weak he was. Now that Josiah is the alpha, he has to work against that."

Luther shook his head. "I want to see him. I know that he was forced to become alpha because of our presence here, and I feel guilty."

"You're right. He *was* forced. He never wanted to become alpha, but you insisted, and there was no other solution."

"Did I ruin his life?"

Luther sounded serious, and Chris was surprised. He hadn't expected Luther or any other human to care that much about Josiah and what he had to do. "I don't think so." Chris had to be careful. "We're friendly, but we're not best friends or anything like that, so you should probably ask someone else. From what I saw when I last visited him a few days ago, though, he's settling in. He never wanted to be alpha or to go back to the band, but he has, and he's strong. Eventually, he'll manage to do what he's planning, which is to have a flourishing band. It's going to take hard work, much more than any other alpha has to face when they become alpha, but he can do it. Besides, he's not alone. The council stands behind him, and they'll help him if he needs anything."

Luther slowly nodded. "I think we should go. I'd like to see him."

Jacob cleared his throat. "We can head there right now. I'm sure Chris can call him to warn him we're coming. That way, it won't be a surprise."

They headed toward Thomas's house. Both Chris and the humans had parked there, so they could grab their cars and drive to the band.

Chris watched Jacob as they walked. He hadn't said much during the conversation Chris had with Luther, but Chris knew he'd been listening. He hadn't intervened, and Chris was both surprised and grateful. He hadn't told the humans he was one, but that was only because it hadn't come up. If he had a chance, he *would* tell them.

"We can take my car," Chris said, still looking at Jacob.

Jacob turned around. He didn't look happy, but he had to see how stupid it would be for him and Chris to take different cars. Still, he tried. "We can both take one car. That way, you won't have to drive me back here once we're done."

"It's not a problem."

"It's not for me, either. I'd rather have my truck."

Of course he would. He didn't want to spend any length of time alone with Chris. Chris's stomach churned, but he didn't insist. They'd both made their decision, and they had to live with it.

Once they got to the cars, the humans climbed in theirs and drove away, leaving Chris and Jacob behind. Chris bit his lower lip. He wanted to talk to Jacob, but what could he say? "I really can drive you back. It's not a problem."

Jacob sighed. "I know it's not. I just don't want you to have to do it. It's not easy for me, and I know it can't be easy for you, either."

Chris shook his head and stepped closer. "It's not. But I miss you. It's almost like I lost an arm or a leg. I feel incomplete without you." The words tumbled out of Chris's lips before he could stop them. He was mildly horrified, but he suspected Jacob already knew how he felt.

"I know. I feel the same way."

Chris blinked up at Jacob. "I miss you so much."

To Chris's surprise, Jacob reached for him. One second, they were standing apart. The next, they were in each other's arms, kissing.

Chris had no idea what they were doing, but he didn't care. He closed his eyes and kissed Jacob as if was the last time he would do so.

Because it might be.

CHAPTER SEVEN

They hadn't talked about the kiss, and Jacob wasn't planning on it. It had been a mistake for both of them. Jacob could only speak for himself, of course, but he knew that even though he'd enjoyed the kiss and had wanted to drag Chris inside his truck and do much more than that, now that he had kissed him again, he wanted what they'd had back.

That wasn't possible, though. They'd broken up for a reason, and that reason still stood. They also still had to work together, which made everything more complicated.

Chris bit his lower lip and looked down. They'd decided to meet to talk about the skunk and rodents situation. Luther had been happy to visit coyote territory, and he'd spent over an hour chatting with Josiah, but he wouldn't forget about the skunks and rodents anytime soon. That meant that Jacob and Chris had to reach out and try to convince them to allow the humans in.

Jacob cleared his throat. "I think you should try contacting Jasper."

Chris frowned. "He's the skunk alpha heir, isn't he?"

"He is."

"Why do you think we should contact him?"

"Well, I know he used to have a crush on Dimitri. He was jealous of Levi for marrying him. I also know that he might not be as averse to the humans' presence as his father will be."

"You don't think he's like his father?" Chris seemed to find that surprising, although maybe he shouldn't. He wasn't like his father, either. Of course, his father wasn't evil, but still.

Jacob tapped his fingertips on the railing. They were stand-ing on Thomas's porch, which had somehow become the place where they met. It was neutral, even though it was in cete territory. "I don't know him personally, but I've heard things."

"What have you heard?"

"I was told that when his father made a fuss about the council turning their way around, he didn't. Instead, he stayed back to talk to a council member after his father left. I don't know what they talked about, but I think it shows that he wants things to change."

"But his father is in charge, and I doubt he's going to retire anytime soon. Jasper might be willing to change things, but that doesn't mean things *can* change."

"Maybe not. We do have to find a way into skunk territory, though. We can waste as much time as possible, but Luther won't stand for that much longer. He wants to visit skunk and rodent territories."

"And since we already know Jasper might be inclined to help us, it would be easier to start with the skunks."

"Exactly."

Chris nodded. "You have his phone number?"

"I think we should drive there." It was the last thing Jacob wanted — being in a car for that long with Chris was going to be hell — but he truly thought that if they managed to see Jas-per and talk to him, things would go better. If anything, Jasper wouldn't be able to forget about it like he might a phone call. He'd *have* to talk to Chris and Jacob.

Jacob would have done this on his own, but he couldn't. He and Chris were working together, and Chris would pitch a fit if Jacob did anything on his own. He would be right to do so. They were coworkers, and Jacob had to keep that in mind — and to forget about the kiss.

Chris sighed. "I suspected you'd say that. All right. When

do you want to go?"

"We can go now."

Chris blinked, but he nodded. "All right. Do you want to take separate cars?"

It was tempting to say yes, but things would be easier for both of them if they only used one. "We can take my truck."

Chris looked surprised, but he went along with it. "Let's go, then."

Jacob had parked his truck in front of Thomas's house, like always. Chris's car was next to it, but Jacob barely looked at it as he and Chris climbed into his truck. He turned the engine on, checked that Chris had his seatbelt on, and headed out.

The silence grew heavy between them. He knew they needed to talk, but he didn't want to. They had a fragile equilibrium, and it felt like anything they did or say might break it.

Jacob couldn't stop thinking about how well they worked together. It was as if things between them were fixed, as if they were in a relationship again, even though they weren't. They were too careful around each other, neither of them wanting to say something to upset the other after the kiss. But working with Chris had made Jacob see that if he had agreed to become alpha mate, they would have worked well together.

He couldn't see a way to make things better between them, though. Chris was still the bobcat alpha heir, while Jacob was still head of security for the cete. He would never be a good alpha mate, even if he and Chris worked things out.

Neither of them had changed their mind, and Jacob doubted they would. Chris couldn't, not when he was still trying to make his father proud and happy. Jacob couldn't, not when he didn't want to move and when he knew he would be a terrible alpha mate. He couldn't be what Chris needed, and Chris couldn't be what he needed. It was sad, but it happened, and they had to wrap their minds around that and accept it. They also had to stop kissing. Even though it felt incredible and had made Jacob's heart race, it was the worst way for them to solve this.

They had to keep their distance. It made Jacob wonder if this was what Thomas had intended when he'd decided to put them together. It would make sense, since he was playing matchmaker, but what did Dan want from the situation? He couldn't want Jacob and Chris to get back together, could he? It didn't make sense. He was the alpha, and he no doubt wanted Chris to have a decent alpha mate. Jacob would be anything but.

"What does your father think about the situation?" he blurted out.

Chris frowned. "You mean about the skunk thing?"

"I mean about us. I know why Thomas wanted us to work together, but I don't understand your father."

"Why do you think Thomas wanted us to work together?"

"Because he wants us to get back together. I thought it was obvious."

"Now that I think about it, I guess it is."

"Your father can't want the same thing."

"Why not?"

"Because he already knows why we broke up. You told him, didn't you?"

"I told him that I couldn't stay and that you couldn't leave."

"So why has he agreed to this? It would have made things easier on you if you hadn't been the one working with me."

"That's probably exactly why he wants me to do it. He wants me to be strong and to learn how to deal with my feelings. He knows that this is hurting me because I can't stop thinking about what we had, but he's not going to allow me to step down."

Jacob tightened his hands around the steering wheel. "He's an asshole."

"He's just trying to do the best for the clowder." Chris hesitated. "That's also why he wanted me and the daughter of the fox alpha to get married."

Jacob was going to break the steering wheel if he tightened his hold onto it any more. "He wants you to marry the daughter of the fox alpha?"

"In his dreams, I would. He and her father tried to stick us together and see what happened, but she didn't want to marry me, and she was very obvious about it. We told our fathers it would never happen, and they dropped it."

The situation made even less sense now. Dan was trying to find a decent partner for his heir, and it wasn't Jacob. Why had he insisted they work together, then? Chris might be right when he said that his father wanted him to get over the feelings he had for Jacob and power through them, but Jacob found that hard to believe. Maybe he shouldn't, though, after what he'd just learned about Dan.

But whatever the reason Dan had for doing this, it didn't help the situation. Jacob doubted anything would. He and Chris were stuck together even though they didn't want to be, and nothing had changed between them.

Chris was thinking of the unthinkable. He was thinking about leaving everything behind — the clowder, his family, the alpha heir position, everything he'd learned over the years.

He wasn't over Jacob. He'd tried convincing himself he was, but he couldn't deny the obvious, not now that he'd spent time with Jacob and they'd kissed.

He didn't know what to do with that knowledge, though. He didn't even know if Jacob still wanted him. They'd kissed, and Jacob had been into it, but that didn't mean he wasn't still angry and disappointed at what Chris had done. Besides, even though Chris was thinking about leaving his family behind, it didn't mean he was going to do it. He couldn't just dump everything and throw himself into Jacob's arms, no matter how much he wanted to.

What he did know was that the love he had for Jacob wasn't going to change anytime soon. He was miserable, and he knew Nico was right. Eventually, if nothing changed, Chris would come to resent his father, the clowder, and even himself.

It wasn't only because of Jacob, though. Chris had never wanted to be an alpha. He'd never wanted the authority and responsibilities of being alpha, but he'd been taught it was his duty, and he'd gone along with it. Having Jacob in his life had threatened that, and Chris had been quick to go home and get back into his routine. He'd been quick to be unhappy again, but now that he and Jacob were working together, he was starting to see that maybe there was more to life than doing what his father wanted him to do.

He'd give up the alpha position easily, especially if it was for Jacob and to give them a future together. Things weren't going to be easy, though. Chris's father would never agree to have him step down, even though he had another son. Chris didn't want Nico to become the heir if he didn't want to, but he wondered if maybe his brother did. They'd never talked about it. They hadn't needed to, not when everyone knew that Chris would take their father's place one day.

But maybe he wouldn't. Maybe Nico could, and Chris could have a peaceful life with Jacob in cete territory.

Chris couldn't get ahead of himself, though. For now, he and Jacob had to focus on meeting with Alpha Rhodes and convincing him to open his territory to the humans. Even though Chris wanted to make decisions right away and talk to Jacob, it wasn't urgent. Actually, he should probably take his time. Rushing into making decisions would make things harder in the long run. People would think that he hadn't thought things through, and they would try to convince him to change his mind. He knew he wouldn't, but there was more to it than just deciding to move in with the cete. For one, he had to make sure Jacob still wanted him, and he wasn't a hundred percent sure that was the case. They'd kissed, and Jacob had been into it, but he was still working on the assumption that Chris wouldn't sacrifice anything to be with him. What would happen if Chris told him he would?

"Are you still thinking about her?" Jacob asked.

Chris blinked. "Who?"

"The fox woman. The one you're supposed to marry."

"Gwen? No. Why would I be thinking about her?"

Jacob stared straight ahead as he drove. "She would be a suitable wife for you. She's an alpha's daughter, and you're an alpha heir. She could become alpha mate without too many problems. She'd be good at it, too. It would solve all your problems."

It wouldn't, not when Chris's biggest problem was finding a way to be with Jacob. "I didn't even know her before we met that one time. I haven't seen her since then, and I'm not planning to see her ever again. We're not friends or anything like that. Our fathers thought we could work well together, but neither of us was willing to try."

"Is your father going to find you another alpha mate, then?"

Chris forced himself not to smile. He was pretty sure Jacob was jealous, even though he would never admit it. "I don't think so. I told him that I'm only nineteen and that I'm nowhere near ready to getting married to anyone."

Jacob finally looked at Chris, albeit briefly. "Anyone?"

Chris had to swallow. He knew it wasn't a proposal, but he could too easily imagine him and Jacob being married. "Not that anyone has asked, but no. I think I'd like to wait a few years before getting married. I'm not saying I will never get married, but it's not a priority."

"Makes sense."

"What about you? Have you ever thought about getting married? You're thirty-four, and most people your age are already in a serious relationship or married."

"I thought about it once. It fell through, though, and I'm nowhere near ready to try again."

Chris wondered if their relationship was the one Jacob was talking about. Had Jacob thought about marrying him? Chris's heart raced. He wanted to ask, but he couldn't. He was too afraid of the answer.

"We're here," Jacob said, interrupting Chris's freak out.

Chris looked ahead, and sure enough, they'd reached the entrance to surfeit territory.

Chris had never been inside, but his father had driven him past every single territory when he was a teenager. He'd wanted Chris to see where the other alphas lived, and even though they hadn't explored any of the territories—the shifters in the forest hadn't been as friendly with each other as they were now—it had given Chris a good idea of how the forest was set up. "What now?"

Jacob hesitated. "I think we should talk to the guards. We can ask them about Jasper and see what they say. If he's not here or unwilling to talk to us, we can go directly to Alpha Rhodes."

Chris wasn't looking forward to that, but Jacob was right. They had to work things out, and they had to do it now. Luther wouldn't be kept away from the surfeit, no matter what Chris and Jacob told him.

Jacob parked just at the entrance. They didn't have to wait long. After a few moments, a man appeared at the edge of the forest. "Who are you?" he asked.

"My name is Jacob Smith. I'm the chief of security for Alpha Steele. This is Chris Wiley, the future bobcat alpha. We'd like to see either your alpha heir or your alpha."

"Why?"

"Private business. It has to do with the human team."

The man stared at them for a moment. "I'll call. Wait here."

He left them alone, stepping back into the forest. Chris couldn't help but wonder whether they would succeed. He doubted it. It would take more than him and Jacob to convince Alpha Rhodes to open his territory to the human team. Still, they had to try. It was their job, and they would do their best. Unfortunately, their best might not be enough.

"What do you think is going to happen?" he asked.

Jacob didn't look away from the spot in which the man had disappeared. "I have no idea."

"I don't think Alpha Rhodes is going to be happy to see us."

Jacob snorted. "I doubt he's going to be happy about anything in this situation. We'll have to try to convince him, though. He has to see that it would be a bad thing even for him if the human team doesn't get what they want and pulled their superiors into this. The entire forest is at risk, and hopefully, Alpha Rhodes will understand that."

Chris wanted to believe he was right, but he couldn't. Alphas were notorious for being stubborn and incredibly protective of the territories. Some of them managed to open them up through marriage, like the cete and the sleuth had, but the surfeit was different. It had kept itself isolated even when most of the other territories relaxed their rules about letting other shifters in, and more importantly, Alpha Rhodes was one of the bad guys. To Chris, that was a sign that he wouldn't give up anytime soon. He was protecting his privilege, and Chris had no idea how to deal with that.

"No."

Jacob had to resist the urge to huff in frustration. He'd expected Alpha Rhodes to say no, but he'd hoped that the alpha would at least allow him and Chris to explain.

"You should hear what we have to say," Chris said.

Alpha Rhodes glared at him from his side of the desk. "I don't want to hear whatever you have to say. My answer will be no, regardless."

Jacob had been surprised when they'd been allowed into surfeit territory. He'd hoped to be able to talk to Jasper, but instead, Alpha Rhodes had greeted them in front of his home. He'd led them to his office, where they'd sat around the desk. Jacob had barely managed to tell him that he and Chris were there to talk about opening his territory to the human team that he'd snapped his *no* at them.

"You don't understand. The future of the forest rests on this. The human team was sent to keep an eye on the shifters in the forest, and if they don't get what they want, they'll leave and come back with an army. Is that really what you want?" Chris asked.

His voice was strong, and for the first time, Jacob could see the future alpha in him. Chris might not want that, but it didn't mean he wouldn't be good at it.

"I don't want anyone in my territory, and that includes the two of you and the humans."

"Yet you let us in."

"Because I was curious. I wanted to find out why you are here. I didn't expect this, but my answer won't change. No, I won't allow the human team to come into my territory."

Jacob didn't know how they could convince him to change his mind. Chris had just explained why it was important that he opened his territory to the human team, and it hadn't changed anything.

A knock on the door made Chris jump. He tried to hide it, but Jacob had noticed, and he gave him what he hoped was a reassuring smile. Chris was nervous, and so was Jacob.

They'd been lucky that Alpha Rhodes had agreed to see them at all, and hopefully, they would be able to leave surfeit territory without a hitch. Jacob wouldn't put it past Alpha Rhodes to keep them there and try to use them as pawns in his game, though. They were different kinds of shifters, which meant that he could use them against two different shifter groups. Thomas and Dan would be pissed, but there would be nothing they could do if they wanted Chris and Jacob back.

"Who is it?" Alpha Rhodes called out.

The door opened, and Jasper peeked in. Jacob had never talked to him, but he knew him.

Jasper looked to be in his late twenties or early thirties. He was tall and handsome, with dark hair and dark eyes, although he wasn't Jacob's type. No, Jacob's type was shorter and blond, and Chris happened to be just that.

"What do you want?" Alpha Rhodes snapped.

Jasper didn't seem intimidated, though. He stepped into the office and closed the door behind himself. "I think you should listen to them."

Alpha Rhodes's eyes narrowed. "You know why they're here? Was this your idea?"

Jasper shook his head. "I don't even know them. I can guess why they came, though, and it's important."

"The human team wants to visit surfeit territory," Chris said. "They have to. They're obeying orders, and if they don't get what they want, the humans will send reinforcements. It will be dangerous for everyone in the forest, and that includes skunk shifters. Do you really want to put your entire surfeit in danger when it could be so easily avoided?"

Alpha Rhodes glared at Chris. "You might be your father's heir, but it doesn't mean you can talk to me that way."

"I apologize, Alpha Rhodes, but this is vital. If you continue saying no, the human team *will* have to report to their superiors, and those superiors will send other humans. The forest will be invaded, and possibly torn apart."

Alpha Rhodes crossed his arms over his chest. "I don't want any human sticking their nose where it doesn't belong."

"I could stay with them," Jasper offered. "It's not a perfect solution, but I'll be able to make sure that no one goes where they shouldn't be going." He turned his attention to Chris and Jacob. "What do the humans want to see?"

"Mostly, that the skunks aren't being abused," Jacob said. "They're here to make sure that the shifters in the forest can live peacefully together. What happened with the coyotes triggered that, but now, that situation is under control. We need them to see them that we're all happy and friendly."

Jasper snorted. "They'll guess it's a lie unless they're idiots."

"I'm pretty sure they will, but that shouldn't be a problem. Luther, the team leader, isn't a bad person. He's trying to make the best with the situation he was given, and while he has to do his job, he's ready to turn a blind eye on smaller skirmishes and things like that. He does have to explore every single territory, though, and make sure that the shifters are treated well. That's all there is to it."

"So I'll take you and the team around and explain how things work, and that's it?"

"Pretty much. Luther will probably ask a lot of questions, but all he and the team want is to make sure the skunks are treated well and are happy."

Jacob waited. The only one who could make this decision was Alpha Rhodes, and even though Jasper had intervened, he could still say no. Jacob didn't know what they would do if that was the case.

"If I don't agree to this, other humans will come?" Alpha

Rhodes asked.

"A lot of humans," Chris confirmed. "Possibly the army. You know how humans are. They want to keep us under their heels, and unfortunately, we don't have the manpower to fight them. If you want to be left alone and continue living your lives as you've been, you need to give in, at least this one time. Trust me. No one likes it, but we don't have a choice."

"All right," Alpha Rhodes grudgingly agreed. "But I want to know when they'll be here, for how long, and what they're going to see. I won't let them stomp around the entire territory, not without our control."

"We can keep Jasper with us when we come. Besides, Jacob and I will be there, too. We've been assigned to the team to help smooth things out."

And Chris was doing an excellent job of that. Jacob was impressed.

"Fine. Get Jasper's phone number and call him when you know more. I don't want to be involved."

That was a lot more than Jacob had expected, and there was a spring in his step as he and Chris headed back to their car. They'd parked in front of Alpha Rhodes's house, and Jasper walked them out.

"You did a good job," he said.

"We wouldn't have convinced him if you hadn't intervened," Chris answered.

Jasper shrugged. "I don't know about that. He's not stupid. He knows that if we want the humans to leave the forest, he has to go along with this."

"And I bet he's going to make sure there's nothing unsightly to see when we come back," Jacob said. He didn't dislike Jasper, but he didn't know him, and as far as he was concerned, Alpha Rhodes was an abusive piece of shit. Jasper was his son, and even if he wasn't abusive, he still didn't intervene to stop his father. People had been hurt, and Jasper hadn't said anything about it.

Jasper sighed. "He will. I know what you're thinking, and trust me, I'm trying. I don't want anyone to be hurt. It's not easy, though. My father is set in his beliefs, and he won't change them."

"He's an asshole," Jacob snapped. He'd heard what had happened to Turner and Easton. They were both carriers, and they were both skunk shifters. They'd been treated badly, and that was all on Alpha Rhodes's head. Alpha Rhodes had even been arrested for it, but he'd argued that he'd abused Turner before there was no law that he couldn't, and he'd been released. Having to bargain with him had made Jacob want to vomit, but it was necessary.

"He is. I'm trying to change things, but it's not easy. I can promise you I'm not like my father, although of course, you don't have to believe me. I hope you'll give me a chance, though."

Jacob wasn't sure it was a good idea, but since he and Chris were going to have to work with Jasper for at least a few days, they had to go along. "Fine. Show me I'm wrong. Show me you're not like your father, and I'll treat you accordingly."

Things had gone decently well, and Chris hadn't expected it. He hadn't thought Alpha Rhodes would even talk to them, let alone agree to let them in. The man was an asshole, just like Jacob had said, but Chris supposed that even he understood that the forest would be in trouble if the humans didn't get what they wanted. He would no doubt clean up the surfeit as best as he could before the humans came, and Chris wasn't sure how he felt about that.

He wanted Alpha Rhodes to be exposed to the humans as the monster he was. Chris had lived with Turner and Easton, and he knew what had happened to them. He'd seen how

Easton had nightmares every night and how he couldn't forget what had happened to him. Turner was in pretty much the same state, although he was doing better. He still didn't like small spaces from when Alpha Rhodes had kept him chained in a shed behind his house, though.

Chris had wanted to help them, and he still did. He felt guilty about cooperating with Alpha Rhodes, but there was nothing he could do about it. They needed this to go well and for the human team to eventually leave.

They said goodbye to Jasper and climbed into the truck. Chris leaned his head against the window as they drove away, wondering what was next. They still had the rodents to convince, but no one knew what was happening in that territory, so it wouldn't be easy. They probably wouldn't even be allowed in, and they didn't know who the alpha was right now.

"That went well," Jacob murmured.

"It really did. I'm glad Jasper decided to help us."

Jacob hummed. "You said you didn't know him, right?"

"I don't. I've seen him before, mostly because both our fathers are alphas, but we've never really talked."

"Did you expect him to step in like he did?"

"I was hoping he would. He had a better chance to convince his father, and he did."

"I don't think we can trust either of them."

Jacob was probably right. "We won't. We'll explain what happened to Luther and point out that even though Alpha Rhodes is opening the surfeit to him, it doesn't mean he's complying. I don't know what Luther will do, but I do know that he won't be happy with seeing only part of the territory. It's something we'll have to deal with when it happens, though."

Jacob grimaced. "I am *not* looking forward to that."

"Neither am I, but there's no way out of it."

"You did a good job."

Chris couldn't help but smile. "So did you. We work well together, don't we?"

"We do."

And that was one more reason for Chris to leave everything behind and be with Jacob.

He wanted more than what they had right now. He was done fighting his feelings and the knowledge that he shouldn't do this. He was ready to give everything up for Jacob, and for the first time, he thought it was the right choice to make. His father wouldn't be happy—hell, he would be *pissed*—but even if Chris left his family, he would always have Jacob. Jacob, who hadn't demanded Chris move in with him. Jacob, who was still willing to talk to him, work with him, and even kiss him, even though Chris hadn't chosen him. He'd never demanded or had expected anything from Chris, not the way Chris's father did.

Jacob was willing to accept Chris the way he was, but Chris's father wasn't. It wasn't that hard a choice after all.

Once they were back at Thomas's house, they went inside to tell him what had happened. He was both surprised and happy to know how things had gone with Alpha Rhodes but also worried about what would happen when the human team explored the territory. Like Jacob had said, though, it was something they would have to deal with when it happened. Right now, there was nothing they could do.

Jacob walked Chris outside to his car, but Chris wasn't ready to go. Still, he didn't know how to bring it up. "Are you going home now?" he asked.

Jacob nodded. "I am. I might go back to work later, but I think this was enough for the morning. I'll have lunch and rest for a bit."

"Good. You deserve it."

Jacob smiled. "You deserve to rest, too. Go home. We'll talk tomorrow."

Chris nodded. He stared at Jacob as Jacob climbed into his truck. Jacob had told him to go home, but he couldn't seem to make his feet move. He didn't want to.

Jacob didn't look behind as he left, and Chris was alone. He looked at the sky. He'd made his decision, but the thought of actually doing this was terrifying. What if Jacob rejected him? What if he changed his mind and didn't want Chris anymore? They'd kissed, yes, but they hadn't talked about it, and Jacob had behaved normally since then. Of course, so had Chris, so that didn't mean anything.

Chris had to take a chance. Jacob might reject him, but he also might not, and Chris would only know if he tried.

He climbed into his car and headed toward Jacob's house instead of going back to clowder territory. He knew where it was because Jacob had shown it to him once after things had calmed down and the carriers had been allowed to leave the Bishop house. His heart raced and his mouth was dry, and he was praying that Jacob wouldn't kick him out as soon as he saw him. There was only one way to find out, though.

Once he got to Jacob's house, he parked next to Jacob's truck. The door opened before he could walk up the porch steps, and Jacob stood in front of him. He'd taken off his shoes and his t-shirt, and he was now wearing a pair of shorts — and nothing else. He looked delectable, and Chris licked his lips.

"Chris? What are you doing here?"

Chris shook his head. He wanted to explain, but he didn't think he could. His mouth felt like a desert, and even if it hadn't, how could he find the right words? He knew he and Jacob needed to talk, but right now, he needed to feel Jacob more.

So instead of saying anything, Chris rushed toward Jacob. He threw his arms around him, and even though Jacob was surprised, he managed to keep both of them up. He hugged

Chris to his chest, looking down at him, no doubt to ask what was going on, but Chris didn't let him. Instead, he pressed their lips together.

Jacob gasped, but he didn't push Chris away. Instead, he instantly started kissing him back. Chris's heart felt like it exploded, and together, they staggered inside the house. Chris reached back with his hand, never stopping kissing Jacob, and slammed the door shut.

"What are we doing?" Jacob asked.

"What we should have been doing this entire time. I'm sorry. I shouldn't have left."

Jacob shook his head and kissed Chris again. "Talk later. Kiss now."

Chris laughed. "That's fine with me. Where's your bedroom?"

Jacob blinked. "You want to go to my bedroom?"

"More than anything. I've missed you. I want to."

Jacob stared at him for a moment, but thankfully, he didn't ask if Chris was sure. Chris was, but it wouldn't stop him from changing his mind if he was given too much time. Doing this was terrifying, and he didn't want to think about it for now.

Jacob reached down, cupping Chris's ass with both his hands. Chris hopped up, wrapping himself around him as he laughed. He didn't know how he could have ever left this. Living without Jacob had been hell, and now, Chris's heart started healing. Hopefully, it would manage to heal all the way through, and Chris would be happy again.

Jacob walked them to his bedroom without even looking where he was going. He slammed Chris against the walls a few times, but Chris didn't even care. He would take the bruises if they meant he was with Jacob.

"This is harder than I expected," Jacob mumbled as they finally stumbled into what had to be his bedroom.

Chris had seen the house from outside, but he'd never been inside. Now he wished he had. They would have had more privacy than in the Bishop house.

Jacob almost dropped Chris when he stumbled over a discarded pair of jeans, but he managed to get them both onto his bed in one piece. Chris stretched out, trying to imagine waking up here every day, but he couldn't, not yet. What he *could* do was kiss Jacob again, so he did. He couldn't believe he was being allowed to do this again. He never wanted to stop.

"What do you want?" Jacob asked. His voice was soft as if he were free to break the moment.

"You. Whatever you're ready to give me." Chris wanted Jacob to fuck him, but he knew it was too soon. They had no idea what they were doing or where they stood with each other, and Jacob wouldn't want to do something so intimate if there was a chance that Chris would leave right after. If Chris had a say in it, he would never go, but he knew it wouldn't be as easy as telling his father that. Even if his dad agreed to let him step down from being the heir, he would have to help Nico take his place. It would take time, time Chris didn't want to waste.

Jacob nodded, then went to work on Chris's jeans. He had them undone in seconds, and together, they pushed them and Chris's underwear down Chris's legs. Chris also tried to take his t-shirt off at the same time, but it was a bit more complicated, especially when he realized he was still wearing his shoes.

He couldn't help but laugh, and it brought him back to the other times he and Jacob had done this. They hadn't had a lot of time or privacy in the Bishop house, so they'd always rushed through it. Chris hoped that one day they wouldn't have to, but right now, he was too eager to feel Jacob's skin against his again.

Jacob threw Chris's shoes against the wall. Chris's clothes followed until he was naked and stretched out under Jacob, who was still wearing his shorts. Chris reached for them, but he hesitated before touching them. "I love you," he said. "I never stopped loving you. I'm sorry."

Jacob arched a brow. "I thought you didn't want to talk about this?"

"You're right. I don't. I just wanted you to know that I still love you."

Jacob's expression softened. "I love you too. Like you, I never stopped."

They didn't say anything else. Jacob leaned down to kiss Chris again, and Chris let go. They were wrapped around each other, and Chris wished it would never stop. He'd missed Jacob so much, and now, he had him again.

He was never letting go.

They fought with Jacob's shorts, but they were easier to get off than Chris's jeans. They continued kissing and rutting against each other, and Chris wasn't ashamed that it took him almost no time to come against Jacob's stomach. He'd been hard since their first kiss at the door, and Jacob had always known how to play his body. Besides, the yearning Chris had felt for this moment was so much that Chris wasn't surprised it had only taken him a moment to come.

At least Jacob wasn't far behind him. He grunted as he thrust harder against Chris, pushing him into the mattress and spilling over his stomach.

Chris almost expected Jacob to roll away once they were done, but instead, he moved to his side and pulled Chris with him. They stayed there, plastered against each other without talking. Chris wanted to live in this moment. He never wanted it to stop. It would have to, but it could wait. He and Jacob would have to talk, but for now, this was perfection, and he didn't want to break it.

CHAPTER EIGHT

Chris kept peeking at Jacob. Once again, he and Jacob had taken Jacob's truck to head out with the human team. They were driving right behind them, and Chris wondered what would be waiting for them once they got to skunk territory.

They'd managed the impossible. They'd convinced Alpha Rhodes to open his territory to the humans, and Chris was nervous about what would happen. His mind cycled through several options, all of them bad. It was hard to focus on what was next for the human team, though, considering what was happening in Chris's private life.

Chris and Jacob had had sex. They hadn't talked after that, neither of them wanting to break the fragile balance between them. They should have, but Chris had been terrified, and he'd gone home without asking Jacob what they were doing, or without telling him that he'd made a decision. Now, things were awkward between them. That morning Jacob had acted as if nothing had happened, saying hello to Chris like they were friends and nothing else, but maybe that was because Chris had been slightly late and the human team was already there.

Chris didn't know what to think. He wanted to believe that Jacob had wanted what they'd done as much as he had, but he wasn't sure. He wasn't sure of anything anymore. Now wasn't the right moment to talk, either. They needed time, which was something they didn't have this morning. Hopefully, once they were done with the skunks, the humans would go back to whatever hotel they were staying at, and Chris and Jacob would finally be able to clear things up between them. Chris didn't like the way they'd been behaving as if they barely knew each other, and he wanted that to change.

He wanted a lot to change.

So far, he hadn't told anyone what he'd decided. He was too afraid. He knew his father wouldn't take it well, and while Nico would be happy for him, he would also have to take his place when it came to becoming the next alpha. Chris wasn't sure how Nico felt about it, and he was going to have to ask him. He had a lot of meaningful conversations in his near future, and he wasn't looking forward to any of them. He *would* have them, though. He wanted to start the next part of his life with Jacob, and that would only happen if he was honest with everyone involved.

"Well, there aren't any guards outside, so there's that," Jacob said as they neared skunk territory.

Chris peered out of the windshield. They'd arrived at the entrance, just like they had the only other time they'd come. There was no one there, even though Jasper had been alerted to the fact that the humans were coming. It made Chris nervous, but he tried to convince himself he shouldn't be. Not only had Alpha Rhodes decided to open his territory, but Jasper had promised nothing bad would happen to the humans. Chris wasn't sure how much he trusted Jasper, which was a problem, but in this case, he was going to have to deal with it and accept it.

The humans parked behind Jacob's truck, and they all waited.

"Do you think someone is going to come?" Chris asked.

"Probably. Jasper never answered the text, so I don't know what's going on."

"You mean Alpha Rhodes might have changed his mind

and we're here for nothing?"

Jacob grimaced. "I hope not. I was also hoping that Jasper would text back or call me if something went wrong. He didn't, though, so I decided we might as well come."

"Risky."

"I know. There's a lot of risky stuff in this situation, unfortunately." Jacob hesitated. "If something happens—"

"If something happens, I'm not going anywhere. You don't have to protect me."

"You don't know that. We might be attacked, and you're the only one who doesn't know how to defend himself."

Chris was slightly offended, but he couldn't deny Jacob was right. Jacob had tried to teach Chris some self-defense when they'd both been at the Bishop house, but Chris wasn't good at it. If they were attacked, he would be the one in the worst shape.

"Fine. If something happens, I'll run to your truck. I'm not going anywhere without you, though."

That got a smile out of Jacob. "What about the human team?"

"No offense, but I don't really care what happens to them. As long as you're safe, I'll be fine."

Jacob opened his mouth to answer, but Chris noticed movement by his window, and he tilted his chin toward it. Jacob snapped his mouth shut and turned toward a man who had appeared at the window. He lowered the window. "We're here to see Alpha Rhodes."

The man looked at the car behind Jacob's truck. "You brought the humans?" He sounded like he wasn't quite sure what to do about them, more curious than angry. He probably had never met a human.

Chris hadn't until he met these.

"We did. We've already talked to your alpha, so he knows what's going on. He agreed to let them in."

"I know. His son let me know that you'd be here. You can go ahead and park in front of Alpha Rhodes's house. Jasper will be waiting for you."

Chris was relieved to hear that. He couldn't believe Jacob hadn't called Jasper, or at least demanded an answer to the text. It wasn't like him, but then, he'd been distracted. Chris couldn't blame him for that.

They were still doing their jobs, but he couldn't deny they were both more focused on each other rather than on that. Hopefully, it wouldn't be a problem. The skunks and the rodents were the only groups who would give them trouble, while the other shifter groups were welcoming. Still, they were in skunk territory right now, and they had to be careful. Chris should probably stop thinking about Jacob and focus on that.

Jacob drove slowly until they reached the alpha's house. Sure enough, Jasper was standing on the porch. He waved at them when he saw them and hopped down the steps to meet them. Jacob parked, and Chris got out.

The tension was so thick he could have cut it with a knife. It was cliché, but that didn't mean it wasn't the truth. Chris and Jacob headed toward Jasper, who nodded at them. "Good morning."

"Good morning. You could have answered Jacob's text," Chris told him.

Jacob hissed, but Chris was focused on Jasper.

They were equals, in a way Jacob probably hadn't thought about. But Chris and Jasper were future alphas, and if Chris changed his mind and decided to stay with the clowder, they would one day have to work together. Even if that didn't happen, Chris wanted Jasper to respect him and Jacob.

Luckily for him, Jasper didn't look offended. "I should have, yes. I apologize. I tend to read my texts, tell myself I'll answer later, and never do it, even if it's important."

"You should probably get rid of that habit before you take your father's place."

Jasper laughed. "Don't let him hear you say that, or he'll think you're threatening him."

"I'm not. I'm sure he'll be the alpha for years to come."

"But you and I will eventually have to work together as alphas, and you want to make sure I answer my texts."

"Exactly." Chris looked at Jacob. He still hadn't told him he'd decided to leave everything behind, and now wasn't the right moment to do that.

Jasper's gaze moved to the humans standing behind them. "Why don't you introduce me?"

That seemed to shake Jacob into finally saying something. "Of course. Jasper, this is the human team in charge of making sure the forest is at peace. This is Luther, their leader. Then you have Marlowe, Miriam, Suzanne, and Dean."

Chris was only slightly surprised when Jasper shook their hands. He had to remember that Jasper wasn't his father. Chris knew what Silas had done, and while Jasper hadn't tried to stop him, it didn't mean he was like him. More than anyone, Chris knew what fatherly expectations felt like, and his dad hadn't been abusive. He could only imagine what Jasper's life had been like. Had he wanted to stop his father from abusing Turner? Had he wanted to free him and the others before he was sold?

Chris had to believe so. He didn't know anything about Jasper, and he didn't want to assume. The forest needed better men than who had been in charge until now, and hopefully, Jasper would be one of those.

Jacob observed as Jasper said hello to the human team. He wasn't sure what he'd expected, but it wasn't that.

He'd thought Jasper would be as opposed to this as his

father had been, even though he'd convinced Alpha Rhodes to do it. Knowing it had to be done didn't mean he had to be happy about it, though, so it *was* a surprise to see him acting as if nothing was happening.

"If everyone is ready, we can start walking around," Jasper said.

Jacob could tell the human team was tense. They knew what had happened in surfeit territory when Kari had led them to find Turner chained to the ground in a shed behind the alpha's house. As soon as they walked around the house, Jacob looked, but the shed was nowhere to be seen. It had been taken down, and he was relieved.

He was sure the surfeit had worked hard to make sure nothing strange would pop up. They didn't want the humans to have anything negative to say about the surfeit. They wanted them to leave, and the best way to make that happen was to make sure nothing amiss was happening.

Still, Jacob couldn't help but wonder if that was the truth or if they were acting for the humans. It wouldn't surprise him if that was the case, but he couldn't exactly ask Jasper if his father was abusing another carrier.

Unfortunately, there was no way to know how many carriers the surfeit had. They'd known about Turner because of Kari, and there had been others, but they'd been sold a while ago. There could still be other, younger carriers, and they might be in trouble if Alpha Rhodes didn't change his behavior. Jacob doubted he had. He knew the humans were coming, so he'd have made sure they wouldn't find anything strange, but Jacob knew better, and he suspected everyone else in the forest did, too.

"As you can see, everything is fine." Jasper waved around as they walked. "Most of our territory consists of forest grounds, which comes in handy when we shift."

"Are all of you skunks?" Suzanne asked.

"We are. My father, well, he's very traditional. He doesn't like mixing with other shifters."

"Why not?" Luther asked. "Does he think other shifters aren't good enough?"

"Not exactly, no. But he's a man of his time, and that's what his father taught him. You know, twenty or thirty years ago, things were different in the forest. We didn't mix. It just wasn't done, and that's the way my father still thinks."

"What do *you* think? You'll be the alpha in his place one day."

"I will, and I have nothing against mixing with other shifters. Not that I'm going to tell my father that. He wouldn't be happy with me, and I like my teeth where they are."

Jacob blinked. He wanted to ask what Jasper meant, even though it was quite obvious. He was pretty sure Luther hadn't missed it, either. The man grimaced, but thankfully, he didn't push.

Jacob was sure Luther and his team wanted to make sure the forest was peaceful, and it was. There was nothing they could do against abusive men, though, especially not alphas. They'd been warned that the skunks weren't easy to deal with and that their alpha wasn't a good person. They'd promised to keep their thoughts to themselves as long as the surfeit was in a good state and its members were treated well. Jasper obviously wasn't, but Luther wouldn't do anything for only one person.

Still, it made Jacob wonder. If Alpha Rhodes had hit his son, and of course, had chained carriers in that shed, what was he doing to the other surfeit members?

"Where do the surfeit members live?" Luther asked.

"They have houses scattered in the forest. My father doesn't want them to live near his house, so they choose their own place and build their homes there."

"So it's every man for himself?"

"Not entirely. My father pays for the materials and any repairs that need to be done. But for the rest, yes. We're very independent. He does rounds to talk to everyone once a month, but for the rest, he lets them do what they want."

"What about the carriers?"

Jasper grimaced. "I'm sure you've already found out about those through the council."

"Your father abused them."

Jasper took his time answering. "He did. I'm not going to deny that, because I can't. But again, he's a product of his time. I know it's not an excuse, especially considering that most of the alphas didn't act that way. He's not doing it anymore, though. I can promise you that."

"Is it because he changed his behavior, or because he knows the council will take care of him if he does?"

"I don't have an answer to that. I'm sorry. I'm focused mostly on the fact that he's not abusing carriers anymore. I'm sure you noticed that the shed wasn't there. It's because I took it down as soon as I could."

Jacob was pretty sure Jasper wasn't telling them everything, but that was okay. If he wanted, he could ask later.

Luther frowned. "So what happens to the new carriers? I was told they only realize what they are once they reach puberty. I'm sure you have children and teenagers in surfeit territory. What happens to them if you find out they're carriers?"

Jasper hesitated. "So far, we haven't found any other carriers in the surfeit. I'm not sure what my father has in mind if or when he finds them, but I won't hold back the way I did the other times."

"You allowed carriers to be abused." Luther sounded angry, and Jacob shared that emotion.

"I didn't even realize what was happening was wrong until I was a teenager myself. And yes, I allowed him to do that. I was afraid of him. I still am, some days. But I'm an adult now, and even though he still tries to hit me sometimes, I can defend myself. I'm stronger than I was before, and I won't allow him to hurt anyone else. You have my word."

There was enough passion in Jasper's tone that Jacob wanted to believe him. He knew the council would keep an eye on what was happening here anyway, but he was glad that Jasper seemed to have realized how wrong his father had been. Hopefully, if they found other carriers, he would contact the council for help.

The rest of the visit went smoothly. There was nothing wrong with the surfeit, although Jacob was pretty sure that it was because they'd hidden everything rather than because nothing weird was happening. Still, the humans were satisfied, and Jacob was relieved when they were able to go back to the car and drive away.

The humans went directly back to Rosewood, no doubt to write their reports and send them to their superiors. Jacob, on the other hand, headed back to cete territory.

Chris had taken the habit of driving to the cete and leaving his car there so he and Jacob could drive together in Jacob's truck. Jacob didn't know what that meant, and he hadn't asked. He didn't care much, not as long as it meant he could spend time with Chris.

And spend time with Chris he did, because once they got back to the cete, Chris asked Jacob to drive right to his house, and he walked inside as if he belonged there.

Jacob wanted him to.

He never wanted Chris to leave, but he knew it was a foolish hope. Instead, he focused on the way Chris kissed him, and he forgot everything else for a bit. They had to talk, but it could wait.

They tumbled into the bedroom, their clothes flying until they were both naked. Chris was panting, and Jacob felt similarly out of breath.

They both wanted this, and apparently, they were done fighting it.

This time, Jacob sucked Chris off. He loved having Chris writhing under him, and he knew they weren't ready for anything more. *That* was one thing they had to talk about before they did, and he couldn't wait.

He knew he was setting himself up for more pain, but he couldn't help it. He loved Chris, and he didn't want to let him go. Being without him had been hell, while having him back in his life was heaven.

Chris buried his hands in Jacob's hair as he pushed up and fucked his face. Jacob didn't tell him to slow down because he didn't *want* to slow down. He wanted Chris to come down his throat, for things to go back to the way they had been before they'd broken up. He wanted both of them to forget how much pain they'd caused each other and focus only on this.

He rutted against the mattress, pleasure mounting inside of him. He'd always loved sucking Chris off. Chris was so responsive, hiding none of what he felt when Jacob did it. He was like putty in Jacob's hands, under his fingers, and Jacob wanted to wring orgasm after orgasm from him.

He settled for one, and once they'd both come, they wrapped around each other in his bed as they focused on breathing.

Jacob could have stayed here forever, not saying anything, but he knew they couldn't. "We should talk," he murmured against Chris's hair.

Chris sighed. "I agree. Do you want to do this now?"

"Why not? Or did you want to go home?"

Chris shook his head and sat up. His hair was all over the place, and he looked well-kissed. He looked like he belonged to Jacob.

He turned around and sat cross-legged, staring down at

Jacob. "Let's talk, then."

Jacob sat up, too. "I still love you. I don't think I'll ever stop, and I don't want to. I want to find a way to make things work between us. I know it's not going to be easy with you having to go back to the clowder and me having to decide whether or not I'm ready to be alpha mate, but that's not going to happen for years, is it? I don't have to make that decision now. We can just be together and see what happens. We have time, and I should have realized that before we broke up. I wanted everything, and I didn't want to compromise. It was wrong of me."

Chris stared at him. Jacob waited for him to speak. He wanted Chris to agree to this, but he didn't know whether or not Chris would, and it made him nervous.

Thankfully, Chris nodded. "You're right. We do have time. And you already know I still love you and that I want to be with you."

"That's all we have to talk about for now, then."

"I'm pretty sure that's not the case."

"Maybe not, but everything else can wait." Jacob reached for Chris again, and Chris didn't protest when he pulled him closer and kissed him.

CHAPTER NINE

Chris was surprised by what Jacob had said. He hadn't expected what had happened, and he still didn't know what to make of it. Jacob had never wanted to be alpha mate, but now, he was willing to consider the position as long as it happened years in the future. Was Chris really that important to him? Chris wanted to believe he was. He *needed* to believe it. Jacob was doing something he hadn't been willing to do before, so maybe there was hope for them.

Chris hadn't told Jacob what he'd been thinking of doing, but maybe he should have. He hadn't changed his mind. He was leaving everything behind, and that wasn't going to change.

It would take a while, though. Not only did Chris need to talk to his father, but he also had to talk to his brother. He didn't know what Nico's reaction would be, even though he knew Nico would probably be happy for him. He might not be as happy once he realized he would have to become the next alpha, though.

But Chris wanted to be with Jacob, and he wanted to be away from the clowder. He'd never wanted to be an alpha, and while he loved the clowder, he knew it wasn't his future. Working with the humans and Jacob had made him realize that. He wouldn't be happy if he became the alpha. He didn't know what that meant for his future or what he would do, but he was only nineteen. He would find something, and hopefully, it would make his father happy and proud, even if it wasn't what he'd had in mind for Chris.

Chris had to find a way to make this work, but he didn't know if he would manage. He hoped Jacob would be happy, though. He also hoped Jacob would give him a place to stay. Chris doubted he would be able to stay with his parents when his father found out what he was planning. His dad wouldn't kick him out, but he would be angry, and Chris didn't want to deal with that or with how pushy his dad would be. He was finally making his own decisions, and his father would have to get used to it.

Even if Jacob didn't want Chris to stay with him, Chris knew he wouldn't be homeless. He could always go back to the Bishop house, and he was tempted to do just that. He loved living there with the other carriers, but he wanted to stay with Jacob more. Still, he had options.

"You wanted to talk to me?" Nico asked from Chris's bedroom door.

Chris had left the door open after he texted his brother. He nodded and gestured at Nico to come in. "Close the door."

Nico's eyebrows shot up. "That sounds serious. What's going on?" He obeyed and closed the door.

"I'm about to tell you. I'd rather Dad not hear, though. Not yet."

"I don't know whether or not I'm going to like what you're about to say, but I *am* curious."

Chris had been planning this, but now that he had his brother in front of him, he wasn't quite sure how to say what he had to say. He supposed he should just say the words and see what happened. "I wanted to talk to you about Jacob and the situation with him."

Nico's eyes widened, and he sat on the bed in front of Chris. "So there *is* something going on with Jacob. I was wondering. You've been happier over the past few days."

"There is. We're back together. We, well, you know. A few times, and we talked."

"You shouldn't be having sex if you can't say the words."

Chris grabbed his pillow and hit his brother with it. "I *can* say the words. I'm just uncomfortable saying them to you. You're my brother."

"So? Don't you think I'm aware that you and Jacob were fucking all over the Bishop house?"

Chris's cheeks heated. "Oh my God. Can we not talk about that?"

"Sure. You have to admit you weren't discrete, though."

"I'm aware, and I regret it."

"It's fine. Everyone was happy for you and Jacob. You shouldn't worry too much about it. What's going on with Jacob, then?"

Chris bit his lower lip. "Well, we talked. He admitted that he acted impulsively, and that he should have tried to work out a compromise with me. He's realized that I'm not going to be alpha anytime soon, and he wants to try being with me and see what happens. If we're still together by the time Dad retires, well, we'll see." This was *not* what Chris had been supposed to say, dammit. Why were those words so hard to get out?

Nico looked happy, though, and he hugged Chris. "I'm happy for you. I'm glad Jacob finally realized how stupid he was."

Chris swallowed and looked away. He *had* to do this. He wanted to leave, and he needed his brother's support. "There's something else, actually. Something I haven't told Jacob yet."

Nico frowned. "What is it?"

"I've been thinking. I'm happy Jacob finally accepted being with me even though I'm supposed to be next alpha."

"But?"

"But I never wanted to take Dad's place. I never wanted to be an alpha. Everyone's been telling me I had to be one since

127

I was a kid, but I don't want that kind of power. I don't want to make those decisions. I don't want to hold people's lives in my hands. I don't know how Dad does it, but it's not for me."

Chris peeked at Nico, who was staring at him. He wasn't saying anything, and it made Chris worry. He had to continue explaining, but he didn't know if he could or what would happen.

"I didn't make this decision easily," he continued. "I've been thinking about it for days. It would be easy to ignore how I feel about this now that Jacob's in my life again, but I can't. Being with Jacob doesn't change how I feel about being an alpha."

"So you've decided to step down from that position?" Nico asked slowly.

"I'm going to talk to Dad and tell him I don't want to take his place. I know I'm the firstborn son, but it doesn't mean I have to be the alpha. After all, I'm a carrier, and that should make it impossible for me to be."

"That's never stopped you. It *shouldn't* stop you."

"It wouldn't if that was the only problem. It's not, though. I don't want to be an alpha. I don't want that kind of responsibility. I want to move in with the cete, with Jacob, and live my life there like a normal person. I want to build something that I want, not what's expected of me."

"And you're sure of that decision?"

"I am. I've been thinking about little else for the past few days. I've always known I didn't want to be the alpha, but this is the only time I've had the courage to think about what would happen if I decided to tell Dad that." Chris bit his lower lip. "But stepping away from that role would mean that *you* would be the next in line. It would make you the next alpha, and I don't know if I can do that to you if you don't want it."

To Chris's surprise, Nico rolled his eyes. "You should have

talked to me about it. You would know I don't mind if you had."

It was hard for Chris to wrap his mind around the fact that someone would *want* to be an alpha. "You wouldn't mind taking my place?"

"I wouldn't. I understand that being alpha isn't for everyone, and thank God for that. There would be way too many of them in the forest if that was the case. Besides, I've always known you weren't happy. I didn't think you would have the courage to do something, but I'm glad you do. I'll be there when you talk to Dad, and hopefully, we can convince him this is for the best. I'll be happy to take your place. You don't have to worry about that."

But Chris had many other things to worry about, and the first one was his father's reaction to the news. He could delay it for a bit, thankfully, although his next conversation would be even more nerve-wracking.

He had to talk to Jacob.

Jacob wasn't expecting anyone, so he was surprised when he heard someone knocking on his door. He expected it to be Thomas, although Thomas would have called.

It wasn't him. It was Chris, and he was standing there, looking nervous. "Had we agreed to see each other and I forgot?" Jacob asked as he let him in.

He could see from Chris's expression that something had happened, and it was terrifying. Had Chris changed his mind? Had he decided that he couldn't be with Jacob after all?

"What's going on?" Jacob asked.

"We need to talk."

Jacob's stomach dropped. He'd been right, hadn't he? Chris *had* changed his mind, and he didn't want to be with him anymore.

"Of course. Where do you want to talk? Living room or kitchen?"

Chris shook his head. "It doesn't matter."

"Tell me what's going on."

Chris scraped a hand through his hair. "I should have told you this before you decided you wanted to be with me." He wasn't looking at Jacob, as if he were afraid of what would happen if he did.

"You're scaring me. Just tell me what you have to say, and we'll take it from there, all right?" Jacob felt shaky, but he knew he had to ignore the fear and focus on Chris. Whatever was happening, Chris needed him. Even if he decided that he and Jacob couldn't be together, it wouldn't change how Jacob felt about him. Jacob loved Chris, and he would be there for him, whatever happened.

"I want to be with you."

Jacob blinked. That wasn't what he'd expected. "I know. I want to be with you too, which is why we decided to be together."

Chris shook his head. "That's not what I mean. I've been thinking for a long time, ever since I realized that I wouldn't be able to forget you. I talked to my brother, and he agreed with this. I'll step down from the alpha heir position. He'll take my place, and I'll be able to move here with you."

Jacob jerked back. This was *not* what he'd been expecting. "What happened to make you make that decision?"

"I just told you. Once we started working together and I realized I wouldn't be able to forget you, I started thinking about what would happen if I decided to move in with you in cete territory rather than stay with my father. You know I've never wanted to be the alpha. I didn't say anything because my father wanted me to, and it's still uncomfortable for me to think I'm going against his wishes. I'm nineteen, though. I still have time to change my life and to decide what I want to do."

Chris stepped closer. "And what I want to do is be with you."

"We can be together even if you're the alpha heir."

"You're not listening. I don't *want* to be my father's heir. I want to be Chris, a normal guy who lives with his boyfriend. That's it."

"Have you talked to your father about it?"

Chris grimaced. "That's my next step. I'm not looking forward to it, but I know it needs to be done. And I *will* talk to him. I wanted to tell you first, though. Nico is more than happy to take my place, and I wasn't sure how that conversation would go. It's why I didn't talk to you before." He peered at Jacob. "Aren't you happy?"

"Of course I am." Jacob opened his arms and stepped closer, and Chris dove into them. Jacob kissed the top of his hair, relieved that he was still able to do this.

He'd expected Chris to break up with him, but instead, he'd told him that he wanted to be with him. Jacob had a hard time wrapping his mind around it, but he was over the moon happy. "I can't believe you made that decision."

Chris chuckled against Jacob's chest. "I can't believe I did, either. I'm terrified about what my father is going to say, but I won't change my mind. I want to be with you. I want us to build a life together, and I don't want to make decisions for the entire clowder. It's not me."

Jacob kissed Chris's hair again. He was happy, but he was also worried. "I just don't want you to resent me in a few years."

Chris tilted his head up. "I won't. I'm not making this decision for you. I'm making it for me. You were just the change that triggered it."

Jacob wanted to believe that. He'd known Chris didn't want to become alpha, but also that Chris wanted to make his father happy and proud. He had a hard time believing that had changed. It had been Chris's only goal until recently, and it was hard to trust that it had changed so much in such a short time.

Jacob wanted to believe Chris, though. Chris was giving him everything he'd ever wanted. They could have a life together, build a family eventually. It was too easy to imagine Chris living here with Jacob, sharing his home and his life.

But there was the niggle of doubt in the back of Jacob's mind. What if eventually, Chris *did* come to resent him? What if Chris's father couldn't accept that Chris was making his own decisions and refused to see him again? What would Chris do then? Would he still try to make his father happy? Or would he stand his ground and be with Jacob?

"So there," Chris said. "You know everything that's happened. You know what I've been thinking about since we saw each other again. I should probably have talked to you before making this decision, but it had to come from me, not from you. And you don't have to agree to be with me or let me stay here if you don't want to. I'll understand. I'm not doing this for you. I'm doing it because I never wanted this, and because it's time for me to stand up to my father."

He stared at Jacob, and Jacob tried to find something to say. He was happy. Chris was giving him everything he'd ever wanted.

But still.

Jacob supposed there was only one way to find out whether or not Chris could actually do this. Even though he had his doubts, he wasn't going to push Chris away. He couldn't.

Chris held his breath and waited. He didn't know what Jacob's reaction would be.

He understood why Jacob was wary of accepting this. Chris had pushed him away so many times that he probably thought that Chris would change his mind eventually, especially once he talked to his father.

Chris wouldn't, though. He'd thought about this. He knew he was making the right choice—for himself and for Jacob.

They could be together now. His father would no doubt try to stop them, but he wouldn't be able to. Chris wasn't changing his mind, no matter what his father had to say about it.

The thought of talking to him was terrifying, though. Chris knew his father wouldn't be happy, and he'd have to face that. He was ready for it, or at least, he hoped so. He wanted to be with Jacob, and even though Jacob had agreed to be with him even when he'd still thought Chris was going to be the next alpha, Chris knew it was only a temporary solution. Jacob might be willing to try, but Chris wasn't the alpha yet. What would happen if he had to take his father's place? Would Jacob still want to be with him then?

They wouldn't have to find out. Chris should have decided this a long time ago, but he'd been afraid. He still was. He wanted his father to be proud of him, and he knew that wouldn't happen now that he wouldn't take his place as the alpha. He would find another way to make his dad proud.

But Chris's father was proud of Chris's sisters, and none of them would be the next alpha. They were happy, and that was all that mattered, wasn't it? They were living their lives. They were in love, had children, had built their own space. Why should Chris have to stick to the space his father wanted to give him? It wasn't fair. It had never been, especially when Nico was willing to take Chris's place.

Still, Chris wasn't sure what Jacob thought about it. Jacob was hesitant, even though he also seemed happy. Chris didn't know what to make of it, and the only thing he could do was wait.

"As long as you're sure you won't regret it once your father retires, I'm happy for you," Jacob finally said.

"I'm sure." Or at least, as sure as Chris could be.

He doubted that thinking more about it would change anything. He'd made his decision, and he would have to stick with it. He knew that even when his father retired, he wouldn't want to be the alpha. He might feel like he had to do it, but that was another problem, and a problem he would have to deal with. "It's not like my father is going to retire next week. Even if I hadn't made this decision, it would have taken years, probably ten or more. I don't think that once he does retire, I'm going to drop everything and move back to the clowder. I'm doing the right thing, Jacob. I'm convinced of it."

Jacob smiled, and it was a real smile, a smile Chris had missed when they hadn't been together. "All right. You're stepping down from that position, then."

"I am. My father doesn't know about it yet, but that's only because I wanted to know what you thought of it first. Now that I know you're okay with it, I'll go home and talk to him."

Jacob's arms tightened around Chris. "Stay for a bit longer? We still have things to talk about."

They were both more relaxed now, so Chris didn't have a problem doing just that. "I know. I don't have to move in here with you if you're not ready for that. I can even stay with the clowder if you'd rather have that kind of distance between us. I just wanted you to know what was going on."

"Don't be stupid. I've wanted you to move in with me since we both lived at the Bishop house. If you're ready for it, this can be your home."

Chris was relieved. He hadn't really thought Jacob would kick his ass out, but it had been a possibility. "All right."

"I'm just worried that you won't be able to get over your sense of duty toward the clowder."

And they were back to talking about whether or not Chris was sure of what he was doing. It was a big thing, though, so

Chris wasn't surprised. "I can't promise you that I won't ever think I made the wrong choice. I'll always wonder. But I know my brother. He's a good person, and he'll be a good alpha, probably better than me. If anything, he'll be better because he actually *wants* to do this."

"You would be a good alpha, too."

"I'd be decent. I've learned enough from my father to know how it works and to be able to make the right decisions. It doesn't mean I would have been happy, though."

"What will you do now?"

"I don't know. I have my entire life to figure it out. I'm nineteen. The only thing I know for now is how to be an alpha. I'm going to have to learn other things, but that's fine with me. I can't wait to find out what else I'm good at." That was the truth. Chris had been so focused on learning from his father that he hadn't allowed himself to find out what else he could do in life. Maybe he was good at drawing or singing. Maybe he would be a good potter. There was no way for him to know except by trying, and he couldn't wait to have the time to do that.

"And if everything else fails, I'm sure Thomas won't mind giving you a job of responsibility."

Chris snorted and swatted Jacob's chest. "So you think I'm going to fail at everything else?"

Jacob smiled. "I think you can be anything you want to be. But you're right. You're young, and you have time to find out what you're good at and what you want to do with your life. If everything else fails, though, I want you to know that you'll always have something to fall back on. Thomas will help you if you ask him."

"I know." It was one of the reasons that some days, Chris had wished Thomas was his father. He loved his dad, but he knew how uncompromising he was. He was so focused on Chris being an alpha that he didn't know anything else about

Chris. That was the only side of Chris he could see, and Chris had resented that. He still did, but making this decision had helped him feel better.

He knew his father wouldn't be happy. He suspected his dad would yell at him and try to convince him to take his place back. He might even threaten to kick Chris out and stop talking to him. Hell, that would probably happen regardless. He *was* going to be angry, and he'd put distance between them. Chris knew all of that, but he hadn't changed his mind. He was doing it for himself, more so than for Jacob. He was finally standing up to his father, but hopefully, they would be able to fix things in the future. He couldn't imagine never seeing his father again.

If that was what it took, though, Chris would have to deal with it. It was scary, but he wasn't alone. He had Jacob, and he knew that Jacob would be there for him whatever happened.

That was all that mattered.

CHAPTER TEN

Chris took a deep breath, but he didn't move. He stared at the door in front of him, wondering if he would have the courage to face his father.

He had to have it. He couldn't just act as if nothing had been happening in his life. He and Jacob were back together, and he wasn't sure his father would be happy about that. There was also the tiny detail that Chris had decided not to take his father's place when he retired, and of course, he would have to tell his father that, too.

He didn't know where to start, but he knew that procrastinating wasn't going to help. Eventually, he would have to tell his father about this, and the sooner he did it, the better it would be.

He took another deep breath, then raised his hand and knocked on the door of his father's office.

"Come in!"

Chris didn't want to go in, but he forced himself to push open the door. His father was behind his desk, and he smiled when he looked up. "I was just thinking about you. Are you here to report about how that thing with the humans is going? I heard you went into skunk territory, and I'm surprised they allowed you to."

Chris closed the office door and went to sit in front of his father. "It took a bit of convincing. We had to talk to Jasper, Alpha Rhodes's son. He pushed his father to agree, and I guess that both of them realize how important it was. No one wants the humans to stick around for longer than they have to."

"Still. It was surprising, and a good job. I'm proud of you."

Chris's chest felt tight. This was what he'd always wanted. He wanted his father to be proud of him, and now, he'd finally managed to make that happen.

He was also going to destroy all of that with only a few words.

"Who's next on your list?" his father asked.

"For now, we're going over the territories of the alphas who are eager to work with us. We still have to talk to the rodents' alpha, and we will, but it's a bit more complicated than the skunks."

Chris's father shook his head. "We still don't know what's going on in there, do we?"

"We don't, not as far as I'm aware. That's why Jacob and I are careful when it comes to the rodents."

"You're right to be. They're sneaky, and they won't hesitate if they can hurt you. Be careful with them, Chris. I don't want you to get hurt."

"I will."

Chris's father stared at him. "There's something else. What aren't you telling me?"

Chris wasn't surprised his father had noticed it. He was observant. He had to be, since he was alpha. "There *is* something else," Chris confirmed. "Jacob and I, well, we became closer as we're working together. We're together again, as in, we're a couple."

Chris could see his father was hesitant, and he waited, curious to see what he would say. It was the least of his father's problems, but he didn't know it yet.

"I know you missed him when the two of you weren't together," Chris's father began.

"I did."

"Then I'm happy to hear you're together again. Has Jacob

gotten over the fact that he'll be alpha mate if the two of you stay together?"

This was it. Chris was about to tell his father that everything they'd worked toward for the past five years had been for nothing. "Actually, he won't be. I've decided that I want to step down from the alpha heir position."

Chris's father stared at him. For once, Chris wasn't able to read his father's expression, and it scared him. He doubted his father would hit him, but he wouldn't be surprised if he started yelling, and he didn't want that, either.

What Chris wanted was for his father to accept his decision, but he knew that wouldn't happen. His dad would try to get him to change his mind in any way he could, even if it was an underhanded one. Chris was wary, but he was also angry.

His father had so many expectations for him, and he'd never understood that Chris didn't want this. Chris was ready to bet it had never crossed his father's mind that Chris wouldn't want to be alpha. He never considered Chris the man, just Chris the future alpha. Now, he was faced with the fact that he'd been wrong.

"What are you talking about?" he finally asked.

Chris swallowed. "I never wanted to be your heir. I never wanted to be an alpha. I want to move to the cete with Jacob. I already talked to Nico, and he's okay with taking my place."

"But he's not the firstborn son. You are."

"I know. It doesn't matter, though. I still don't understand why one of my sisters couldn't be the alpha."

"Because girls don't become alphas."

"Neither do carriers."

"You can't do this, Chris. *You* are the next alpha, not Nico. I understand that you want to spend time with Jacob, and I don't mind. You are *not* going to move in with him, though. If you two want to live together, he'll have to move here."

It was hard to push back. Chris was used to obeying his father, especially when he was talking that way, so it felt like the words wouldn't be able to cross his lips. "Are you ordering me as my alpha?" he asked.

His father's expression shifted. "Would it work? You don't know what you're doing. You're back with Jacob, and you want everything to be perfect. It's not realistic, though. The two of you have to realize that."

"Why can't it be? Thomas wouldn't force any of his children to become the alpha if they didn't want to."

Chris's father slammed a hand on his desk, making Chris jump. "I don't care what Thomas would or wouldn't do. I'm not him. We're not badgers. You are my son, my *heir*, and you're going to do what I tell you to do."

Chris wanted to say yes. He wanted to fall back into line and make his father happy. He'd been proud of Chris until now, but that was long gone.

Saying yes would be the easiest way out. Chris's father would stop being angry, and Chris would go back to his normal life.

It wasn't what Chris wanted, though. He rose to his feet, facing his father. "Are you going to kick me out if I continue saying no?"

"It would be my right to do so. You're my son. You should obey my orders."

"I'm nineteen. I'm not a child anymore. I'm an adult, and I can make my own decisions." Which he had. It was terrifying, but he was finally doing what he wanted instead of what was expected of him.

"You might technically be an adult, but you're still a child. The fact that you're with Jacob doesn't change that. I shouldn't have allowed the two of you to work together."

"Why did you, then?"

"Because I want you to be happy. I thought that if you and

Jacob got back together, he would move here. I never imagined that you would give up everything for him. It's ridiculous. You can't give up your life and your future for a man. You can have any man you want, most of them better than him, but there's only one alpha position."

That made Chris angry. So far, he'd been content to let his father yell at him because he knew he deserved it. His father had no right to talk about Jacob that way, though. "He's a good man. I won't stand here and listen to you talk about him like that. I've made my decision. I hate disappointing you, but I need to live *my* life, not the life you want and chose for me. I never wanted it. I never said anything because I wanted to keep you happy, and now I realize that while you were, *I* wasn't. Is that really what you want? For one of your sons to be unhappy? Because I already was, and I'll continue to be if you force me to stay."

"You're being ridiculous. Stop acting like a child. You just told me that you were an adult, but you're not acting like one. I won't stand for this, Chris."

Chris sighed. He'd hoped his father would want him to be happy, but apparently, he didn't care about that. The only thing he cared about was that he was losing his heir.

Jacob had to talk to Thomas. Now that he and Chris had decided that Chris would move in with him, he needed his alpha's approval. He was pretty sure Thomas would give it without too many problems, but still. He had to talk to him.

He knocked on the office door and waited for Thomas to tell him to enter to open the door. Thomas was behind his desk, but he smiled when he saw Jacob. "I wasn't expecting you."

"That's because I have to talk to you about something that's not work. Although if you want, I can give you a report on what's going on with the humans."

"Whatever you think is more important. I'm sure the humans can wait."

This was one of the reasons Jacob loved Thomas so much. As the alpha, he *had* to find out what was going on with the humans, but he was more interested in what was happening in Jacob's private life. He wanted Jacob and everyone else in the cete to be happy.

Jacob sat on the other side of his desk and stared at his alpha. "I'm sure you'll be happy to find out that Chris and I are back together."

Thomas's smile widened. "I am. It's what I was hoping for when I got both of you to work together."

"So you *were* playing matchmaker."

"I admit I wasn't sure it would work. But I knew that you and Chris still loved each other, and I wanted both of you to be happy. I'm glad it happened."

Jacob tapped his fingertips on his bouncing knee. "We talked, and we came to a decision."

Thomas grimaced. "Are you moving in with the clowder? I can't say I'm happy about that, but I won't try to stop you. You have to follow your heart."

Jacob was touched that Thomas would have agreed to it without thinking twice about it. "That's not what I wanted to tell you, no. You *don't* know everything, even though you're the alpha."

Thomas chuckled. "I'm very much aware of that. What is it, then?"

"Chris wants to move in with the cete, into my house."

Thomas blinked. "I have questions."

"I'm happy to answer them if I can."

"When you say that Chris wants to move in with you, what's that going to mean for his position as his father's heir?"

"He wants to give it up. He's never wanted to become

alpha, but he was forced into it because he wanted to make his father happy. He wanted him to be proud, and he thought that was how we would manage that."

"I'm sure Dan *is* proud of him."

"He probably won't be once Chris talks to him. But anyway, Chris never wanted it, and he's finally decided to tell his father that. We want to be together, but he doesn't want us to be with the clowder. He wants to be a normal person and move in with me. That is, if you're okay with it."

"I am. I wouldn't have been trying to get the two of you together again if I weren't. I'm surprised, but I'm more than happy to welcome him here. You don't even have to ask."

"Thank you."

"I *am* a bit worried about Dan, though. He won't be happy about this. There's also the fact that Chris might regret giving up that position eventually. Have the two of you talked about it?"

The niggle of doubt was back in Jacob's mind, but he did his best to ignore it. "We have. Chris insists that he's not doing this for me, or to be with me, but for himself. This is his chance to leave all of that behind. We both know his father won't be happy, but hopefully, he'll get over it eventually. Chris *is* his son, after all. He should want him to be happy."

"That, and Chris is an adult. I hope you're right when you say he won't regret it. But if he made his decision, then I won't try to change his mind, and I doubt you will, either. I'm truly happy for both of you."

"So he can move in?"

"Of course. Let me know if he needs help, whether it's to move his things, or to talk to his father." Thomas hesitated. "I know how harsh Dan can seem to you in this situation. He's not a bad man, though. I've known him for decades. He wants the best for the clowder, and that's what he's been working toward."

"I understand wanting what's best for the clowder since he's the alpha, but does that mean that he can't want what's best for his son, too? Look at you. I know you wouldn't have forced Alex to take your place if he wasn't okay with it, just like you didn't force Levi to get married even though he was twenty-six and in danger. You won't sacrifice your sons' happiness for the cete."

Thomas smiled. "And Dan probably thinks I'm an idiot because of that. I agree with you. But like I said, I don't think Dan has been doing this because he was trying to hurt Chris. He has a one-track mind, and that track is the clowder's safety. Now that Chris won't be his heir anymore, he'll have to find someone else, and as I'm sure you're aware, it's not that easy."

"In this case, it is. Chris's twin brother has already agreed to take Chris's place. He was happy about it. He wants more responsibilities, and he doesn't have anything against becoming the alpha."

"Is he aware of the many responsibilities?"

"I'm sure he is. He hasn't been raised focused on it the way Chris was, but he was still around. He knows what he's walking into. I'm not sure Dan will accept it, though, and I'm worried."

Thomas nodded. "I understand. If you need anything, feel free to come to talk to me. That goes both for you and Chris. I can try talking to Dan and make him see that it's for the best. He's been raising Chris as a future alpha, but it doesn't mean Chris would have *been* a good alpha. People who don't want to be sometimes are, but sometimes, they come to resent the position. It's not for everyone. Being an alpha means that you're not as free to be who you are or who you want to be as everyone else is."

"Do you regret it?" Jacob was curious. He and Thomas talked often, but not about this kind of thing. He couldn't imagine anyone else at the head of the cete, although eventually, that would happen. The cete would be in good hands with Alex, who was more than willing to take his father's place.

Thomas sighed and looked out the window. "Sometimes. I loved my father, and I was eager to take his place when I was younger. It's a hard position, though. There are a lot of responsibilities and choices to make, especially in these trying times, when the forest is in trouble. But I'm doing my best, both for the cete and for my sons. I would never demand them to take my place if they didn't want to. It would be too easy for them to resent both me and the position, and to make a mess out of it."

"I understand."

Thomas looked at Jacob again. "I *am* happy, and I've been happy for decades. My father never forced me to marry someone I didn't love, and I think that had a lot to do with it. He was proud of me, even when I put my own spin on the cete, and when I married my wife. But it's easy to imagine a life in which I wouldn't have had to become the alpha. It would have been very different, but this life is good, too. I don't regret it, but I don't want anyone who's not willing to do this to have to do it."

"What would you have done if Alex hadn't wanted to become alpha?" They both knew that neither Levi nor Joey, Thomas's other two sons, would have wanted the position.

"I would have turned to the beta, or to someone else. I would never have expected them to do anything they weren't willing to do. In Chris's situation, though, it's different. Chris agreed to it for a long time."

"Because he thought was the only way to make his father proud." And Jacob suspected that was the case.

"Dan should be proud of whatever Chris does with his life, as long as Chris is happy." Thomas clicked his tongue. "If he causes any trouble, come to me. I'll talk to him. And tell Chris that I might not be his father, and this might not be his home, but he *is* welcome here. Everyone will be happy to have him around."

Jacob had known this was how the conversation would go, but he was still relieved. Now, Chris had to face his father, and there was no way to know how *that* conversation would go.

Chris was a mess when he knocked on Jacob's door. He hadn't told Jacob he was coming, but he'd needed to walk away from his father.

Things had got even worse after they'd talked. Chris's father had refused to listen to anything Chris had to say. He was convinced Chris was making a mistake, and that eventually, he would regret it.

Chris couldn't help but wonder if maybe his father was right. He didn't want to regret choosing Jacob and a life free of responsibilities when it came to the clowder over being the next alpha. He knew he never wanted to be an alpha, but he'd gone along with it for many years. Was his father right, then? Would Chris regret giving up the position once he found himself without it? Would he want to take that spot back?

That was Chris's father talking, and Chris knew it. Even though his father hadn't known it, he'd never wanted to be alpha. That hadn't changed. It was *never* going to change, especially now that Chris had a better grasp on what being an alpha was like. His father couldn't understand it because he'd never felt that way.

The door swung open, and Jacob stood there. His hair was damp, and he was bare-chested, wearing only pajama pants. "Chris?"

Chris shook his head and stepped right into Jacob's arms.

Thankfully, Jacob didn't ask what was going on. He just wrapped his arms around Chris and held him until Chris felt steady enough to explain.

"I told my father."

Jacob's arms tightened around him. "I take it that it didn't go well?"

"Well, it could have gone worse. My father didn't kick me out of the clowder or anything like that, so I guess there's hope."

Jacob pulled Chris inside the house. "Tell me."

Chris didn't want to talk about it, but Jacob had to know. "I told him that I wanted to be with you, and he thought it meant that you would move in with the clowder. When I explained that wasn't the case, he wasn't happy. He told me I was making a mistake and that I would regret it."

"That's what Thomas is wondering, too."

Chris looked Jacob in the eyes. "I won't. You know I won't. I want this, and I'm happy to be rid of that weight on my shoulders."

Jacob's expression was gentle. "I know that's what you think now, but things might change. You might never have wanted to be an alpha, but you do want to make your father happy. It's something that's always influenced you, and this situation isn't any different. For now, you're happy to be with me, and that eclipses every other feeling. Eventually, though, if your father keeps pushing, you might decide that you did make the wrong decision."

Chris opened his mouth to tell Jacob that wasn't the case, but Jacob shook his head.

"Don't say you won't ever regret it because you can't know what the future will be like. I hope you'll stay with me, but I won't try to stop you if you want to go back to the clowder. I hope you won't, and I want to believe you when you say it, but you can't make any promises, and neither can I."

He was right. Chris wanted to swear that he would never change his mind, but he already almost had. It had been hard to go against what his father was saying. Jacob was right— Chris wanted to make his father happy.

He wasn't sure why. He'd never been a rebellious teenager, even though he'd wanted to do just that. It didn't make sense. But his father had a way of making him feel important and seen when they worked together, and Chris wanted more of that. The only Chris his father saw was the future alpha, not his son, and it hurt. It hurt especially now that Chris had probably lost that, but he couldn't go back on it.

He didn't want to. What he wanted was to be with Jacob, which was why he was here. He loved Jacob, and that wasn't going to change.

But Chris couldn't promise that, either.

Neither he nor Jacob could tell what the future would be like for them, but they *could* work toward making it a good one. If they wanted to be together, they would have to work for it, but that was okay. Neither of them was afraid of hard work. Hell, Chris had just done something he'd never thought he could do, and while it hadn't been easy, he didn't regret it. It had shown him that he was stronger than he thought, and that was a good thing. It meant that he could stand up to his father, no matter what his father said.

"Did he yell at you?" Jacob asked.

"Not really. But he was disappointed, and he made sure I knew."

Jacob snorted. "Of course he did. He wants you to change your mind, and he knows that's the best way to make it happen."

A few months ago, Chris would have been offended that Jacob talked about his father that way, but now, he realized how right Jacob was. Chris had no doubt his father loved him, but now, he could see how manipulative he was. He used his knowledge of Chris and how he wanted to make him proud to his advantage. "Well, it's over. I told him I was moving here."

"Thomas agreed. He also said that if you want to talk about your father or anything related to the situation, he's always available."

Chris's chest felt tight. Why couldn't his father be more like Thomas? Thomas was a good person, and he was a good alpha. He would never force his sons to do anything they didn't want. Chris knew his father loved him, but he didn't love him *enough*. He didn't want Chris to live his own life, and now that Chris had accepted that, it hurt. Why didn't his father want him to be happy? Why were the alpha position and the clowder more important than Chris?

Chris doubted he would ever get an answer.

"Are you staying for the night?" Jacob asked. He was gentle, as if he expected Chris to break down.

"If you want me to."

"I always want you to."

"I'm staying." Chris was going to have to go back home to pack his things, and hopefully, to talk to his father again. He prayed that if he let his father stew in his anger, he would change his mind, or at the very least, accept that Chris wasn't his puppet anymore. He wasn't sure that would happen, but he could hope.

Still, before that happened, he wanted some time to think. He wanted his father to realize what was going on. He wanted his dad to understand how much he was hurting him.

"I can go back home with you if you want. I can help you pack and keep your father away from you." Jacob looked like he was going to do just that, and Chris was touched.

Yes, Chris's father loved him, but Jacob loved him more. He'd shown that when he'd been ready to let Chris go — when he *had* let him go. It was the opposite of what Chris's father was doing.

"I don't think that will be necessary, but thank you."

"Don't even mention it. I know how hard this is for you."

"It is. I hoped my father would have a different reaction, but I knew that wouldn't be the case. Don't worry too much about me. I'll be fine."

"I know you will. You're strong, stronger than you think, and stronger than your father thinks. But you don't have to be, not when you have me in your life. If you need me, I'll be there. I'll help you stand up, face your father, whatever you need from me."

"Thank you." This was why Chris knew he'd made the right decision. Not only had Jacob let him go because he thought it was the best thing to do, but he was ready to fight for Chris, to keep Chris happy.

Chris's father wouldn't even consider that possibility.

CHAPTER ELEVEN

It wasn't the first time Chris woke up in Jacob's arms, but it was the best one so far. He wasn't afraid of what would happen next, of what his father would say. He already knew. His father was angry, but what had happened yesterday felt almost like a dream next to the position Chris was in now.

He wanted to wake up in Jacob's arms every day. He wanted this to be the rest of his life.

"Isn't it too early to smile the way you're smiling?" Jacob grumbled.

Chris laughed. "It's never too early to smile. Good morning."

Jacob kissed the back of Chris's neck. "Good morning."

Chris twisted until he could turn around and face Jacob. "How did you know I was smiling?"

"I could feel it. You're vibrating."

"It's because I'm happy."

Jacob peered at Chris. "No regrets?"

"Are you going to ask me every morning?"

"Until I'm sure that you don't have regrets. So?"

"No regrets," Chris confirmed. He couldn't promise he *never* would have regrets, but for now, he felt happy and like he'd made the right choice.

"Good." Jacob kissed Chris's forehead. "You have anything planned for today?"

"Not really."

"You want to go home and grab some of your stuff?"

"Not yet." Chris would have to eventually, but he wasn't

ready to face his father yet. He was lucky he'd started moving some of the stuff in Jacob's house once they'd gotten back together, so he wouldn't have to go naked or wear Jacob's clothes.

"Once you're ready, we can go together. Or I can stay here if you want me to. This is your show, so you're the one making the decisions."

"I know. But thank you for offering to go with me. I'm going to need the support, even if you don't come."

"Your father is an idiot." Jacob dragged Chris closer. "I don't know why he can't see what's right in front of his face."

Chris didn't want to talk about this again, but he was curious. "What do you mean?"

"You look so much happier and relaxed. Your father should be able to see that. Instead, he's only focused on what he's going to lose when it comes to the alpha position. He might lose you as a son if he doesn't accept your decision, but he doesn't seem to care about that. I don't like it. I don't like *him*."

Chris laughed. "You've made that abundantly clear. You don't have to like him. It's fine. Right now, I don't like him very much, either."

"But he's your father. That's never going to change."

Chris sighed. "I know. And I don't *want* it to change. He's not an easy man, but he's still my dad, and I love him. I hope that he loves me enough to allow me to do this and not kick me out of his life."

"Even if he does, you'll always have me."

"I know." It was one of the reasons Chris had been strong enough to talk to his father. Still, thinking about it made his stomach churn, and he wanted to stop, at least for a bit. "Want to shower together?"

Jacob blinked. "That was a strange change of topic. First we were talking about your father, and then you want to shower with me."

Chris grimaced. "Can we not talk about my father and us having sex at the same time? Those two things don't go in the same conversation."

"Sex? You said you wanted to shower together, not that we were having sex."

Chris rolled his eyes, but he couldn't stop smiling. "You knew what I meant."

"Maybe. Still up for it?"

Chris took one of Jacob's hands and pushed it under the blankets until his fingers touched Chris's hard cock. "What do you think?"

They raced each other to the bathroom, Chris almost slipping on the carpet in front of the shower. He turned the water on, and two arms wrapped around him from behind. Jacob's hard cock pressed against Chris's ass, and Chris sucked in a breath.

This wasn't something they'd done. Chris had wanted to, and he still did. He wasn't sure he was ready, though. It felt like a huge step, even though it wasn't. He wasn't a virgin after all. Having Jacob fuck him wouldn't change that, or anything else.

"Relax. I'm not going to take you like this," Jacob murmured.

"I know."

"Then why are you so tense?"

"I was just thinking that we haven't done *that* yet."

"And we never have to do it if you don't want to. I love what we have, Chris. I love *you*. Having or not having penetrative sex isn't going to change any of that."

And *this* was another reason Chris knew he'd made the right choice. Jacob cared about him and what he wanted. He would never push him to do something he was against, which was more than Chris could say about his father.

But he didn't want to think about his dad right now.

When he and Jacob got out of the shower, Chris was much more relaxed. His knees felt like they would buckle at any second, and Jacob had to hold him up. "Maybe next time, we can do that in bed," he said.

"I don't know. I like touching your naked wet skin."

"I'm sure we can come up with something. Maybe we can buy a stool for the shower or something."

Chris wrinkled his nose. "That's not very sexy, though."

"Maybe we can update the bathroom and make it bigger so we can include a bench inside it or something like that. It could be our first project together."

Chris's heart raced—although it could be because of the sex they'd just had. He could see both of them working together on the shower. He could see them making this house their home, for both of them, not only Jacob.

"I'd like that."

Jacob smiled softly. "So would I."

They went back to the bedroom to dress, and Chris's phone beeped, catching his attention. He was wary, but he didn't want his family to think he dropped off the surface of the earth. He didn't want to talk to his father, but he could talk to his siblings.

It wasn't any of them, though. His mom had texted him, and she was asking when he would be home. He hadn't talked to her before leaving yesterday, and he felt guilty about it.

"Breakfast?" Jacob asked.

"Please. I'm starving."

Jacob looked at the phone. "What's going on?"

"It's my mom. She wants to know when I'll be home."

"What did you tell her?"

"Nothing yet. I know I have to go home eventually. I haven't even talked to her. The only one I talked to was my

154

father, and I left as soon as that was over because I couldn't stand sitting there for one minute longer. She's no doubt worried, and who knows what my father told her. Probably that I'm a disgrace or something like that."

"She's your mom. She loves you, and I'm sure she'll see this is the best for you."

"I hope so." But Chris couldn't be sure. His father didn't want that, so why would his mother?

"Do you want to call her?"

"Not right now."

"What do you want to do, then?"

"I want to have breakfast with you. I want to forget about everything else for a bit. I'm going to have to go back home soon, but I don't want to think about that one second before I actually have to do it."

Jacob stared at him for a moment. Then, he nodded. "All right. Let's get breakfast."

Chris gave his phone another glance. His mom hadn't texted again, but he knew how worried she had to be. Instead of ignoring it, he snatched it from the dresser and quickly wrote an answer.

I'll be home later this morning. Don't worry about me. I'm fine. I'm happy. I'm sorry I didn't talk to you.

Once that was done, he put his phone down again. He was going to have to tell Jacob that he would go home today, and he wasn't looking forward to it. He wished he could stay in this happy bubble he and Jacob had, but he couldn't. He had to face reality, even though it was much sooner than he wished to.

But once that was done, it would be over, and he would be allowed to stay here with Jacob for the rest of his life. *That* was what he had to focus on.

Life couldn't get any better. Jacob had been happy before, or rather, he'd been content. He had a home, a job he loved, and friends. This was so much better, though. Now he also had Chris, and he couldn't believe how much happier he was.

He was walking on clouds. That was the only way he could describe it. He knew some people would make fun of him, but it would be all in good jest. Everyone wanted to see him happy, and that wasn't going to change. The cete was home, and its members were his family.

He wished he could have gone with Chris. Instead, Chris had headed home on his own, and Jacob couldn't help but wonder what was going to happen. He could only imagine what Chris's father would have to say, which was why he'd wanted to go with Chris. Chris had told him he needed to do this on his own, though, and Jacob wasn't going to argue that. It wasn't his place. Just like Chris was adult enough to make the decision to step away from his family and the alpha position, he could make the decision of going home and talking to his parents on his own. Besides, it was probably better this way. Dan wouldn't be happy to see Jacob.

Jacob was wary. He was afraid Chris's father would manage to change Chris's mind. He would definitely try. That was one thing Jacob was sure of. Hopefully, Chris would be strong enough to resist his father.

Since Jacob didn't have anything to do today and was feeling angsty because of Chris being gone, he decided to take a walk in the forest. Maybe he would cross paths for someone he could talk to. If he didn't, he could always go to the Bishop house and see what was going on there.

He shifted for a bit, sniffing around and making sure no one had been around his house who shouldn't have. The only things he could smell were badgers, with a hint of other shifters. They were familiar, though, and Jacob knew that he and his house were safe. It soothed his instincts, and it made it easier to deal with Chris being gone.

He found a patch of sun behind the house and curled up in it, sighing as he closed his eyes.

He couldn't wait until his and Chris's scents were mixed. It was going to be strange, with Chris being a bobcat, but Jacob couldn't wait. He knew the cete would welcome Chris, just like they'd welcomed every other shifter who had become part of their family. They'd *already* welcomed Chris when he had been staying at the Bishop house. Things had changed, but not that much. Jacob knew that the cete members would be happy for him and that they wanted him to be happy.

He was.

"Who is that, do you think?" a voice asked.

Jacob had been dozing, but he blinked open his eyes and stared at the men standing above him. They were both pregnant and holding hands. They looked gorgeous, and Jacob smiled — or at least, he smiled as much as he could since he was still in his badger form.

Kaspar shrugged. "How am I supposed to know who that is? They're all the same."

"I would be offended if I were him. Or her? I didn't check," Julian answered.

Jacob rolled his eyes and shifted back. Neither man seemed to care that he was naked, but Jacob still grabbed his jeans and pushed his legs into them. "I'm not offended. We do all look alike."

"See? I told you." Kaspar sounded smug.

"I suppose that all shifters look like each other if they shift into the same animal."

"Not you. You're the most gorgeous weasel I've ever seen."

"You're so sweet, you're going to make my teeth rot," Jacob told them.

Luckily, they weren't offended. "We're still in the honeymoon phase," Julian said. "Just like you and Chris."

Jacob wasn't surprised Julian and Kaspar were aware of

the fact that he and Chris were together again. "Does the entire cete know?"

"Of course they do. He's been seen coming and going from your house."

Jacob put his shoes on and got to his feet. "It could be because we're working together."

"He wouldn't need to come to your house if that were the case. You don't have to tell us if you don't want to, but we're happy for you. Everyone is."

Jacob *wanted* to talk to someone. Raven had done another of his disappearing acts, and he was nowhere to be found. Jacob had tried to find him, to no avail. Raven was his best friend, but they didn't spend a lot of time together. Raven was too wild for that. He disliked staying in one place for long, and in the past few months especially, he'd been disappearing for days at a time. Jacob wanted to ask him why, but he hadn't. He didn't want Raven to feel like he had to explain himself.

That left him a bit lonely, though, and with no one but Chris to talk to. He supposed he could talk to Thomas, and he had, but it wasn't the same thing. Thomas was a friend, but he was also Jacob's alpha.

Julian and Kaspar, on the other hand, weren't. They were friends, and Jacob had spent enough time with them at the Bishop house to know they would keep whatever he told them to themselves until Chris was ready for the entire world to know what was happening.

"We're together again," he confirmed. He couldn't help but smile at Julian's beaming smile.

"So we were right," Kaspar said.

"You are. We talked, and we decided to try a second time."

"What about the entire situation, though? There's a reason you broke up in the first place. Has any of that changed?"

"It has. Chris told his father that he wanted to move here

with me and that he wouldn't be his heir anymore."

Julian gasped, while Kaspar sucked in a breath.

"He really did?" Julian asked.

"He did. He talked to his father yesterday, and he went back this morning to talk to his mother. He also needs to pack his things. He's coming back, though." Julian and Kaspar looked happy, but Jacob could see they were also hesitant. "What's going on?" he asked.

Julian and Kaspar looked at each other. Kaspar shook his head, but Julian was more forward, and he explained, "I can't help but wonder if Chris is going to regret it. I'm happy for both of you, and I hope he won't, but we all know how important it was for him."

"He's never wanted to be an alpha," Jacob said. He wasn't sure whether or not they were aware of that.

"Even so. He might never have wanted it, but he's been training for it for years. I'm not saying he *will* regret it or anything like that, but I'm a bit worried. I know how important his father is to him, and how much influence he has over him."

Jacob had been trying to stay positive, but Julian's words hit hard. "He can do it. I know he can," he forced himself to say.

"I'm sure you're right. Chris isn't the kind of person who would make this decision on impulse. He's no doubt thought about it for days, if not longer. I'm sorry. I didn't mean to make you worry. I shouldn't have said those things."

Jacob shook his head. "I'm glad you did, because it means you care."

"I do care. I never had anyone before I moved here, and I can't believe how many friends I found." Julian looked at Kaspar, who smiled at him. "And not only that. I found friends, but also a man to love and a family. I'd like to think you're part of that family, Jacob. That's the only reason I felt free to say that."

Jacob reached for Julian, gently squeezing his arm. "Of course I'm part of your family." It broke his heart a little to hear Julian say that, because he knew how important it was to him. Julian had spent most of his life alone in the woods, and now he didn't have to anymore. "Don't worry about it. I know you brought up those doubts because you want to make sure I'm happy and that nothing will disturb that happiness. Chris will be fine, though. I'm not saying it will be easy for him to go against his father, but he can do it."

Jacob couldn't think of the situation in any other way. He didn't want to lose Chris again, especially not to Chris's father.

He had to stay back and see what happened, though. The situation was out of his hands, no matter how much he hated it.

It was an intervention. There was no other word for it, and Chris wasn't looking forward to it.

He should have known this would happen when his mother had reached out to him. He'd felt guilty about not telling her what was happening, and he hadn't thought beyond making her feel better. Now that he was home, his parents were waiting for him in the kitchen. They both looked up at him when he walked in, and his father gestured at one of the chairs at the dining table.

"Sit down."

Chris almost rolled his eyes. Still, it was ingrained in him to obey, and he knew they would have this conversation anyway, so he settled in front of his father. His mom was next to his dad, and together, they were trying to show a united front to Chris.

"Where did you go?" Chris's father asked.

"I spent the night at Jacob's. You already knew the answer to that, though, didn't you?"

His father ignored the question. "We need to talk about what's going on."

"We've already talked about it. I told you what I wanted, and you ignored it. You decided you knew better than me what I should do with my life, just like always."

"You're my firstborn son. I've been training and teaching you for the past five years. Are you really willing to throw all of that away for a man?"

"I'm willing to throw it away for *Jacob*. He's not just a guy. He's the man I love, and he loves me, too." Chris was nervous. He'd never stood up to his father this way, and even though he knew his father wouldn't be violent, it didn't mean he wouldn't yell at him. He didn't want that to happen, but for once, he was ready to face it if it did.

"All right. Let's say you actually do this. What will you do with your life? You're nineteen, but the only skills you have are the ones I taught you. If you can't be the next alpha, what will they be good for?"

"I don't know. But like you said, I'm only nineteen. I have the rest of my life to figure out what I want to do."

"What will you do for a living, then? Don't expect me to pay for you once to move out. Will Jacob do it? Will you be a kept man?"

Chris bit his lower lip. He hadn't thought that far, but he knew that Jacob would help him out if he asked for it. And Jacob wasn't the only one. Thomas would help, too, even if it meant going against Chris's father. Still, Chris wasn't looking forward to being a kept man, like his father said. He didn't *want* to be one, but it might be necessary until he found out what he wanted to do with his life. He doubted his father would understand that, though. "If that's what it takes for a bit, then, yes, I'll be a kept man. It's not a bad thing. I mean,

Mom is technically a kept woman, isn't she?"

Chris's father's eyes narrowed. "Don't talk about your mother that way."

"But you can talk about *me* that way?" Chris sucked in a breath. He couldn't allow this to escalate. If things went too far, he and his father would end up yelling at each other, and it was the last thing they needed. Chris wanted to go back to Jacob. He wanted to go *home*. That wouldn't happen if he started fighting with his father. "I apologize. I shouldn't have been disrespectful."

Chris's father nodded. "Damn right. You weren't happy without Jacob, but with him, you're another man. I don't recognize you, Chris."

Chris looked away. "That's because you never saw me. The Chris you knew was the one I was showing you, not the real one. You don't recognize me because that was never me. *This* is me, and you're going to have to get used to it."

"What your father is trying to say is that he's worried," Chris's mother intervened.

"I know he is. I'm worried, too. Leaving everything behind is terrifying, but I know I have to do this. I want to be happy, Mom. I don't know why Dad can't see that, but I've never wanted to be an alpha, even though I never told you or Dad about it. I am now, though, and you're not listening. How should I feel about that? You'd rather have me unhappy, *miserable*, and doing what you want rather than allowing me to live my life the way I want."

"We want you to be safe and happy. You have to understand that this is a big change, though."

"I know it is. I'm moving out. I'm leaving the life I knew behind. I'm moving in with my boyfriend. None of this is going to change my mind, though. I'll do this, whether you like it or not."

"If you do, we won't take you back," Chris's father warned.

Chris's mother gasped, but Chris kept his attention on his father. "You're kicking me out?"

"You don't belong here if you're not the future alpha."

"Will I be allowed to come back to visit? I mean, my sisters technically don't belong here, either."

"Stop talking to me that way. You know what I'm referring to, and you *will* obey. Either you stay and stay my heir, or you leave, and I never want to see you again."

Chris swallowed. He got to his feet, staring at his father. "All right. But remember, you were the one who made this decision, not me. Don't complain when I don't come back. I love you, Dad, but you're making it hard. You've never seen me, not beyond the fact that I would become the next alpha. You're kicking me out because I want to live *my* life, not the one you want me to live. You're not in the right here. You're going to hurt a lot of people by doing this, but I guess we all have to go along with it, since you're our alpha."

He had nothing else to say, and he knew his father wouldn't change his mind, so he turned around to leave. Chris's mother was sobbing, but he didn't look at her. He wanted to comfort her. He wanted to hug her, to tell her everything would be okay.

But she hadn't stood up for him like she should have. He was her son. She should want him to be happy, and she should stand up to his father for him. She wasn't, and even though it hurt and it was terrifying, Chris left both of them behind.

He didn't know what to do, so he headed to his bedroom to pack a bag. He grabbed everything he thought he would need in the next few days and everything important enough to him that he didn't want to leave it behind. Once that was done, he headed to his car. He climbed inside and stared at the windshield. Nico had been nowhere to be found, and Chris wondered where he was. He took his phone out and called his brother, who sounded happy when he answered.

"Chris! I don't think you'd call anytime soon. I thought you were still in bed with your boyfriend or something like that."

Chris licked his lips. "I need you."

Nico's tone changed. "What happened? What's wrong? Is it Jacob?"

"It's not. It's Dad. He kicked me out."

There was a pause before Nico swore. "Of course he did. And he waited for me to leave the house to confront you. God, I hate him sometimes."

Chris chuckled, but it was a wet sound. He was about to cry, and he didn't want to do that in front of his parents' home. "You're not alone. Where are you?"

"At Josiah's. Why don't you come here? Unless you want to go home to Jacob?"

It touched Chris that his brother thought of Chris's home as being with Jacob rather than in the house they both grew up in. "I'll come to you. I need to see you." He also needed to see Jacob, but Nico would understand more than Jacob ever could.

Nico had grown up with Chris. He'd always been put to the side because he wasn't the heir, and it was a wonder he didn't resent Chris for that. Chris didn't think he would ever be able to make up for it, but he was grateful his brother wasn't kicking him out of his life the way their father was.

"We're at Josiah's house. Come whenever you want. We'll both be here, and you can talk to us, or cry on my shoulders, or whatever you need. I'm sorry Dad did what he did."

"I'm sorry, too. I'll be there as soon as possible."

"I'll be waiting for you."

Chris knew this wouldn't solve anything. Nico wouldn't be able to make their father change his mind, but it didn't matter. Chris *didn't* need their father to change his mind. He needed to be supported through this, and he had a lot of people who could do that—Jacob, Nico, but also Josiah, and a long list of other people. Chris wasn't alone, and he would survive this.

CHAPTER TWELVE

Chris looked at the bathroom. "We did a good job, didn't we?"

Jacob stood next to him. "I don't know. I think the tiles could have been straighter."

Since Chris had been the one to put them down, he took that as a critique of his work. "It's the first time I've worked with tiles. What did you expect?"

Jacob turned to smile at him. "You're right. It's perfect."

"We can probably pull them and try again if you hate it."

Jacob shook his head and hooked an arm around Chris's shoulders to drag him closer. "It's perfect." He kissed the top of Chris's head. "Really. I'm glad we did this. I want this house to be your home, too, and I know it's not a given since I was here before you."

He wasn't wrong. It was taking Chris a while to get used to living here. He'd lived his entire life in his parents' house, and now he wasn't there anymore. He was sharing Jacob's home with Jacob, but he wanted it to be his home, too.

He didn't have a lot of things with him, which meant it was hard to see his imprint on the house. That would change, too. Once he settled down, he would start buying things like books and trinkets, and he would make this place his home. In the meantime, though, it felt good to help Jacob renovate the bathroom.

The shower was bigger now, and it included a bench. Chris was planning on using it as soon as possible, and he couldn't help but smile. They hadn't done all of this just because they wanted to have sex in the shower, although that had been a big reason. The shower was more comfortable now, and Chris couldn't wait to use it.

"You did a good job," Jacob said. "Maybe you could make this your job."

Those words made Chris's stomach churn. "I don't know what I want to do with my life."

"I wasn't trying to be pushy. I'm just saying you were good at this."

"You just said the tiles were crooked."

"It doesn't mean they don't look good. You have all the time in the world to decide what you want to do. Ignore what I just said."

But Chris couldn't. He'd been worried about finding a job since he'd moved in with Jacob a few weeks ago. He hadn't talked to his parents during that time, and he missed them, but he knew it was for the best. His father still hadn't accepted that he didn't want to be his heir, and that wasn't going to change anytime soon. Chris had better get used to not having his parents in his life.

At least he still had Nico and their sisters.

Nico especially had been close to him, but then, they'd always been close. They'd been born at the same time, and they spent all their lives being close. Still, Chris had been surprised and relieved when his sisters had agreed with him. He knew Lucy had always resented the fact that even though she was the firstborn, she couldn't be the alpha. She was thirty-two now, and she would have been a great heir to their father. It would never happen. Their father was strange that way. He didn't see a problem with Chris being an alpha even though he was a carrier, but he didn't want a woman to lead the clowder.

It was stupid, and Chris was even more grateful that he'd left all of that behind.

He missed it, though. He missed his father and his mom, and even his home. He was working hard on making Jacob's house his, too, but it wasn't enough, not yet. It would take time, but it was time he had. It wasn't like he had anything else to do. Jacob had tried to reassure him by telling him that he didn't care if Chris never found a job, but Chris couldn't depend on him for the rest of his life. He'd depended on his father too much, and now that his father had kicked him out, he saw how wrong that had been. He wasn't going to repeat that mistake with Jacob.

"What do you say about having lunch?" Jacob asked.

"That's a good idea. I'm starving."

They headed downstairs. Chris's phone vibrated in his pocket as he walked into the kitchen, and he took it out, smiling when he saw it was his brother. "What? Jacob and I are busy." He and Nico had been teasing each other. For whatever reason, Nico seemed to think that Chris and Jacob had sex all the time, and he always asked if he was interrupting them.

This time, though, he didn't answer with a joke. "I need you to come home."

Chris froze. "Why? What happened?"

"Someone shot Dad."

Chris didn't understand the words. He knew them, recognized them, but they didn't make any sense. "What do you mean?" It had to be a joke.

Nico sighed heavily. "Just what I said. We don't know who did it yet, but Dad is in the hospital in Rosewood. You have to come. We need you."

"Why? Why would someone shoot him?"

"I don't know. We need an alpha, and the beta wasn't trained for it." Nico hesitated. "And neither was I. We need *you*, both as family and as an alpha. I know you never wanted this, but it'll be only temporary."

"I'll be there soon as I can." Chris didn't even care about everything else his brother was saying. He just needed to get to his father and make sure he was okay.

"Call me once you're at the hospital. I'll come downstairs to get you."

"Do I have to pick up Lucy or someone else?"

"No. Everyone is here already. Don't worry about that. Just worry about getting here."

Chris hung up. He was still frozen, and he didn't know what his next step should be.

It was his fault, wasn't it? His father wouldn't have been shot if he hadn't left.

Jacob appeared in front of Chris. He grabbed both of Chris's shoulders. "What's going on? I only heard part of the conversation. Someone was shot?"

Chris nodded. He felt numb. "My father. I don't know anything else. Nico just told me that he was shot and that they needed me. I need to step into my father's shoes. I need to make sure he's okay."

"Of course. He's in the hospital in Rosewood?"

"He is. I have to go there."

"I know. I'll drive you."

Chris nodded, then shook his head. "It's not your problem. You don't have to do this."

"It *is* my problem. No matter how little I like it, your father is my father-in-law. Besides, I doubt you're in any state to drive right now. It will be safer if I drive." Jacob hesitated. "Do they know what happened yet?"

Chris shook his head. "They don't know anything." He swallowed. "I should have been there, though. If I hadn't left, maybe my father would be okay."

"You can't know that, and you shouldn't blame yourself for something you didn't do. The only person at fault here is the person who shot your father. You don't know whether or not you could have stopped this from happening if you'd been there. As far as you know, you would have been shot, too."

Chris swallowed. "Maybe it would have been better. I don't know what to do now. I have to take my father's place until he heals, but I don't even know if he will. What if he dies?" Nico was right. Neither he nor the beta knew how to be an alpha. Chris did, though, and if something happened to his father, he would have to go back. There was no way out of it.

Jacob grimaced. "We'll think about that if we have to, all right? They couldn't tell you how bad your father's condition is?"

"No."

"Then maybe it's nothing. Maybe it was just a scratch, and your father will be fine."

Chris could tell Jacob was trying to convince himself of that, but neither of them believed it.

Chris was freaking out, and it was entirely understandable. Jacob was glad they'd been together when Chris got the call. Chris would probably have tried to drive to the hospital otherwise, and it could have been a disaster. As it was, he kept bouncing his knee as he looked out the car window, and he was wringing his fingers.

Jacob didn't like how Chris thought it was his fault. He wasn't surprised, though. Chris already had so much guilt when it came to his father, and this was just another drop in the bucket. His father had tried hard to make sure that Chris felt indebted to him, and he'd succeeded. Now Chris felt guilty, even though he wasn't the one who had shot his father, and Jacob dreaded how things would end.

He also hated that apparently Chris was thinking about

moving back to the clowder, at least for now. He understood why, and in any other circumstance, he would have been more than happy to support Chris when it came to that. Jacob suspected that if Chris went back to the clowder and stepped into the alpha role, he wouldn't be coming back to him. He couldn't even begin to imagine what would happen if Dan died.

The situation was a mess, but he was going to be there for Chris as long as Chris wanted him to. The question was— would he?

Jacob already knew he was going to lose Chris, whether or not Dan died. He dreaded that moment, but in the meantime, he would be there for his boyfriend. He hated that Chris was blaming himself. He understood it was because Chris was terrified, but he wanted Chris to realize that he had nothing to do with this. His father would probably have been shot even if Chris had been there, and Jacob couldn't even think about how Chris might have died or been shot, too, if he'd been present.

Jacob didn't like that, but he didn't want Dan to die. If he had to choose between Chris and his father, though, he wouldn't even have to think about it. He'd want Chris to live, and to live with him.

All of that was pointless, though. Jacob could already tell he was losing Chris, and he didn't know what to do or how to stop it. He doubted he could.

"You don't have to stay once we're at the hospital," Chris suddenly said. He was still looking out the window, obviously not wanting to face Jacob.

"Do you *want* me to leave?"

"I don't know. Maybe. I don't, not really, but I'm technically the alpha now. I have to show everyone that I'm strong, and it's not going to happen if I have my boyfriend there hugging me and comforting me."

"You might be the alpha, but you're also a human being. You're obviously in pain. Your father has been shot, and you don't know what's going to happen to him. Anyone in your place would need to be comforted. It doesn't make you weak."

Chris chuckled darkly. "Maybe not in your eyes, but a lot of people will think it does. I can't afford for that to happen. Even though no one knows that I stepped down from the alpha heir position as far as I know, they'll be looking up at me. I can't allow any of them to think I'm weak. I have to do this the right way until my father gets better and can take his place again."

"What if it doesn't happen?" Jacob didn't ask what would happen if Chris's father died, but they both knew that was what he was referring to.

Chris swallowed. "I have no idea. I can't think about that right now. I have to believe he'll be okay eventually."

"I'm sure he will." Even though Jacob didn't know what had happened exactly, Dan was a fighter. He wouldn't leave the clowder behind, not if he had a say in it.

Jacob had to believe that this was only for now. He already knew Chris would move back in with the clowder, but that was okay. They hadn't lived together long, and they were used to being apart. Chris would come home once all of this was over, and they would go back to their life as a couple. Hell, they didn't have to break up for Chris to go home. He wasn't going to stay away forever.

Or at least, that was what Jacob was trying to convince himself of. He knew better, though. Even if Dan didn't die, he might have months of rehabilitation in front of him. During that time, Chris would have to be in charge, and that would keep him away from Jacob. His place was with the clowder right now. Jacob couldn't deny that, and he didn't want to. Chris needed to be with his family, and unfortunately, since he was still his father's heir, with the clowder. He would have to guide them and to make sure nothing happened to them. He would have to step into his father's shoes, something he'd never wanted. He would have to be an alpha, something he hated.

But there was nothing either of them could do about it.

"Just remember that I love you," he murmured.

Chris finally looked his way. "I know. I've never doubted that."

But it wouldn't be enough. Sometimes, love wasn't. Jacob couldn't blame Chris for choosing his father. How could he? Chris's father had been shot, and he might die. Jacob would forever feel guilty if he tried to take Chris away from this.

He was going to lose Chris, and they were both aware of it, even though Chris hadn't said anything. He was focused on his father, as was right.

"Do you want me to stay with you at the hospital?" he asked again. He needed to know.

"I told you I don't know."

"I'll stay for a bit, then. Just the time to find out what happened. That way, if you need me, I'll be close."

"You don't have to do that. I know you don't like my dad."

"I might not like him, but it doesn't mean I want him to die. What happened to him is hurting you, and that's the last thing I want. I want you to be happy."

Chris snorted. "How can I be happy when my father's just been shot?"

"That's not what I meant, and you know it. I know you're not happy right now, and I wish I could fix it. I'm just trying to help, Chris. There's no reason to fight with me. I'm here for you."

And he always would be. It didn't matter what happened between him and Chris. Now that Jacob knew what Chris really wanted, he would always be there for him, even if it was only as a friend. Chris wanted to be with him. He wanted them to build a life together. They wouldn't do it because of the circumstances happening around them. They couldn't control those, and they would have to go along with them, but Jacob knew the truth now. Chris loved him, and if he had a choice, he would stay with him. The problem was that he *wouldn't* have a choice, at least not for now.

This was going to hurt so badly. Jacob wanted to be there for Chris, but he could already feel his heart breaking in his chest. He could do nothing to prevent it. He loved Chris, and losing him would be hell.

But Jacob wasn't alone. He'd survived losing Chris once, and he could survive it a second time, too. He knew Chris would want to continue to try being together for a while, but he could see how guilty Chris felt, and eventually, that would reflect on their relationship.

In the meantime, though, Jacob wasn't going anywhere.

As soon as Jacob parked the car in front of the hospital, Chris rushed inside. He didn't even wait for Jacob, and he hoped Jacob wouldn't be offended. He needed to get to his father, and he needed to get there now.

Nico was waiting in the entrance, and as soon as he saw Chris, he rushed toward him. "Did you drive here? You shouldn't have. You look horrible."

Chris snorted. "Thanks for the compliment. I didn't drive, though. Jacob did."

Nico looked behind Chris. "Where is he, then?"

"I don't know. He might have gone home."

Nico arched a brow. "Did you *ask* him to go home?"

"I didn't. I just told him I wasn't sure whether or not I wanted him to stay."

Nico stared at Chris for a few moments. "You're an idiot,

aren't you?"

"Stop insulting me and tell me how Dad is."

Nico sighed. "I'll take you to him. We should wait for Jacob, though."

"I just told you I didn't know if Jacob was staying."

"If you think he's going home, you're wrong. That man loves you. Of course he's going to want to be with you when you need him most."

"I wasn't nice to him. I wouldn't be surprised if he left."

"He won't. I can promise you that."

"I just want to see Dad and find out what happened. Please."

Nico focused on Chris again. "Dad was in Rosewood. He had a meeting. I'm not sure what it was, but he hadn't asked me to go with him."

"Even though technically, you were his new heir?"

"I don't think he considers me that. He hasn't told anyone, and he hasn't talked to me about it. I think he still has hope you'll come back."

"Even after I told him I wouldn't?"

"You know how stubborn he is. Anyway, he was here in Rosewood. Someone shot him. That's all I know. I wasn't with him, and we only have the information we were given."

"Is he conscious?"

"He is. He'll be fine. He has to stay in the hospital for a bit, and it's not going to be easy, but he'll be okay."

The tension that had held Chris up until now flooded out of him, and his knees buckled. He thought he was going to fall until two strong arms wrapped around him from behind and held him up. He allowed himself to press against Jacob's chest, knowing it might be one of the last times he could do it. He didn't know what would happen next, but he doubted it would be good for either of them.

"Are you okay?" Jacob asked. "What happened? Is it your

father?"

"He'll be fine," Nico told Jacob. "He's conscious, and he wants to see Chris as soon as he arrives. Let's go."

Chris felt slightly better, but he was still grateful when Jacob took his hand. Together, they followed Nico through the hospital until they reached a room. The door was closed, and Nico stood there, watching Jacob and Chris. "I think you should wait outside," he told Jacob.

Chris knew he should have been defending his boyfriend, but he agreed. He turned to Jacob. "I'll be quick. I promise."

Jacob stared at him. He looked sad, almost as if he'd lost something. "Take all the time you want or need. I'm not going anywhere, not until you tell me to."

Chris wanted to kiss him, but he didn't. Instead, he let go of Jacob's hand, and he pushed open the door.

Nico was right behind him as they stepped into the room. Chris was surprised to see his father was alone, and he turned to Nico, frowning. "Where are Mom and the rest of the family?"

"I sent them to get something to drink," Chris's father said.

Chris turned his attention back to him. He'd never seen his father so pale. He was obviously in pain, and Chris looked at his body, trying to understand where he'd been shot. "What happened?"

Chris's father waved his words away. "What happened doesn't matter. It's in the past. What does matter is the future." He looked Chris straight in the eyes. "You're going to have to take my place."

Chris had known this was coming. He wouldn't have expected anything different from his father. "I'm not your heir anymore."

"Of course you are. I didn't tell anyone about that stupid decision you made. No one knows what you did, and it's going to continue that way."

"Someone else could do it."

"There's no one else. The beta can't work both his position and mine. Besides, he doesn't know how to be an alpha. You do, though."

"I still don't want to do it."

Chris's father tried to sit up, but he winced, and Chris rushed to his side. His father pushed him away before he could touch him and shook his head. "No one else can do it. Stop acting like a child, and face your responsibilities. Right now, *you* are the clowder's alpha, and you *will* act like it. I won't allow you to be selfish."

Chris swallowed and took a step back. "I'm not selfish."

"What do you call it, then? You're ready to leave everything behind just because you don't want to do something. You're ready to put the clowder in danger because you're in love."

There was scorn in Chris's father's voice, and every single word hit Chris like a blow.

"I just wanted to be happy." Chris's voice was barely more than a whisper, but he knew his father could hear him.

"Your happiness doesn't matter right now. I'm going to be out of commission for a while."

"Where were you shot?"

"In the chest. I've already had surgery, and I'll be fine. I need you to stop acting like a child and take care of the clowder for me."

Chris wanted to say no. He didn't want to go back, not now that he'd finally managed to escape. He knew there was no way out of it, though. His father was right—the beta couldn't take his place, and neither could Nico, although their father hadn't even mentioned him.

Chris swallowed. "All right. I'll come home for now."

His father's gaze was hard. "I suppose I can't get anything more than that. It's going to take me a while to get better, though. You won't be able to leave the clowder during that time."

"I won't. I'll take care of the clowder."

"At this point, I'm not sure I can trust you with it, but I don't have a choice." He sucked in a breath. "Now go. I have to rest, and I can't do that while listening to you."

Chris walked to the door. He paused once he got there, looking back at his father, but his father wasn't looking at him. He was staring at his phone, no doubt working already.

Chris didn't know what was going to happen. He had to help his father, though. There was no one else that could do it, and no matter how much Chris hated it, he was going to have to do this.

Jacob was still in the hallway when Chris and Nico stepped out. He was leaning against the wall, but he straightened as soon as he saw Chris. "What happened? I heard raised voices."

"He'll be okay. He was shot in the chest, but he already had surgery." Chris turned to his brother. "How long ago was he shot?"

"Early this morning."

"And it's past lunch. Why did no one tell me about it sooner?"

Nico shuffled his feet. "He told us not to. I think he wanted to see whether or not he would be able to get back to work right away. When it became obvious he couldn't, I decided to call you."

Chris shook his head. He was angry, but he couldn't take it out on Nico, who had only been obeying their father's orders. "You should have called me."

"I know. I'm sorry I didn't."

"It's fine." Chris turned his attention back to Jacob. "You should go home."

"I want to stay here with you. You don't have to do this

alone."

"I'm not doing it alone. I have Nico. I'll be fine, I promise." He hesitated. "I'm going to have to go back to the clowder. I can't come home. My father will take a bit of time to heal, and I need to take his place in the meantime."

"I understand." Jacob stared at Chris. "Just remember that you'll always have a home with me, no matter what happens. I love you."

Those words felt like a goodbye, like Jacob thought they were going to break up.

Chris was about to cry, and he couldn't say anything.

He suspected Jacob was right.

CHAPTER THIRTEEN

Chris was exhausted. He'd only been doing this for a week, but he felt like he could sleep for just as long and not being rested enough to face the amount of work he had to do.

He'd always known that being an alpha was a lot of work. He'd watched his father do it for years, so he'd been prepared for it. It was a lot more than he'd expected, though. He didn't know how to deal with most of it, even though his father had done his best to teach him. Chris had never wanted this, and sometimes, he hadn't listened the way he should have.

Now, he was in trouble because of that.

Between everything he had to do for the clowder, talking to the other alphas and reassuring them that his father would be okay and that the clowder wasn't indefinitely in a nineteen-year-old's hands, and worrying about his dad and Jacob, Chris didn't have any more brain space. It was too much, and several times a day, he could feel panic rise in his chest. When that happened, he had to sit on the floor under the desk, curling himself into a tight ball and trying to breathe.

It didn't always work, unfortunately.

He was under the desk when someone knocked on the office door. He didn't want to answer, but it could be important. He couldn't ignore it, so he got to his feet, tried to plaster a decent expression on his face, and went to open.

It was Nico. Chris relaxed when he saw his brother, but he still didn't want his twin to see how distraught he was. "What is it?"

Nico looked inside the office. "I wanted to see how you

were doing."

"I'm perfectly fine. Do you need anything that pertains to the clowder?"

Nico's eyebrows rose on his forehead. "I don't. I wanted to talk to you, though."

"I don't think I have time. I'm sorry."

Chris expected his brother to back down, but instead, Nico pushed him to the side and strode inside the office. The only thing Chris could do was close the door behind him and turn to face him. "What is it? I don't have much time."

Nico looked at Chris. He put his hands on his hips and stared until Chris wanted to squirm. "What are you doing?" Nico finally asked.

"I'm trying to keep the clowder in one piece. What did you think I was doing?"

"You're isolating yourself. You're only focusing on the clowder and Dad, and while I was grateful for the first few days, I can see how much it's tormenting you. What's going on in that brain of yours?"

Chris shook his head and went to sit behind the desk. He felt out of place there, and he was. This was his father's place, and Chris shouldn't be sitting there. It was his place for now, though, and he had to deal with it. "If you don't need anything, I have to get back to work."

"I do need something. I need you to stop acting like an idiot. Where's Jacob? I can't believe he hasn't come around yet, and I know it's not because he didn't want to. What did you tell him?"

"Nothing. You were with me the last time we talked."

Nico's eyes widened. "You mean you haven't seen him in a week? Have you at least called him?"

"I just told you I haven't talked to him since the hospital. We texted, but that's it."

"What are you doing? You finally managed to leave all of

this behind. You chose love, and now, you're giving it up?"

"I don't want to do this right now." Chris didn't want to think about everything he'd left behind, let alone talk about it.

"Pity, because we *are* doing it. You being the alpha for now doesn't mean you have to break up with Jacob. I know you don't have much time, but you should at least call him."

"I don't have time."

"You're retreating from him. You're isolating yourself. I know what you're doing, Chris. Eventually, you're going to break up with him because you feel guilty."

"What should I feel guilty about?" But Nico was right. Chris *did* feel guilty. Every time he talked to his father—and it happened several times a day—that guilt churned in his stomach. His father never missed a chance to tell him that all of this probably wouldn't have happened if Chris had been there, and Chris couldn't help but wonder if that was the truth. He'd thought about it, too, and maybe he could have done something to help his dad when he'd been shot. Instead, his father had been alone, and now, he was in the hospital.

"*I* should be doing this," Nico said.

"You can't. You haven't been trained."

"But you could help me. I could try doing it with you by my side, and it would give you more time to be with Jacob."

"I can't be with him, not right now. I also don't have time to deal with you."

Nico took a step back. "That was harsh."

"I'm sorry. I don't want to fight with you. I need your support."

"And you have it. You would have more support if you still talked to Jacob, though. Don't break up with him. He makes you happy, and there's no reason for you to."

But Jacob didn't want to be alpha mate, and Chris couldn't go home. He couldn't leave the clowder. His father relied on him, and he couldn't break the trust between them, not again, not so soon after his dad had been shot.

"Chris." There was urgency in Nico's voice. "Don't do it. Don't ruin the best thing you've ever had for Dad."

"How can you tell me that? Can't you see what's going on?"

"I see *exactly* what's going on. I see that you feel guilty. I see that Dad is using that to keep you here. He knows that if he plays this right, once he comes home, you won't be going back to Jacob. It's what he wants. He wants you to leave Jacob behind and come back home, but it's not the right thing."

"What *is* the right thing? The only right thing now is what I'm doing."

"Maybe so. You're right, I don't know how to be an alpha, and it doesn't make sense for me to try doing it now. You have a life outside the clowder, though. Don't ruin it by isolating yourself from Jacob. You'll be able to go back once Dad comes home."

Chris had to look away. He could tell his brother truly believed what he was saying, but Chris didn't. "I should have been there."

"What do you think would have happened if you had been? Dad would have been shot anyway. You wouldn't have been able to do anything to stop that from happening. If you had, *you* could have been shot, and you could have died. You think that would have made things better?"

"Of course not. But I could have helped after it happened."

"Stop thinking about that and focus on what he's doing to you. You can't allow him to control your life now that you've finally managed to escape."

But Chris hadn't. As soon as his father had needed him, he'd come running back. It was telling that even his love for Jacob hadn't been enough to get him to stand up to his father.

He sighed. "I have a lot of work to do, and I'm tired. I

understand what you're telling me, but it doesn't change anything. Let me do my job, Nico. Please. I need your support, not for you to yell at me."

Nico stared for a moment. Chris expected him to say no, and he was relieved when Nico nodded.

"Fine. I'll do everything I can to help you. This isn't over, though. I won't let you ruin your life."

Chris wasn't sure anyone could stop him from doing just that, though, not himself, and certainly not his brother.

Jacob parked in front of the alpha house. He looked up at the place in which Chris had lived all his life and was living again.

He missed Chris. They hadn't talked since Chris's father had been shot. They'd only texted, and even that, they'd only done so sporadically. Jacob felt that Chris was slipping through his fingers, and he didn't know how to stop it. He hoped that his presence here would help remind Chris what waited for him once this was over and that he had a home with Jacob.

If Jacob's house and cete were still his home. Jacob wasn't sure. He wasn't sure of anything anymore.

He got out of his car and headed toward the front door. He knocked, expecting someone to open right away, but it took ten minutes. He almost left, but he wanted to see Chris.

The door opened, but it wasn't Chris. It was Nico, and his expression didn't bode well. "Does he know you're here?" he asked.

"Hello to you too. No, he doesn't. He's not answering my phone calls." Jacob could have texted, but he was pretty sure Chris would have found a reason for him not to come. This was his only way to confront Chris, and while he wasn't looking forward to it, he suspected they both needed it.

Nico grimaced. "I'd like to tell you everything is going

well, but I'm sure you know that's not the case."

Jacob frowned. "Is it your father?"

"No, although him being back home isn't helping. It's Chris. He's exhausted himself, and even worse, he's isolating himself from everyone except our father. It's not going to end well. Either he's going to explode, or he'll collapse."

"Is there anything I can do to help?"

"I doubt it. The way I see it, he's going to push until he can't anymore. He won't even allow me to do anything. I'm really sorry, Jacob."

Jacob had expected this to happen but hearing it from Nico's lips made everything worse. "It's all right."

"It's not. He's fucking up his life, and he's doing it for nothing. He's allowing our father to get his claws into him again. I wish I could do something, but I tried, and there's no getting through to him. Maybe you'll manage."

They both knew that wouldn't be the case. Jacob had only half expected that today would end in him and Chris making up, but he wasn't surprised it apparently wouldn't. Chris had been distant since his father had been shot, and Jacob should have pushed. He hadn't because he'd thought Chris needed time, and now he regretted it. "Where is he?"

"The office. Let me show you the way."

Jacob followed Nico inside the house. He looked around, curious and hoping he wouldn't cross paths with Chris's father. He didn't know what he would do if that was the case. The man was probably resting, so Jacob tried to relax. It wasn't easy.

Nico stopped in front of the closed door and turned to face Jacob. "We both know what he's going to try to do. I'm not asking you to insist or to push back. There's only so much you can take. He's not doing this because of you, though. I know he still loves you."

"It's just not enough. It never was."

Nico grimaced. "Again, it's not because of you. I hate what my father did to Chris, but no matter how many times I try, I can't break through. Even my father won't listen to me."

"Because he has what he's always wanted."

"I suppose." He raised a hand and knocked on the door. "Good luck."

Jacob suspected he wouldn't be lucky today.

"What?" Chris called from inside.

Jacob and Nico looked at each other again. Then Jacob pushed the door open.

The first thing he thought was that Dan's desk was too big for Chris. The second was that Chris had been thin to begin with, but now, he was *too* thin. He looked like he wasn't eating well, which was probably the case.

Chris looked up when the door opened, and his eyes widened. "What are you doing here?"

"I wanted to check in on you and your father. How are you doing?" Jacob answered as he closed the door behind himself.

"As well as I can. My father is healing well, though." Chris paused and bit his lower lip. "I'm sorry, but I don't have time to talk to you. I have a lot of work to do."

"I know. But I've missed you." Jacob desperately wanted to touch Chris. He wanted to drag him into his arms and shield him from everything that was happening. He suspected Chris wouldn't allow him to, not in this room. Here, he had to be the alpha. He had to be strong and not need anyone, or at least, that was probably what his father thought. It was ridiculous, but Jacob couldn't fight against that.

He was starting to wonder whether or not he could fight against anything in this situation.

"You should have called. I hate that you came here for nothing."

Jacob didn't miss the fact that Chris hadn't told him he'd missed him. "It's fine. I have the day off. I thought I could take you away from a few hours, just some time to relax."

"I can't. I have too much to do."

"It's not going to help if you collapse because you're exhausted. Have you been eating and sleeping?" There were dark shadows around Chris's eyes, and Jacob knew the answer to that was no.

"When I have time. Look, I'm happy to see you, but you can't stay. I don't have time for you."

Jacob crossed his arms over his chest. "When will you? We're boyfriends, remember?"

Chris raked a hand through his hair. "And as my boyfriend, I hope you understand that I have to do this."

"I do understand, which is why I didn't come around sooner. You're not taking care of yourself."

"That's because I have too many other things to take care of. What do you want, Jacob? You already knew I wouldn't have time to see you. Why are you here?"

"I want to know what's going on. You haven't been talking to me. Nico told me that you're not talking to anyone but your father, and we both know that's not a good thing. He's going to push you into taking your place as heir back, and it's not what you want."

Chris got to his feet. "How would you know what I want? You're not around."

"And why is that? You haven't been *allowing* me to be around."

"It's because you don't belong here. This is a bobcat clowder. You're a badger."

Chris couldn't have hurt Jacob more if he'd physically hit him. "It doesn't mean we can't be together."

"Have you changed your mind, then? Do you want to be the alpha mate? Because right now, I'm the alpha, and I don't know when it's going to stop."

"Once your father feels better, he can retake his place."

"What if he never gets better? He's been shot, Jacob. It's not something he's going to heal from in a week or two."

"I'm just trying to be here for you. I'm trying to support you, but you can't see it."

"I wouldn't have been away in the first place if it weren't for you," Chris snapped.

Jacob took a step back. He knew it wasn't really Chris talking, or at least, he hoped so. It was the exhaustion, the sadness, the fear. Still, those words hurt, and Chris had said them as if he meant it. "You wouldn't have been able to do anything even if you'd been there when he was shot," he said.

"Maybe not, maybe yes. That doesn't take away from the fact that I wasn't there, and I should have been. I'm my father's heir."

"Not anymore."

Chris stared at Jacob. Jacob knew what it meant, and he could feel his heart breaking.

"I think I made a mistake," Chris said. "I've been talking to my father, and he showed me that. I should never have left. We can be together if you agree to be the alpha mate, but otherwise, I have other things to focus on."

Jacob shook his head. "You don't actually want any of this. You know it. You want to come home, and you can do that anytime you want, no matter what your father says. He's trying to use you. He's manipulating you and using the situation to his advantage. Don't let him do it, Chris."

Because if he did, he and Jacob truly were breaking up, and Jacob didn't know if he could deal with that.

Chris knew Jacob was right, but it wouldn't change anything. He was aware that his father was using being shot as a means to keep Chris here, and it was working. Because even though Chris was aware of all of that, he was still doing what his father wanted instead of what *he* wanted.

What he wanted was to go home with Jacob and never look back. What he wanted was for their relationship only to be father and son. Instead, his father was manipulating him, and Chris hated it. Right now, he hated his *father*.

He was doing better. He was still on bed rest, but it wouldn't last forever. Hell, knowing his father, Chris knew it wouldn't last another week. Soon his dad would be back on his feet, and even though he would need help, he would be able to retake his place.

He wouldn't allow Chris to go home. If it helped, he would act as if he was on his deathbed to keep Chris here. Chris couldn't even blame him. He'd been shot because of Chris, because of how foolish Chris had been, and it wasn't something Chris could do anything about except what he was already doing.

"I can't leave," he said.

He knew what this conversation was leading to, and his heart was breaking even more than before. He'd known the situation was going to end this way right from the beginning, but it still hurt. He should have talked to Jacob sooner, but he hadn't wanted to give him up, not when he'd already given up everything else. He had to face the situation now, though.

"I'm not asking you to. I'm just asking that you not let your father ruin your life."

"I'm not. I shouldn't have left to begin with."

"You left because you wanted to live your life. What changed?"

"My father was shot. It made me realize that I needed to help him."

"And you can do that until he feels better."

"What if he never feels better? No." Chris shook his head. "I'm the future alpha. Right now, I *am* the alpha. I can't let anything distract me, not even you. When and if my father manages to heal enough to take his place back, I'll take a step back and allow him to, but I can't leave him anyway."

"This is it, then?"

Chris stared at Jacob. He was pretty sure this was the last time he would see him, and he didn't know how he would deal with it. "Unless you want to be alpha mate." He had to try, even though he already knew Jacob's answer.

He couldn't blame Jacob for saying no. Chris might be losing everything he'd ever wanted, but Jacob didn't have to. It would only make the two of them miserable instead of only one. He wanted Jacob to be happy, even if it wasn't with him. It would hurt, and Jacob would always have Chris's heart, but this was the right thing to do. Chris couldn't drag Jacob down along with him. He couldn't make Jacob unhappy, not any more than he already had.

"I can't," Jacob said.

Chris sucked in a breath. "Then I'm sorry, but this is the end. I have to focus on my father, and since our relationship isn't going anywhere, we might as well end it."

"You're going to regret it. This isn't what you truly want. It's what your *father* wants."

"What I want right now is for my father to heal. Yes, I want to make him happy. I can't have him stressed because it would delay his healing. I'm not forcing you to stay with me, though. You'll do what you have to do, and so will I."

Jacob nodded curtly. "All right. I'm leaving, then. I'm sorry things had to end this way. I never wanted them to."

Neither had Chris, but he felt like if he admitted it, he would break down. "Thanks for coming."

Jacob shook his head, clearly frustrated. "I shouldn't have."

"Maybe not, but we cleared things up, and it was what both of us needed. Be happy, Jacob. I might not be in your life anymore, but you deserve to have everything you want."

Jacob started Chris for a moment. "I just *lost* everything I wanted."

Chris's eyes prickled. Jacob didn't add anything. Instead, he turned around and walked out of the office — and of Chris's life.

Chris waited until the door closed behind Jacob to slump onto the chair behind him. He buried his face into his hands and tried to breathe. He couldn't cry, no matter how distraught he was. Alphas didn't cry.

Chris had known this would end the way it had since his father had been shot. He'd hoped against all odds to be wrong, that he and Jacob would manage to work things out, but he'd known. It was one of the reasons he hadn't allowed himself to talk to Jacob and had limited their interactions to texts. He hoped that by keeping Jacob's at arm's length, things wouldn't hurt this badly.

His heart felt like it had been torn out of his chest. Jacob had just left with it.

But it was better that way. Chris couldn't leave, not when his father was hurt, even though he knew his dad was using it to keep him here. Chris knew, but he couldn't change things anyway, no matter how much he wanted to. Jacob didn't deserve to be stuck in this situation. He deserved to live with the cete, in his home, and to be happy. Chris was going to have to make sure he never found out whether or not Jacob had met someone else. He doubted he would ever be strong enough to deal with that fact. He knew it would happen eventually, but he couldn't help but hope.

He loved Jacob, and he knew Jacob loved him. Right now, there was no future for them, and even though Chris knew that wasn't the case, he couldn't help but hope that eventually, they could fix things a second time.

But no. Jacob had forgiven him once. He wouldn't do it twice, not when Chris had chosen his father over him both times.

The office door creaked open, and Chris straightened. He tried to appear as if he hadn't been on the verge of crying and plastered a smile on his face. It broke down when he saw Nico peeking in. "What's going on?" he asked, hoping for something to distract himself.

Nico stepped into the office and closed the door behind himself, then, for good measure, locked it. "I should be the one asking that. What happened with Jacob? I just saw him leave the house, and he didn't look okay."

Chris looked out the window. "He will be eventually."

"What did you do?"

Chris's eyes prickled again, and he was pretty sure he was going to end up crying in front of his brother. At least it was Nico, who'd seen him cry many times before. "The only thing I could do."

Nico sucked in a breath. "Please tell me you haven't broken up with him?"

"You already know I have. Why are you even asking?"

Footsteps told Chris that Nico was coming closer. He half expected his brother to yell at him for ruining the best thing that ever happened to Chris, but instead, Nico turned Chris's chair around and crouched in front of him. Chris tried avoiding looking at him, but Nico would have none of that, and he waited until Chris finally did.

"What did you do?" he asked again.

"I had to break up with him. I know Dad is manipulating me. I know he's using being shot to do that. There's nothing I can do, though. I have to be here for him. I have to take my place by his side again. Thank you for offering to do it for me, but it's *my* duty."

"You're letting Dad ruin your life."

"What else can I do? I can't go back to Jacob, not when Dad needs me."

"I'm not going to be able to change your mind, am I?"

"No. Jacob couldn't either."

Nico chuckled. "Right. And since he couldn't, no one can." He sighed. "I hate Dad right now. He's ruining your life, and you're letting him, but it's mainly his fault. He's using you, and he shouldn't."

"There's nothing I can do." Chris's eyes were filling with tears, and he let them fall. He knew his brother would have his back.

When Nico straightened and wrapped his arms around Chris, Chris leaned against him. He buried his face against his brother's stomach and let go.

This was the only time he would be able to do this—the only time he would be able to show someone else how much he was hurting. He was glad he had his brother.

He would feel even better if he had Jacob, though.

CHAPTER FOURTEEN

"You need to eat more," Chris's mother said.

He didn't even look at her, focused on the document he was reading. "I'm eating plenty."

"You look tired."

"That's because I *am* tired, Mom." Chris sighed and put down the document. "What's going on?" Because he knew his mother wasn't only here because she wanted him to eat.

She stared at him from the other side of the desk. "You've changed."

"What did you expect? I'm doing all of Dad's work."

She shook her head. "That's not what I meant. When you were training with your father, you were still a happy man. You ate, slept, and laughed. Now, all of that is gone. You look like a zombie. I haven't seen you smile in days."

"Again, what did you expect? This is what you and Dad wanted. I'm taking my rightful place, and you should be happy."

She shook her head. "I want you to be happy. It's clear you're not."

Chris snorted. "I doubt I will be again." That was a tad dramatic, but Chris couldn't help it.

He hadn't been able to stop thinking about Jacob since they'd broken up the week before. He even dreamed about it, and in the dreams, he couldn't find Jacob. He ran around, trying to get to him, calling out, but he never found him.

That was why Chris wasn't sleeping. He was terrified of having those dreams again, and when he did close his eyes

194

because he was exhausted, he woke up in a panic because he couldn't find Jacob. He had to remind himself that the only reason he couldn't was that he'd told Jacob to leave.

He regretted it. He'd regretted it seconds after he'd said it, but he knew there was no way to change it. He'd done the only thing he could do, both for himself and Jacob.

He had to focus on his duty. He had to focus on keeping the clowder strong while his father healed. Jacob didn't have the same duty, though. He could go back to sleep and be happy, which was one of the reasons Chris had broken up with him.

He'd known Jacob would wait for him if he didn't. He'd yearned for that, but he knew it was selfish. He couldn't demand Jacob wait, not when he didn't know what would happen next. He was in charge until his father felt better, but he wasn't sure when that would happen, and by then, his father might have found another way to make him stay. It was easier to give in, to go back to his old life—a life without Jacob.

"Maybe we got it wrong," Chris's mother said, interrupting his thoughts.

"What are you talking about?"

She hesitated, and Chris waited. "I talked to Nico. He told me Jacob was here the other week."

"He was. If you're wondering why, it's because we broke up."

"I never wanted the two of you to break up. I could see how happy he made you, and now you're unhappy."

Chris shrugged. "I wasn't happy before him. Nothing has changed much."

"But I don't like that. You're my son. I want you to be happy, and if Jacob makes that happen, then you should be with him."

"But I can't. You already know that. If I have to be here and be dad's heir, I can't be with Jacob. He won't be alpha mate. I can't force him to do that."

"But—"

"Nothing is going to change. You and Dad got what you wanted, and you should be happy about it. I'll be fine." He would have to be.

It was obvious Chris's mother wanted to insist, but thankfully, she didn't. Instead, she said, "I'm going to get you a sandwich."

Chris wanted to tell her he wouldn't eat it because he wasn't hungry, but he knew it would make things worse. He might as well let his mom do what she wanted and focus on his work.

She'd only been gone a few moments before the door opened again. Chris huffed and looked up, cringing when he saw his brother standing there. "I'm busy," he said. He and Nico hadn't talked since last week when Chris had cried in his brother's arms. He hated feeling weak, and he hated that his brother had seen it.

"I don't care." Nico closed the door behind himself and crossed his arms over his chest. "This isn't working."

"What's not working? Do you need anything? Is someone giving you problems?"

Nico rolled his eyes. "That's not what I was referring to. I was referring to *you*."

"You don't think I'm doing a good job?" That was Chris's main fear right now. He'd already lost Jacob, so *that* fear was gone. In its place were regrets and pain, and Chris needed to be doing something well.

"Of course you're doing a good job. You know what you're doing, even though you don't have experience. I'm talking about you, not about the alpha stuff. You're not eating. You're not sleeping."

"I am."

"My bedroom is right next to yours. I can hear you crying

at night. You've woken me a few times with your screams." Nico paused, and his tone was softer when he continued, "You're calling for Jacob."

Chris briefly closed his eyes. "I'm sorry I woke you up."

"I don't care about being woken up. This isn't working, though, Chris. You're in pain. You don't have to be. Call Jacob. Tell him you changed your mind."

"Even if I had changed my mind, and I haven't, why would he take me back? I broke up with him twice. I chose Dad over him both times. He doesn't have a reason to welcome me back into his life."

"He does. He loves you. That's the only reason he needs."

Chris hated the flash of hope that went through him. As long as he told himself that Jacob didn't want him back, it was easier to stay here instead of running away and back into Jacob's arms. He had to continue convincing himself of that. Otherwise, he would break down, and he couldn't.

"Come on, Chris," Nico continued. "This isn't the life you want to live. You're overworking yourself. Eventually, something is going to break, and that something will be you. You've never wanted his life, and you had a chance to leave it."

"Do I have to remind you that Dad was shot?"

"I'm very much aware of that since he's been using it to control you ever since. He's playing with you."

"He's not. He's still healing."

"I saw him the other day. He was in the hallway peeking downstairs, probably hoping to get a peek at you. He's spying on you."

Chris shook his head. "Even if that was the case, I can't go back. My duty is to do Dad's work until he feels well enough to do it himself again."

"And by the time that happens, your life will be in shambles. He doesn't care about your happiness. He only wants you to do what he wants you to do."

"That's what duty is, isn't it?" But Chris couldn't help but wonder. What would his future be like? He didn't have Jacob anymore. He'd moved back home and had taken his father's place, although only temporarily. Could he continue like this?

Nico wasn't wrong. Chris *was* exhausted.

He wasn't eating enough because he wasn't hungry. He wasn't sleeping because he had nightmares. He could feel himself weakening, and that wouldn't help.

But then, nothing would. The only thing Chris wanted was to leave the clowder behind and go home to Jacob, but he'd ruined that possibility for himself. There was no way Jacob would take him back, no matter what Nico said.

Chris was home now, and he had to forget about the brief peek he'd had of another life. He had to focus on the things he could do, which was helping his father. Everything else wasn't worth thinking about. He couldn't afford to be distracted.

"I hate watching you ruin your life," Nico murmured.

Chris hated doing it even more, but he wasn't going to stop.

He couldn't.

Jacob was having a hard time focusing on anything that wasn't Chris and the memories of the time they'd shared together. He knew it was over. Chris had been clear, and Jacob wasn't going to beg. He hadn't the first time, although this time hurt even more.

He'd had a peek of what life with Chris could be like. He'd had hope, much more than he had before the first time they'd broken up. He'd thought they were really going to do this, and then, reality had come crashing down.

Jacob had lost Chris and the life he'd thought he could

share with him. He'd been trying to focus on work, but there wasn't a lot to do. The forest was at peace, and the carriers were safe. He'd gone with the humans to a few shifter groups, leaving Chris behind since his father had been shot and he had work to do. The humans had been understanding, and they probably could tell there was more to it than what Jacob had told them, but thankfully, they hadn't asked. They'd been leaving Jacob alone, and Jacob was grateful.

Still, he needed more to focus on. He wasn't doing a good job of distracting himself, and he was starting to hate his brain. It kept giving him memories of Chris, especially when Jacob was home. He couldn't look at his kitchen without thinking about the times he and Chris had cooked together. He couldn't look at his bed without remembering when he and Chris had slept in it wrapped around each other.

He was a mess, and he knew it. He was pretty sure every-one was worried about him, but no one had confronted him yet, and he hoped things would continue that way.

He decided he had to do something that wasn't moping around, so he headed out. He knew he would always find someone at the gym, and he was grateful that when he stepped in, the trainees were there. They weren't part of cete security yet, but they wanted to be, which meant they had to be tested. They had to be able to defend themselves and the cete, and that would only happen with hard work.

Jacob was going to help them.

He'd changed before leaving home, so he was ready to fight. They all knew him since he would be the one to decide who would be hired and who wouldn't, and they knew they had to impress him.

He came to stand in the middle of the mats and gestured in front of him. "Who wants to fight me?"

None of the trainees seemed to want it, but one of them did step up. He was one of the guys who were doing well, and

Jacob suspected that eventually, the two of them would work side by side. For now, though, Tommy was a trainee, and Jacob had to make sure he knew what he was doing.

Tommy rushed him, and Jacob stepped aside. He struck, hitting Tommy on the back, but Tommy caught himself before his face could hit the mat.

Everything after that was a blur. Jacob punched, kicked, and did everything he could to get Tommy down on the mat. When he finally did, he straddled the man's hips, cocking his arm back to punch him.

Someone grabbed his wrist and stopped him.

Jacob blinked. He was slick with sweat, and his eyes burned. He looked to the side, finding Raven staring down at him. "What are you doing?" he asked.

"Saving that trainee from having to spend a week in the infirmary. What are you doing?"

"Training him."

"You call that training?"

Jacob bristled. "What do *you* call it?"

"Punching his face into the mat. That wasn't training. That was you taking your anger out on him." He pulled on Jacob's arm, and Jacob got to his feet. When he looked down at Tommy, he winced. The man's lower lip was split, and blood ran down his chin. One of his eyes was already starting to swell, and Jacob was pretty sure he was going to be bruised over most of his body. He was staring at Jacob with wide eyes, as if he expected Jacob to punch him again.

Jacob shook Raven's hands away from his arm and held his hand out to Tommy. "Good job."

Tommy blinked and hesitantly took Jacob's hand. "Thank you?"

That sounded like a question, and Jacob knew it was his fault. "You *did* a good job," he repeated. "I apologize if I went too far."

Tommy shook his head. "It's fine. I knew this wasn't going to be easy when I decided to apply."

"You should go to the infirmary." Jacob couldn't deny he had gone too hard on Tommy.

"I will."

Jacob stepped away, and Raven was on him again. He grabbed Jacob's arm and dragged him outside, where he would no doubt yell at him. Jacob didn't care. He was used to Raven yelling at him for one reason or another.

"What the fuck are you doing?" Raven snapped as soon as they were out of sight.

"I already told you I was training him."

"You weren't. You were taking your anger out on him, and that means you weren't being a good superior. You shouldn't have done that."

"Things got out of hand," Jacob admitted.

"You knew they would. You've been angry and sad and everything else, and I get it. It doesn't mean you can do what you just did, though." Raven paused. "You should probably leave the trainees alone until you and Chris solve whatever is going on between the two of you."

"Taking care of the trainees is part of my job."

"Then find someone else to do it or change your attitude. I won't talk to Thomas this time, but if I hear that something like this happened again, I will. I don't care what's going in your private life, but don't take it out on other people, especially not the trainees."

Jacob wanted to snap at Raven to leave him alone, but Raven was right. He shouldn't have done what he'd done. He took in a deep breath, trying to settle his anger. He wasn't angry at Raven, but rather, at Chris and his father. "It won't happen again," he said.

"Good." Raven stared. "Do you want to talk about what's going on?"

Jacob snorted. "There's nothing I want less."

There was a hint of a smile on Raven's lips. "You know that's never stopped me. Talk."

"I thought the entire cete already knew what happened."

"I haven't been listening to gossip. I had things to do."

Raven had been part of the team that had gone around the various shifter territories to free carriers, but that was over now. He still had some work to do when it came to that, mostly to make sure that no shifter group was hiding other carriers, but it didn't take that much time. He'd disappeared for a few weeks, and while Jacob hadn't been worried because Raven often did that, he was curious. He didn't bother to ask because he knew Raven wouldn't answer.

He sighed heavily. "There's nothing much to say. Chris and I broke up."

"Again?"

"Again," Jacob confirmed. "You know his father was shot?"

"I do, and I kind of wished they'd done a better job of it."

That almost made Jacob smile, but even though he didn't like Chris's father, he didn't want the man to die. "That wouldn't have helped."

"It wouldn't have made things worse, either."

"True."

"Have you talked to Chris?"

"I have. Why do you think we broke up? I went to tell him that whenever he was ready, he could come back home, but he told me he would stay, even when his father recovered. His father is using this to get his claws into Chris again, and Chris isn't fighting back." He'd chosen Dan over Jacob again, and Jacob couldn't ignore that, no matter how much he wanted to. He had to let Chris go, but it wasn't easy.

"Is there anything we can do? I could kill Alpha Wiley if it helps," Raven offered.

"I'm forbidding you to. The man is an asshole, but he's still Chris's father."

"Someone should remind him of that," Raven muttered. "You think things with Chris are really over?"

"I'm pretty sure they are. He was clear that his father needs him and that he has to help."

"Maybe he'll come back once Alpha Wiley recovers."

"It didn't sound like he would." But Jacob found himself hoping. What would he do if Chris *did* come back? Would he hold a grudge, or would he welcome him into his life? He still loved Chris, but he wasn't sure his heart could take this again. What if Chris changed his mind a third time? Jacob couldn't compete with Chris's father, and he was done trying.

CHAPTER FIFTEEN

"I don't have time for this," Chris whined.

Nico ignored him. "You're the alpha. You have to welcome guests, especially when it's a future alpha mate."

Chris couldn't deny he was right, no matter how much he wanted to. Seamus would be the next cete alpha mate, and Chris had to keep him on the clowder's good side. "Why is he even here?"

"I wanted to meet his daughter."

Right. Seamus had given birth to a baby daughter, and if Thomas and his son, Alex, had what they wanted, she would one day become the alpha after her father and grandfather. It would be revolutionary, but then, Thomas was exactly that. It made Chris's heart ache to think about it, and he pushed those thoughts away.

"What does it have to do with me?" he asked.

"Nothing except for the fact that you're the alpha and that he's a future alpha mate."

"You couldn't have gone to the cete to meet her? Wouldn't it be better for her and Seamus?"

"Seamus wanted to get out of the house. Are you going to tell him to leave?"

"Of course not." Seamus wasn't just a future alpha mate. He was also a friend. He'd taken care of the carriers when they'd been at the Bishop house, and he knew what some of them had been through. Chris and Nico, along with a few others, had been lucky. They'd never been abused. A lot of them had, though, and they'd needed a gentle hand.

Even though Chris hadn't, he'd been grateful for Seamus's friendship, and he'd been happy when he and Alex had found out they were expecting. They'd gotten married, and now, they were a family.

Nico burst into the living room, where Seamus was sitting on the couch. He was holding his daughter, but he looked up and smiled when he heard them. "I was wondering where you'd gone," he told Nico.

"To get my brother. He had his face buried in some documents, but I'm sure he can take a break."

Chris wanted to say he couldn't, but he didn't want to be rude. Besides, he *could* do with a break. He'd been working himself ragged, doing everything his father wanted him to do and trying to prevent problems before they started. It wasn't easy, not when most other alphas didn't trust him. He didn't have any experience, even though he'd been working with his father for years, and he was only nineteen. Most of them saw him as a child, and they weren't wrong. Some days, he wanted to stomp his feet and leave. The only reason he didn't was that he'd given up everything to do this job, and he wasn't going to ruin this, too.

He plastered a smile on his face. "I didn't expect you to leave the cete so soon after you gave birth."

"I couldn't wait to leave. Alex doesn't have an excuse to keep me home now that the forest is at peace, so I took advantage. Besides, he knows I'm safe here."

"You are."

Seamus beamed. "Thank you. And I know you're busy, so sorry for interrupting you. I was here to see Nico, but I'm glad to see you, too."

"Don't worry about it. Nico isn't wrong. I could do with a break."

Seamus frowned. He looked worried, and it took Chris a second to realize that he was worried about *him*. "You look tired. How are you doing?" Seamus asked.

Why was everyone asking that? "I'm fine. It's more tiring than I thought, but I can handle it."

"I don't doubt that. You can't run yourself into the ground, though. Remember that you're not alone. Even though your father is wounded, you have your brother, and if you need anything, you can reach out to Alex and Thomas. They'll be more than happy to give you tips or anything you might need."

Chris's eyes prickled with tears, something that happened way too often lately. "Thank you. I'm doing fine, though. You don't have to worry. My father is recovering well, so it won't be long before he takes his place back."

Seamus continued staring at Chris until Chris wanted to wiggle. "What are you going to do then?" he asked.

"Continue to train with him."

"Even though you don't want to?"

Chris had to look away. "I do want to. I have to."

There was a moment of silence between them. It was tense, much more than Chris was comfortable with.

He cleared his throat. "Anyway. Do you want anything to drink? I can grab you whatever you like."

Nico shot to his feet before Chris could go. Chris glared at him, but his brother ignored him. "I'll go get something for everyone. You two just talk."

He almost ran out of the room, leaving Seamus and Chris staring at each other.

Chris's gaze moved down to Scarlett. She was sleeping, and she looked adorable. It was hard to believe she'd come out of a person. She was so perfect, and even though she was still young, Chris could see hints of both her fathers in her. "How are you doing? It can't be easy to be a dad."

Seamus looked down, smiling softly. "It's not. Yet at the same time, it's the easiest thing to do. It's terrifying when she cries and I don't understand why, but in moments like these, I'm glad it happened."

Seamus's pregnancy had been an accident, but Chris was relieved to see he was happy with how his life was going. "If you need anything, you can just call. I know you have a lot of people at the cete and that you probably don't need me, but still." Chris wanted to offer. They weren't best friends, but Seamus was a friend anyway.

"Actually, I really need to go to the bathroom. Do you think you can hold her for ten minutes?"

Chris's eyes widened. "I'm sure you can wait until Nico comes back."

"I really can't. Sorry. I can take her with me if you'd rather not, though."

Chris had no idea what to do with a baby. His sisters had children, but he'd stayed far away from his nieces and nephews until they could walk. He couldn't say no to Seamus, though. "As long as you make sure I can't hurt her."

"It's much harder to hurt a baby than you think. They're sturdy." He got to his feet and moved closer to Chris. Chris held out his arms, not sure what else to do. Seamus slowly lowered his daughter into them. Then he manhandled Chris into the right position. It put Scarlett's head just under Chris's chin, and he took a deep breath, smiling at the baby scent.

"There. I'll be back in minutes. Don't move too much, and everything should be fine."

Chris snorted. "It's that *should* that terrifies me."

Seamus smiled. "You're doing a good job. If she wakes up, just try to shush her. She ate recently, so she shouldn't be hungry anytime soon."

Chris was petrified at the thought that the baby might wake up, so he stayed as still as he could once Seamus had disappeared down the hallway. He heard Seamus and Nico talk, no doubt because Seamus needed to find out where the bathroom was. Chris's attention quickly turned to Scarlett, though. He took in a deep breath, and he realized that even though he was still scared, this was nice.

It wasn't that he didn't like babies, just that he didn't know what to do with them. He was only nineteen, and he'd never really thought about having children. He'd always believed he wouldn't carry any. His father would find him a nice girl to marry, and *she* would carry their children. It had to be that way because no one could find out Chris was a carrier.

Things had changed, though. Most of the forest didn't know about Chris yet, but Josiah was an alpha, and he was a carrier. That meant that if Chris wanted, he could have children, even if he was the alpha.

Thinking about that made him think about carrying Jacob's babies.

He had to swallow. He'd never thought about himself being pregnant, but now that he was, he wanted to carry Jacob's children. He wanted to have a family with him, and he'd thought he could have it, but now that was gone. Chris had broken up with Jacob. He was never getting him back. It didn't matter that he wanted children with him.

Chris had ruined his own life, and he couldn't ruin Jacob's, too. Jacob would recover from this. Chris wasn't so sure *he* would, though.

Jacob stared at his beer bottle. He'd taken a sip, but he wasn't in the mood. He wasn't sure why he'd allowed Raven to drag him to a night out with friends, but now, he regretted it.

"You could at least try to look like you're enjoying yourself," Mabel said.

Jacob didn't glare at her, but it was a close thing. "I *am* enjoying myself," he said, plastering a fake smile on his face and taking a sip of beer.

She chuckled. "That was a terrifying smile. But fine. We all know that you're not dealing with the breakup well." The smile slipped from her face. "I'm really sorry things didn't work out with Chris."

Jacob grimaced. "Can we not talk about this?"

"Of course. I'm sorry."

He shook his head. This was one of the reasons he hadn't wanted to come. People were looking at him, knowing that he and Chris had broken up again. They pitied him, and they were treating him with kid's gloves. He didn't want to be treated differently. He didn't want people to know what had happened with Chris. He didn't want what had happened with Chris to be real.

And here he was, thinking about Chris again. When would it stop? He already knew he wouldn't stop loving Chris from one day to another. It would be too easy, and his life had never been easy. He wanted to leave his friends behind and go to the clowder, try to shake some sense into Chris. It wouldn't help, but his mind kept going back to it, and it was tempting. The fact that there were several couples around the tables at which they were sitting didn't help.

Their little group had decided to head to Rosewood for the evening. That idea had probably come from Raven. Jacob thought it would only be the two of them, but Julian and Kaspar had decided to come, along with Callum. The bat shifter looked angry, but then, he always looked angry. Mabel was there, too, along with Graham. There was also Tyson, a bear shifter, and to Jacob's surprise, Calder and Kari. Kari's stomach looked like it was about to explode, but he'd glared at anyone who had tried telling him that this might not be a good idea.

In a fight, Jacob would bet on him, even though he was about twelve months pregnant, or at least, he looked like he was.

Jacob was happy that Kari felt safe enough to leave cete territory even though he was pregnant. He was less happy about watching Kari and Calder making heart eyes at each other, or Julian and Kaspar kissing every few minutes. It reminded him of what he'd lost, and even though he knew he would eventually find love again, he couldn't imagine himself with anyone but Chris.

He still loved Chris. He hadn't stopped since he'd fallen in love with him, and it was hard to imagine a time in which he wouldn't love him anymore. It made it hard to imagine the future. He'd started hoping when Chris had talked about moving in with him. He'd thought that maybe, in a few years, they could have children. They could get married. Jacob had always wanted a family, but he'd thought it wouldn't be easy since he was gay. There weren't a lot of children in the forest, and most of them were kept in their shifter groups, even when they were orphans.

It would have been different with Chris. Chris was a carrier, and he could have had their babies. They hadn't even had the occasion to talk about it, though. Things had been over before they got to that point in their relationship.

Raven knocked his shoulder against Jacob's. "I thought going out would help you, but you look even more depressed."

"I told you it wasn't a good idea."

"I should have believed you."

Jacob finally smiled a real smile. "Why didn't you? You know me."

Raven sighed. He took a sip of his beer, staring ahead. "You're right. I do know you. You're my best friend, even though we don't spend a lot of time together. I know you love Chris, but I was hoping to help you. You're annoyed, though, so you can leave anytime you want. I'll drive Julian and Kaspar home."

It was tempting. Jacob wanted to go home, curl up in his

bed, and think about Chris. He also knew that was the worst thing he could do, though. Chris wasn't coming back to him, not this time, and he had to stop thinking about him. He had to stop imagining the future they could have had together. They wouldn't have any kind of future, and Jacob had to make himself believe that.

But being here *was* a distraction. He'd only been thinking about Chris around ninety percent of the time, against the hundred percent when he was home.

"I have half a mind to go to the clowder and drag him away," Raven confessed.

"It's tempting, but we both know he wouldn't handle it well."

"Do we care? I mean, I'll be honest. I want you to be happy, but I don't care much about him, not after what he's done to you."

"I do care about him, though, and even though I don't like what's going on, I understand why he's doing it."

"Because he doesn't have the guts to stand up to his father."

"There is that, but there's also the fact that his father was shot."

Raven snorted. "So? He's not dead or anything. Actually, from what I know, he's doing well."

Jacob arched a brow. "From what you know?"

Raven shrugged. "I have people everywhere."

"Including in the clowder?"

"Of course. I like to know what other people in the forest are up to, especially in this case. I knew Chris was going to be bad news for you."

Jacob grimaced. "He's not bad news."

"Could have fooled me."

"It's not just that his father was shot. Dan is using that and the influence he has on Chris to keep him there. If I didn't

know he wouldn't do something like that, I'd think he somehow arranged to get shot himself. It came at the right moment." Jacob frowned. "Do you know anything about who
might have shot him?" It was something the clowder was in-
vestigating, and they didn't want anyone else to stick their
noses into it. Jacob knew the council had tried, but they hadn't
had any success. It made him wonder.

"Nothing so far. But yeah, I wouldn't be surprised if he'd
shot himself or something. You want to investigate?"

Jacob almost said yes, but in the end, he shook his head.
"It's not going to help."

"Are you sure? Because I could find stuff. I'm good that
way."

"I have no doubt you are. I don't think it's the best idea,
though. Chris made his decision, and I can't make him change
his mind. Accusing his father of shooting himself isn't going
to help."

"Maybe not, but we need to know if that's the case."

"I don't think it is."

"Okay. Why was he shot, then? The only result so far is that
his son took his place as the alpha. Why would someone try
to shoot him?"

Jacob tapped his fingertips onto the warming beer bottle.
He hadn't thought about it because he'd been too focused on
having lost Chris, but now that he did, he had to admit it was
strange. "I don't know. Maybe they just had a personal
grudge against him."

"Or maybe there's something else going on."

"Don't start seeing conspiracies everywhere. So far, he's
the only one who's been shot."

"It's not going to stop with him, though. Mark my words.
Either he shot himself to keep his son with him, or something
bigger is happening, and we're all going to be in trouble."

Jacob didn't like the sound of that. He wanted to head to

the clowder and grab Chris, drag him home, and make sure he never left. He couldn't, though. Chris had decided to stay with his father. Not even Jacob's love and the thought of a life together had managed to change that.

Nothing would at this point. Jacob could hope, but he knew how stupid it was. He'd lost Chris, and he was never getting him back.

CHAPTER SIXTEEN

Chris stood in front of his parents' bedroom. The door was closed, but he could hear his father talking inside, no doubt on the phone. It was his daily visit, and he knew his father would want to know how the clowder was doing. It seemed to be the only thing they talked about these days, but that was fine with Chris. He didn't want to answer personal questions. He didn't even want to think about his personal life. He didn't have one anymore.

He waited until he couldn't hear his dad anymore before knocking on the door. When his father told him to enter, he opened it and peeked inside.

Chris's dad was in bed, the blankets at his waist. He was wearing a t-shirt, but Chris could see a hint of the bandages peeking from the collar. Just like always, his father looked angry. He hated being on bed rest, but Chris's mom made sure he wasn't going anywhere.

"Chris!" his father said. "Come in. You're here to give me my daily update?"

"Even though Mom doesn't want me to."

Chris's father rolled his eyes. "She's acting like a mother hen. She's never really had the occasion to do that with me before, and now she's taking advantage."

"Or maybe she's worried about you. You *were* shot."

Chris's father waved his words away. "I'm fine. Close the door. Come sit."

Chris obeyed. He took his place in the chair by his father's bed. Then he waited. His father would no doubt have questions about the clowder and what Chris was doing. He always had a lot of them.

"How are things going?" he asked.

Chris forced himself to smile. "Pretty well. I have everything in hand. You don't have to worry about me."

To Chris's surprise, his father frowned. "You look tired. Are you sick?"

"I'm not."

"Your mother told me you haven't been eating a lot."

"I don't have the time, and honestly, I'm not hungry. Don't worry about me. I'm fine."

Chris's father looked down at his hands. It was weird, because Chris wasn't used to him behaving this way, and he didn't understand what was happening. He wanted to ask, but he knew better. Instead, he waited for his father to say something.

"Your mother and your brother came to talk to me," he finally said.

Chris wasn't surprised. "I hope they didn't worry you. I'm fine, I promise. I can do this."

"I know you can. That's not what this is about."

Chris crossed his arms over his chest. He didn't know where the conversation was going, but he didn't like it. "What's it about, then?" he asked.

"They both yelled at me. Your mother especially is worried because you're not eating and you aren't sleeping well. Your brother wasn't far behind, though. He told me I was selfish."

Chris wasn't surprised Nico had been so direct with their father. Chris had never been able to do the same, maybe because he understood better than Nico what being an alpha meant, but he wished he were as brave as his brother. "I'm sorry."

"You shouldn't be. *I'm* the one who's sorry. I should have realized what I was doing, but I didn't."

"I don't understand." And he didn't want to hope, not yet.

"I didn't listen to you when you told me you weren't happy. I didn't listen when you said you didn't want to be an alpha, that I only saw you as my heir rather than as my son. I thought I was doing the right thing, and it's hard for me to admit I was wrong. I only ever wanted the best for the clowder, and I truly thought *you* were the best."

Chris swallowed. "Have I done something to disappoint you?"

"You haven't. You've been perfect through all of this, and I know it came with a huge loss for you."

"Nico told you I broke up with Jacob."

"He did. In between telling me I was selfish and telling me I was an asshole."

Chris barked out a laugh. He pressed his lips together, hoping his father didn't think he was laughing at him. His father was smiling, though, and Chris was confused more than ever. What was happening?

"And he was right. I *was* selfish. I was so focused on you being my firstborn son that I didn't think that you might not want to be the alpha. Even when you told me, I ignored it, thinking it would pass, that you would accept it. You'd never said anything before, and I thought that the only reason you were behaving that way was that you wanted to spend more time with your boyfriend. There's more to it, though, isn't there?"

"There is, but we don't have to talk about that. I'm back, Dad, and I'm not leaving again. You don't have to worry about all of that."

"But I do. You're my son, and you should be *happy*. I ignored that until now, but I'm not going to do it anymore."

"But I want to take care of everything for you. I know it won't last forever, and yes, I might not be sleeping or eating enough, but it's temporary. Once you're back on your feet, you can take your rightful place, and I'll be able to relax."

Chris's father stared at him. "You're not happy, though."

Chris wasn't, but he wasn't about to tell his father that. "It's because everything is overwhelming. It's not only because it's the first time I'm the acting alpha. You were shot, and I was terrified. I still am. I know you're doing well, but still. You could have died."

"What about Jacob?"

"What about him?" Chris did *not* want to have this conversation with his father. He didn't want to have this conversation with anyone, and as soon as he got his hands on Nico, he would make sure his brother knew how he felt.

"You love him. And he loves you."

"I do, and he does," Chris confirmed. It would be pointless to lie.

"And I'm the reason you broke up."

"Of course not."

Chris's father's expression hardened. "Don't lie to me. I know I am."

"I had to come back and take your place."

"But Jacob would have understood. I might not know him well, but I do know something about him. He knows you had to do this, but he probably expected you to go back home to him once it was over. Instead, you broke up with him. Why?"

"Because I'm back, and I'm not moving in with the cete anymore. You need me. It's my duty to be here."

"And that's what I was getting to. You think it's your duty because it's what I told you since you were a child."

"And you are right. I *am* your firstborn son. I *am* the future alpha."

"That's where I went wrong. Yes, the firstborn son usually becomes the alpha, but it doesn't have to be that way. Things are different now. It's too late for your sister to become the alpha, but it doesn't mean I can't make changes. You never wanted to take my place, but you went along with it because you didn't think you had a choice. Now, you do."

Chris blinked. He had no idea what was going on, and he was afraid to ask. "I'm sorry?"

"I won't force you to stay if you don't want to. Almost dying made me see that I wanted you to be happy more than I wanted you to be my heir."

"But you never said anything, even after you were shot."

"I guess I needed your mother and your brother to tell me things the way they were. They both pointed out how unhappy you were. How weak you were becoming physically because of the strain being my heir was putting on you. I'm sorry, Chris. I should have known better. I should have listened to you. I was trying to do my best for the clowder, and as I did so, I almost ruined your life."

Chris had no idea what to say. He hadn't expected this, and it didn't sound like his father. "Are you doing this because they yelled at you?"

Chris's father laughed. "In part. I probably wouldn't have realized what I was doing if they hadn't. But I want you to be happy. I love you, and that's the only thing I want for you. If being the future alpha doesn't make that happen, you should leave all of that behind and try to find your way to a happy life." He grimaced. "Even if it's with the cete."

"But I broke up with Jacob."

His father arched a brow. "Is that going to stop you from trying to get him back?"

Jacob smiled at Luther when he opened the door of Thomas's house. "He's waiting for you," he told the human.

Luther smiled back. They weren't exactly friends—Jacob wasn't sure he would ever be friends with a human—but they were friendly, and they worked well together. He was glad he hadn't made an enemy out of the humans, and he hoped things would continue that way. The forest hadn't been as peaceful as it was now in decades, and in part, it was thanks to the humans. Their presence had forced the shifters who lived here to work together, and they did so strangely well.

"Will you be sitting in on this meeting?" Luther asked.

"Since you want to talk about the few territories we still have to explore, I thought it would be a good idea."

"You're not wrong. How is Chris's father doing?"

Jacob had no idea, but he had to answer. "Healing."

"We'll keep the clowder for last so they'll have time to organize things. Having your alpha shot can't be easy to deal with."

"It's not, but Chris knows what he's doing."

"He's young to take his father's place, though, isn't he?"

Jacob bristled at the words, but it wasn't his job to defend Chris, not anymore. "He might be young, but he's been learning with his father since he was a teenager. It's not easy for him, especially because a lot of people seem to think the way you do, but he's dealing with it. He'll be fine."

Jacob knocked on the door of Thomas's office and opened it to peek in. Thomas was on the phone, though, and he gestured at Jacob to wait. Jacob closed the door and turned to look at Luther. "He's on the phone. Do you want something to drink in the meantime?"

"Why not? You have coffee?"

"Of course. Thomas goes through at least a few pots every day. The kitchen is this way."

Jacob led the way again, hoping Luther was done talking about Chris. "I have to admit I don't fully understand what it's like to be an alpha, or an alpha mate," Luther said.

"It's a lot of responsibilities. Chris has to make decisions for the entire clowder. To keep them safe and make sure that any conflict between two bobcats is resolved. He also has to work with other alphas, and with the council."

"Is that why there's also an alpha mate? To help the alpha share the burden?"

Jacob blinked as he reached for the coffee pot. He'd never thought about being alpha mate that way. When he'd thought about it, the only thing he could focus on was the responsibilities he might have had if he'd married Chris and had become his alpha mate one day. Things were different when he viewed the role this way, though.

He knew Chris wasn't doing well. Nico kept sending him texts that he never answered. Besides, he'd seen the proof when he'd gone to visit Chris the day they'd broken up. Chris wasn't eating, and he wasn't sleeping. He was overworking himself.

He didn't have an alpha mate. He didn't have *help*.

He had his father's beta, of course, but the man had his own responsibilities and things to do. Jacob could have helped Chris, but instead, he'd run away. He'd made sure to stay far away from the clowder so he wouldn't have any responsibility.

Would it have been that bad to help Chris, though? Maybe if Jacob had been there with him instead of staying away, he wouldn't be as exhausted as he was. Jacob could have taken some weight off his shoulders, but instead, he'd dug his heels in.

It wasn't like he would have been alone anyway. He didn't know the first thing about being alpha mate, but he knew he could always go to Thomas's wife, or even to Chris's mother probably. He doubted she would have kicked his ass out for asking for help. Even if he became alpha mate, he wouldn't have to do it alone. He would also be with Chris, something he didn't have right now.

That realization wasn't helping. He and Chris had already broken up. It was as much Jacob's fault as it had been Chris's.

Jacob had been putting all the blame on Chris, telling himself that Chris's father was more important to Chris than Jacob was, but he'd been wrong. Of course Chris had gone back to his father. The man had been shot, and even though he wasn't in danger of losing his life, it still couldn't be easy. Chris had almost lost his father. He'd almost lost his alpha. He was doing his best to keep things together, and instead of helping him, Jacob had tried to take him away.

Jacob had fucked up.

"Jacob?"

He looked up at Luther, who was staring at him, probably because he was still holding the coffee pot but doing nothing with it.

Jacob cleared his throat and reached for one of the mugs in the cupboard. "Sorry. I was thinking."

Luther's smile was gentle. "I could see that. Is everything okay?"

"I don't know." Because Jacob had lost Chris. Both times he'd been unwilling to compromise and more than willing to let Chris do all the work.

That wasn't how relationships worked. They should have tried talking and to find the halfway point in which they could meet. Instead, Chris had been ready to give everything up — the clowder, the alpha position, maybe even his family since his father hadn't taken it well. What had Jacob given up for Chris?

Nothing. That was the answer. He hadn't even been willing to be alpha mate for a short period while Chris's father got better. He hadn't even *tried*. Yes, Chris's father was important to Chris, but why should Chris have chosen Jacob when he wasn't willing to do anything for him?

"You're starting to worry me," Luther said.

Jacob shook his head. "I fucked up."

Luther blinked. "Do you want to talk about it? I know

we're not friends, and that you probably don't trust me because I'm human, but you *can* talk to me."

Jacob hesitated. He wanted to talk to Raven, but he wasn't sure any of the people who knew about him and Chris would be objective when it came to the situation. They were rooting for them, or they thought it was better they stayed away.

"It's about Chris," he finally said.

Luther nodded as he took a sip of the coffee Jacob had finally managed to pour him. "I thought you were acting differently now that he's not working with us."

"He and I were together. As a couple, I mean."

"It was pretty obvious. Has that changed? You said *were*."

"We broke up after his father was shot."

Luther's eyebrows rose on his forehead. "How come?"

"He doesn't want to be the next alpha, but his father doesn't see reason when it comes to that. He doesn't understand that Chris wouldn't be happy. Still, Chris went back because his father needed him. I didn't go with him because I can't be alpha mate, or at least, I didn't think I could be. We already broke up once over this. Neither of us was willing to compromise."

"But you obviously did since you got back together."

"Only because Chris was willing to leave everything behind to be with me. He told his father he wouldn't be his heir anymore. *I* didn't make any kind of compromise, though. I just accepted that Chris was moving in with me and leaving everything he knew. I didn't even think that there were things I could have done, too."

"I see. And now?"

"Now, I realize that I should have worked toward being with him, too."

"He still doesn't want to be alpha?"

"He doesn't. I was hoping he would come home to me once all of this was over, but instead, he decided to stay with his father." And it was Jacob's fault. It was because Jacob hadn't been willing to sacrifice anything for Chris.

"You should try talking to him. And this time, since you finally realized the problem, try actually compromising instead of letting him do all the work," Luther said.

None of Jacob's friends would have told him that. Luther had gone straight to the point, though. He'd told Jacob how things were, and Jacob had needed it.

Now he only needed Chris to listen to him, and he wasn't sure that was possible. It wasn't going to stop him, though. This was the last opportunity they had to be together, and he wouldn't waste it.

CHAPTER SEVENTEEN

Jacob had made his decision. He didn't know if it was the right one, but he wasn't changing his mind. Chris needed him, and he was going to help him, whether Chris liked it or not.

He still hoped Chris would be okay with it, though.

Jacob had no idea what was happening at the clowder. Nico was keeping him informed, but he wasn't sure he could trust the guy to be honest, especially when it came to his brother and his father. Besides, it wasn't like he called Jacob every day. He tended to text, but that was it. If Jacob wanted more information, he had to text back or call, something he hadn't done yet. He'd been trying to distance himself from Chris because it hurt too much, but now, he wished he'd asked.

He had no idea what he was going to be walking into, but whatever it was, he was ready to face it.

He still wasn't entirely okay with the thought of being an alpha mate. It was too many responsibilities for him, especially because he wouldn't be overseeing badgers but bobcats. He didn't know them, and they didn't know him. Still, it wouldn't be that different from the work he did for the cete, and he wanted to help Chris. This was the moment in which Chris needed him most, and hopefully, he wouldn't push him away.

"I'm not sure this is a good idea," Raven said from the bedroom doorway.

Jacob didn't even look at him. "Did I ask what you were

thinking?"

"No, which means your plan is probably stupid. You're really going to leave the cete, your home, and the people you consider family for him?"

Jacob paused. That was another thing he didn't want to do, but if he wanted to be with Chris, he was going to have to do it. "I'm not excited about it," he started.

Raven snorted. "Are you sure? Because to me, it looks like you can't wait. You don't even know whether or not he's going to welcome you back."

"I don't know it, but I'm hoping he will." They still loved each other. They still wanted to be together. Surely Chris wouldn't kick Jacob out for trying to fix things between them?

Jacob hadn't been nice to Chris when they'd broken up, but he'd tried to do what was best for himself and for Chris. He hadn't realized that the best for them was to be together, whatever happened outside their relationship. Now that he had, though, he was going to work toward that.

"What about Thomas? What about your job here? Did you even talk to him?" Raven asked.

"Talk to who? Thomas or Chris?"

"Either. Both."

Jacob shook his head. "Not yet. I don't want to talk to Chris because I know he's going to try to push me away if I call him."

"And Thomas?"

"I'll talk to him if things work out between Chris and me. I don't even know what Chris will want to do."

"He told you he's staying there, even after his father heals. That means you're going to have to stay there. Can you imagine you living with bobcats?"

Jacob couldn't, but he had to start wrapping his mind around it. "I'll make things work." He would have to if Chris welcomed him back into his life. He might not be looking forward to being an alpha mate, or even to seeing Chris's father again, but he was willing to sacrifice a lot to be with Chris. He didn't know how things would go, but hopefully, if Chris agreed to have him back in his life, he would be able to help. He hated how tired Chris had looked when he'd visited last week, and he could only imagine how much more tired he was now.

Jacob might not have any experience when it came to being an alpha mate, but he'd been working for cete security for years. It was a job that came with responsibilities, and he oversaw a lot of people. Hopefully, being an alpha mate wouldn't be that different. Whatever the case, Jacob was going to help Chris. Things couldn't go worse than they were already going anyway.

Raven sighed. "I see that I won't be able to get you to change your mind."

"You thought you could?"

"Not really. I hope he won't hurt you, though. He already has way too many times. I don't think I like him."

"Good thing you don't *have* to like him. I do."

"I'll wait to threaten him until I'm sure the two of you are together again."

Jacob paused. "You don't have to threaten him."

"You're my best friend. You might as well be my brother. I want to make sure he doesn't hurt you again. The two of you have already broken up twice, and it's once too many for my taste."

Jacob wouldn't try to convince Raven not to do it. He knew he wouldn't be able to, so the only thing he could do was warn Chris about it.

That was if Chris welcomed him back into his life. The two of them had hurt each other a lot. It was as much Jacob's fault as it was Chris's, and even if they did get back together, things would have to change. Jacob didn't want to come second to

Chris's father ever again, but he realized it wasn't going to be easy. Maybe if he agreed to be alpha mate, things would be easier to deal with, but he doubted it.

Chris's father wouldn't be happy to see Jacob again. He had full control over his son now, and he no doubt knew that if Jacob was in Chris's life, he would lose that control, because Jacob wasn't going to tolerate it. He might be willing to be alpha mate now, but he wouldn't allow Chris's father to keep control over Chris. Chris knew how wrong it was, and so did his father. Hopefully, Jacob's presence would help smooth things out.

Nothing would happen if Chris didn't want Jacob back, though, so that was the first thing Jacob had to focus on.

He zipped his backpack shut and looked around. He could always come back, of course. He would *have* to come back to talk to Thomas if things went the way he hoped they would. For now, though, he had enough things with him to be comfortable—well, as comfortable as he could be with the clowder.

That was going to be strange. He'd been born in the cete, and he'd lived here all his life. He'd never thought he'd leave. He still wished he didn't have to, but if it meant having Chris, he would.

"Well, I hope you know what you're doing," Raven said.

Jacob faced him. "I do. I know you're worried, but there's no reason to be. What's the worst that can happen?"

"Let's see. Chris's father might kick your ass."

"He's been shot. I doubt he'll have the energy or the capacity to do that."

"Fine. He could have his beta or any other clowder member kick your ass. Or maybe Chris won't want you back after all."

Jacob grimaced. "I'd rather not think about that."

"You should. But if he doesn't want you, I'll be waiting

here for you. You're not alone, Jacob. I know you don't have a family, but I *do* consider you my brother. You'll always have me to come back to."

Jacob looked at Raven. "If you trust me so much, why don't you tell me what's been going on with your life? You've been disappearing, and while I know it's normal for you, I can tell there's something there."

To Jacob's surprise, Raven looked away and his cheeks turned red. It wasn't something Jacob had ever seen him do, and it made him even more curious.

"How about I tell you once all of this is over?" Raven suggested.

"All right." Jacob didn't want to push. Raven was his best friend, and he would tell him what was going on once he was comfortable with it. Jacob just had to wait.

Besides, Raven wasn't wrong. Jacob had a lot going on right now, and that was what he had to focus on. Once he knew which way the situation would go, he could focus on his best friend again.

Hopefully, he wouldn't be nursing a broken heart at the same time.

Chris wasn't even sure what he was pushing into his backpack. The only thing he cared about was that he needed to get out of here and that he needed to do it as soon as possible.

He was going back to Jacob. He had a hard time believing it. He had an even harder time believing that his father was the one who was sending him away. The conversation they'd just finished had come from out of nowhere, and Chris would never be able to thank his mother and his twin brother enough for what they'd done. They'd made Chris's father realize what he was doing, something Chris hadn't thought possible. He'd fully expected his father to demand he stay, and he'd been ready to do just that.

Now he didn't have to, though. He didn't know whether Jacob would be happy to see him, but he hoped that would be the case. If not, well, he'd find a way to make Jacob see that they belonged together.

He knew he'd hurt Jacob. It wouldn't be easy to get Jacob to talk to him, let alone forgive him. Chris was ready to work as hard as he had to make that happen, though. Now that he had his father's blessing, he wasn't going to let anything take Jacob away from him, not even Jacob himself.

His bedroom door slammed open, and Chris jumped. He almost expected it to be his father come to tell him he'd changed his mind and that Chris needed to stay, but it wasn't. It was Nico, and he was standing there, his eyes wide, looking as if he'd run all the way to Chris's room.

"What?" Chris asked.

"What are you doing?" Nico asked. He looked around the room, and there was no way to hide that Chris was packing.

"I talked to Dad. He agreed to let me leave. I should have talked to you, and I was going to, but only after I was done packing."

Nico shook his head. "Never mind that. You need to come downstairs."

"Is it Dad?"

"It's not. Jacob is here, though."

Chris opened his mouth only to close it again. He licked his lips. "Jacob is here?"

"It's what I just said. Come on. He's waiting for you."

Chris had no idea *why* Jacob was here, but he wasn't going to let him wait. Instead, he 'd go downstairs and tell him he loved him and that they could be together. Hopefully, it would be enough.

Chris didn't know what to do or what to tell him. He had a lot of good intentions, but no idea how to put them into work.

"What are you doing?" Nico asked. He snapped his fingers in front of Chris's eyes.

"What do I tell him?"

"Why don't you listen to what he has to say? He's the one who came here. It's obvious he wants to talk to you. Let him do that, and only then tell him what you want to say."

Chris sucked in a breath. "You're right. I need to stop freaking out."

Nico winked. "Use that alpha training you have and control yourself. You don't know why he's here, but I'm sure it's a good thing."

Chris hoped so, too.

His heart was racing by the time he walked down the stairs. Sure enough, Jacob was standing there in the middle of the entrance. He looked up when he heard Chris, and Chris had to tell him how he felt, even though he'd decided to let Jacob speak first.

"I love you," he said.

Jacob blinked. "I love you too."

That was a huge step forward. "I wanted to tell you —"

"I'm ready to be alpha mate." Jacob raised his hand, and Chris noticed he was holding a backpack. "I can move in here with you if you want me to, or I can go back home. Whatever you need. I want you to feel comfortable with me, and I want to help you shoulder the weight of being the alpha right now."

Chris didn't know what to say. It was what he'd wanted to hear, but now Jacob had stolen the thunder from under his feet.

"I'm going to the kitchen," Nico said. Chris hadn't even realized he'd followed him downstairs.

Chris nodded, but he couldn't look away from Jacob. He finished walking down the stairs and came to stand in front of the man he loved. "You mean that?" he asked.

Jacob nodded. "I do. I was selfish. We should have both made compromises, but instead, you were the only one who did. You were ready to move your entire life to the cete, while I didn't do anything to help you. It wasn't fair, and I realize now that I was wrong. I'm just hoping that you want me back. I'm ready to do anything you want me to for that to happen."

There was nothing Chris could say to that. Instead, he stepped even closer and cupped Jacob's face with both his hands. Then he kissed Jacob as if it was both the first and last time they'd share a kiss.

Jacob kissed him back without asking anything or protesting. He dropped his backpack and wrapped his arms around Chris, pulling him even closer.

Chris was panting by the time they stopped kissing. He blinked up at Jacob, trying to put his thoughts back in order. "You don't have to move in with the clowder," he started.

Jacob shook his head. "I want to. I want to be close to you, close enough that I can help you. That's not going to happen if I stay home. Let me do this for you, Chris."

"That's not what I meant. I talked to my father."

Jacob grimaced. "That's never a good thing, at least not for us as a couple. What did he say?"

"Both my mother and my brother yelled at him. That, plus the fact that he was shot, made him see that it wasn't fair for him to expect me to be his heir if it made me as unhappy as it did. He gave me his blessing to go back to the cete."

"You're not lying?"

Chris laughed. Now that he and Jacob were talking, he felt lighter than he had in weeks. He also felt weak and like he could sleep for days, but he had to focus on Jacob right now. "I wouldn't do that to you. I promise I'm not lying. I talked to my father, and he's okay with this. Nico will take my place."

Jacob looked like he didn't want to hope. "You're coming

home?"

Chris could only nod. "I'm coming home. I won't ever have to leave again." He paused. "Well, not once I have all my things there."

"We can grab everything right now. My truck is outside."

Chris leaned forward and kissed Jacob again. "You're in a hurry."

"I don't want you or your father to change your minds. I don't think I could survive losing you a third time."

Those words made Chris feel guilty. "I'm so sorry for what happened. For what I did."

Jacob shook his head. "You don't have to be. You did what you had to do for your family and for the clowder. I should have understood that. I should have given you space and offered to help you, but instead, I stayed away, and when you didn't do what I wanted you to do, I didn't push enough. I should have understood why you were doing what you were doing, but instead I acted like a child who didn't get the ice cream he wanted. I'm sorry."

Chris couldn't stop smiling. "We're both sorry, and that's fine. Let's just leave it at that. You don't need to apologize to me any more. I know you never wanted to be alpha mate, and I understood it. I'm glad you understood why I had to stay."

"I can't believe your father really changed his mind."

"Me neither, but I know he won't get back on his word. This is it for us. We can go home and be happy, and he'll be happy for us."

"That's all I've ever wanted. We'll have to talk more, though. I don't want us to risk something like that happening ever again. I love you too much, and I don't want to hurt you."

"I don't want to hurt you, either. We'll make things work." Chris was convinced of that. He had Jacob back, and he wasn't giving him up.

Not now, not ever.

Jacob didn't know what to focus on—having Chris in his arms, the knowledge that Chris was coming home with him, or that Alpha Wiley had changed his mind and had finally agreed for his son to move out.

Jacob had a hard time believing it, but he couldn't deny it was everything he'd ever wanted. He could take Chris and go home, and hopefully, he would never have to see clowder territory again.

He knew there was a fat chance of that. The Wileys were his in-laws now, and that wasn't going to change anytime soon. He wouldn't allow it to. That meant he'd have to learn to deal with them, and even though the thought was daunting, it was something he was ready to do. He would do that and just about anything else for Chris.

"What about your father?" he asked before he could forget the details and whisk Chris away. "He's still healing, isn't he? And Nico isn't ready to take your place."

That gave Chris pause. "I know. I was going to come back once a week or something like that. I can do most of the work at the cete, if you're okay with it."

Jacob shook his head. "You don't have to do that. As long as I know you're coming home eventually, I'm not going to ask you to dump everything and do it now. If you need to stay for a while, that's fine with me. I know your father needs help, and so does your brother."

Chris bit his lower lip. "Are you sure? Because things aren't going to be easy. My father is healing, but it's going to take him time to feel strong enough to work the way he was before."

"I understand. I wouldn't be offering if I wasn't sure I'm okay with it. I can move here if you want me to, or I can go home. Whatever you decide, I'll do."

"It wouldn't be fair. I can't ask you to move here."

"You're not asking. I'm offering. Or you could come home with me, and I could drive you here every morning. Or you could drive yourself. Whatever you want." Jacob wasn't lying about that. He wasn't going to let anything come between him and Chris, especially not himself, not after he already had. That was over. He had Chris by his side again, and he would do everything he could to help Chris and his family come out of this stronger.

He couldn't deny he felt a bit guilty. He hadn't been exactly eager to become alpha mate, even though he'd been ready to do it. Knowing he wouldn't have to and that Chris was coming home with him made everything easier. It also made him wonder whether or not Chris would regret it.

He suspected the answer to that was no. Chris had never regretted stepping away from the alpha position. He'd gone back to it because he'd felt guilty about leaving his father behind, especially when his father had been wounded, but he didn't want it.

And now, he didn't have to do it.

"We'll work things out," Jacob said. He dug his fingers into Chris's hair and pulled him closer. Chris came easily, snuggling against Jacob's chest, and Jacob kissed the top of his head. He smelled like Chris — like love, like home — and Jacob had never been so grateful.

"I want to go home with you," Chris murmured. He'd grabbed the back of Jacob's shirt, and he was squeezing it tightly as if he was afraid Jacob would step away.

"Now?"

Chris nodded. "Now. I can come back tomorrow. It's not that far. I was driving back and forth when we worked together with the humans anyway. I want to continue doing that until my father heals and my brother can take my place."

"I'll come with you. I don't want you to have to do all this work on your own again."

Someone cleared their throat, and they both looked sideways to see Nico standing there. "You won't have to do it alone," Nico said. "I couldn't do it before because Chris had decided he would be the next alpha again, but now, I can. I want you to teach me how to take your place. I didn't go through the same training you did, but I've been around you and Dad, and I know a lot. I don't think it's going to take long for me to get up to speed. We can work together until Dad is healed, and once he is, I'll fully take your place. That is, if you're okay with it."

Jacob held his breath. Even after everything Chris had told him, he was afraid to hope. He doubted that would disappear anytime soon. He and Chris needed to work things out through more than one single conversation. It would take work and time, but that was okay.

Chris stepped away from Jacob to face his brother. "You're sure about this? Because I don't want you to do anything you don't want. You don't expect it from me, and I don't expect it from you."

"We've already had this conversation, so stop being an idiot. I want this. I want you to go home with Jacob and don't come back for the rest of the day. I'll keep everything under control until tomorrow. Don't even think about the clowder until you come back."

Chris was still hesitant. "Are you sure?"

Nico rolled his eyes. "I wouldn't have suggested it if I weren't. Go home, Chris. Call me later. Let me and Mom know that you're okay. That's all we want."

Chris finally nodded, and Jacob's chest felt like it exploded.

He and Chris were going home — together.

"All right. But let me know if anything happens, either with Dad or with the clowder," Chris told Nico. "I can be back in forty-five minutes."

"I promise. Stop worrying so much, though. You need sleep and a good meal." He winked. "I'm sure Jacob won't have a problem taking care of you."

Jacob was pretty sure he meant more than he was saying, but he wasn't about to ask. Instead, he held his hand out to Chris. When Chris looked at him, he smiled. "Ready to go home?" he asked.

Chris stared at Jacob's hand for a second. Then, thankfully, he took it. "Let's go home."

EPILOGUE

Jacob stepped out of Thomas's office. The meeting had gone well, but he couldn't wait to go home.

He didn't expect Chris to be in the hallway, and he wasn't sure *why* Chris was there, but that didn't stop him from hooking an arm around his waist and pulling him close to kiss him. "I thought you'd be home," he murmured.

Chris shrugged. "I was bored. I thought I could come here, and we could walk home together or something like that."

"Maybe we can shift for a bit?"

"Don't you have work to do?"

"Nothing urgent. What about you?"

Chris wrinkled his nose. "I called Nico, but they have everything under control."

Jacob was glad to hear that. Chris's father had finally healed after spending weeks in bed. He was strong, but he was in his fifties, and he'd been shot. That wouldn't have been easy for anyone to get over, and it wasn't for him, either. But he was fine now, and he and Nico were working together. That meant that Chris didn't have to go back to the clowder every day, which was a relief.

It made Jacob feel selfish, but he didn't want to share Chris with anyone, especially not with his father. Even though Dan had finally seen reason, he'd still kept Chris unhappy for many years, and Jacob wasn't sure he could forgive him for that. Not that it mattered. Chris was the one who needed to forgive his father, and he already had. Jacob wasn't going to protest. It wasn't his place, and he wanted to support Chris.

"How is Nico doing?" he asked because he knew Chris was worried.

"So far, he seems pretty happy with the work he and my father are doing. I don't understand it, but then, I wouldn't be here if I did."

Jacob had never been so grateful for something. "I'm glad you don't understand it." He kissed the top of Chris's head. "So? Shall we go and shift?"

"That's fine with me."

Jacob offered Chris his hand like he had that day, and Chris took it. Together, they walked toward the front door of Thomas's house, but it opened before they could get there. Josiah stepped in, looking around.

"You didn't even knock," Chris teased.

Josiah rolled his eyes. "Why should I? This is home."

It was true, especially for Josiah and most of the carriers. "Thomas is in his office. He's waiting for you."

Josiah nodded. "Thanks."

The front door opened again, and Luther stepped in this time. He froze when he noticed Josiah standing there, and they stared at each other for so long that Jacob wondered what was going on.

Chris cleared his throat, making both of them jump. Josiah looked away from Luther, but Luther didn't seem to be able to do the same. He stared at Josiah, while Josiah's cheeks turned a dark pink.

"We're just going to go to Thomas's office," Josiah said.

Jacob nodded. "He's waiting for both of you. You know the way."

Jacob and Chris waited until the two had disappeared down the hallway to look at each other.

"What was that all about?" Jacob asked.

"I have no idea, but I'll make sure to ask Josiah when I next see him on his own. Shall we go?"

Jacob nodded, but once again, the door swung open. He wanted to huff in frustration, but it wasn't like whoever it was had come here for him.

Kari waddled in. He was even bigger than he had been the last time Jacob had seen him, and Jacob thought it was a miracle he hadn't exploded yet. He was tempted to ask if Kari and Calder were having twins, but he knew better than to do that. Kari would tear his balls off and nail them to the wall, and he needed them right where they were.

Kari looked around. "I need something to drink."

"Do you want us to walk you to the kitchen?" Chris asked. His voice was gentler now, and Jacob didn't miss the way he stared at Kari's stomach.

They hadn't talked about that yet. It was way too soon. Besides, Chris was only nineteen, and Jacob doubted he was ready to have a family just yet. It was something Jacob couldn't stop thinking about now, though. He'd never really thought about having children. He'd known that eventually, he would, once he met the right person.

And he had.

Chris was the right person, and together, if Chris was okay with it, they would have a family.

Kari waved Chris's words away. "Don't bother. I know the way. Go do whatever you were planning on doing."

"Are you sure? You look tired."

Kari grimaced and touched his stomach. "It's because the little bugger has been keeping me up all night. I can't believe I still have a month to go."

Neither could Jacob, given how big Kari was, but again, he kept his mouth shut.

They waited until Kari disappeared into the kitchen to turn to the door again. This time, no one came in, and they managed to escape the house.

"He's really big," Jacob commented.

"His due date is approaching. A month sounds like a lot to him, but it really isn't."

Jacob hesitated, but now that he was thinking about it, he wanted to know what Chris thought of the situation. "Is that something you might want eventually?"

Chris blinked. "What? Children?"

"Yes. We haven't talked about it, and I don't expect it to be anytime soon, but I was wondering."

Chris smiled. "You know, I never thought I would be having children, not children I would carry, anyway. Since I was a teenager, I expected my father to choose someone suitable for me to marry, and for that person to be a woman. I couldn't have been the alpha if anyone had found out I was a carrier."

"Things are different now, though."

"They are. Nico will be able to get married and carry children if he wants. So will Josiah. It's incredible to think about, but in a way, knowing my kids won't ever be the alpha makes me feel freer to have them. I don't want any of them to feel forced to become the alpha, and now, they won't have to."

"So you do want children?"

Chris smiled. "I do. Not right now, because I'm having too much fun getting used to living with you, but somewhere down the road, definitely. I want to have a lot of little Jacobs running around the house."

Jacob beamed. "Only if I can have a lot of Chrises doing the same."

"Deal." This time, it was Chris who offered Jacob his hand. "Let's go home."

Jacob took it.

They'd both had had difficult choices to make, and they'd made the only right one for both of them. Now, they had their entire future in front of them, and Jacob couldn't wait to live it.

ABOUT THE AUTHOR

Catherine is the creator of several series, most of them paranormal, including the Whitedell Pride Series and the Gillham Pack Series. While she graduated in translation, she decided to go the writer's way because it was more fun to create her own stories and characters.

She's been living in Italy for more than twenty years, but she's a daughter of the North—Belgium to be precise—and she misses it so much that she's already planning to move back.

She loves pizza—probably too much—her son, her pets, and of course, books. She sneaks some reading time into her schedule every time she has five minutes free from writing, demands from her various pets and son, and lastly, housework.

Connect with her:

lievens.catherine@gmail.com
BookBub: https://www.bookbub.com/authors/catherine-lievens
Website: https://authorcatherinelievens.com/
Facebook: https://www.facebook.com/catherine.lievens.9
Facebook Group: https://www.facebook.com/groups/411788002341528/
Twitter: https://twitter.com/authorCLievens
Newsletter: http://eepurl.com/c-uvKn

www.ingramcontent.com/pod-product-compliance
Lightning Source LLC
Chambersburg PA
CBHW070601130626
46556CB00001B/238